Melanie Hudson was born in Yorkshire in 1971, the youngest of six children. Her earliest memory is of standing with her brother on the street corner selling her dad's surplus vegetables (imagine *The Good Life* in Barnsley and you're more or less there).

After running away to join the British Armed Forces in 1994, Melanie experienced a career that took her around the world on some exciting adventures. In 2010, when she returned to civilian life to look after her young son, on a whim, she moved to Dubai where she found the time to write women's fiction. She now lives in Devon with her family.

Her debut, *The Wedding Cake Tree*, won the Romantic Novelists' Association Contemporary Romance Novel of the Year Award in 2016.

🐦 @Melanie_Hudson_
f www.facebook.com/melhudson7171

Dear Rosie Hughes

Melanie Hudson

A division of HarperCollins*Publishers*
www.harpercollins.co.uk

Harper*Impulse* an imprint of
HarperCollins*Publishers*
The News Building
1 London Bridge Street
London SE1 9GF

www.harpercollins.co.uk

This paperback edition 2019

First published in Great Britain in ebook format by
HarperCollins*Publishers* 2019

A catalogue record for this book
is available from the British Library

ISBN: 9780008319625

This novel is entirely a work of fiction.
The names, characters and incidents portrayed in it are
the work of the author's imagination. Any resemblance to
actual persons, living or dead, events or localities is
entirely coincidental.

Typeset in Birka by Palimpsest Book Production Ltd,
Falkirk, Stirlingshire

Printed and bound in Great Britain by
CPI (UK Ltd), Croydon CR0 4YY

To Andrew, Edward and Meg

Prologue

From: aggieb@yahoo.com
To: rosie-of-arabia@yahoo.com
Subject: My First Chapter!

Date: 28 June 2003

Hi, Rosie

I know I'm going to see you next week, but I had to write straight away and tell you that I've completed the first few chapters of my new novel – and the words *flew* onto the page! It will probably be cut to pieces in the edit, but all I can say is, 'Thank Christ for that!'

And so, thank you, my wonderful friend, for allowing me to tell your story. I promise to take the very best of care of it. I'm wetting myself with excitement about writing the final chapter, which is going to be so blooming heart-warming, there will not be a dry eye in the house. Just imagine the scene: two old friends meet up for the first time on an achingly beautiful Scottish beach, one having just come back from a war zone in the desert, the other having finally found a purpose to her life, after years of being lost in a desert of her own. We lost many years of friendship (and all because of a man and a misunderstanding) but once you get home, we can crack on with a new bucket list and pledge (in blood, if necessary) to never lose touch again. Anyway, enough mush. Here's the blurb for the book. Let me know what you think:

Life in Rosie Hughes
By
Agatha Braithwaite

Blurb

It all began – as, perhaps, all such romantic stories should – with a miserable heroine, a crazy idea and an epic train journey. Such was the case for Stella Valentine, a beautiful but lonely romance writer who, on a dank December afternoon, decided on a whim to escape to the wilds of the Scottish Highlands, having lobbed her laptop and latest manuscript into the nearest river first. As anyone who has embarked on a 'bugger-it', life-changing journey will confess, at the outset it is impossible to know if the new path will lead to the much-longed-for 'happy ever after' or if it will simply prove to be yet another crappy, pot-holed road leading to even deeper depths of despair.

But as Stella glanced whimsically out of the window of the old steam train as it powered its way down the glen, any lastminute reservations were forced to the back of her mind. She didn't notice the driving wind and rain, but felt her heart lifted – yes, physically lifted - by the deep dark lochs, towering mountains and faded heather moorlands; a landscape surely designed for the swaddling of the lost and lonely. And as she stepped onto the platform at Mallaig station, she had the definite notion – or the 'ken' as her new Scottish friends would say – that the next six months would prove to be the most pivotal of her life.

What Stella did not know, however, was that at the very same moment she stepped off the train and walked across the platform, dragging her case behind her and smiling into the rain, her childhood friend, Rosie Hughes, was not only thinking of her but had, quite coincidentally and on the very same day, embarked on an epic journey of her own, but to a significantly more dangerous corner of the globe.

This is not just Stella's story, then, but a story of rekindled friendship, and of two women who find that every single day matters, and that nothing in life is so bad or so utterly unfathomable, when shared between friends.

With all the love in the world,
Aggie (AKA Stella Valentine – I told you I'd find a use for the name)

PART ONE

Six Months Earlier

Electronic Letter ('E' Bluey)
From: Agatha Braithwaite, Midhope-on-the-Moor, West Yorkshire
To: Lieutenant Rosanna Hughes RN, British Army Headquarters, Kuwait

Date: 7 January 2003

Oh, my Jesus Christ, Rosie. I've just found out you've gone to war!

Before I go on, it's me, Aggie Braithwaite. (I know it's been an uncomfortably long time since we spoke.)

I bumped into your dad in the village shop this morning and I knew something must be wrong because he was turning a squidgy mango over in his hand and staring glassy-eyed into the 'past its best' fridge. Bearing in mind your dad is from that generation of Yorkshiremen who would never dream of buying a mango (not even a squidgy one) I asked him if he was OK and he said, 'Oh, I'm bearing up, lass, considering.'. I thought, shit, someone must be dead. So, I followed on with, 'Considering *what*, Mr Hughes?'. And then he told me how you'd flown to Kuwait yesterday – with the Army. What were you thinking, Rosie? No-one looks good in khaki. Not even you.

The last time I bumped into your Dad was about eighteen months ago in Midhope. He was at the Chinese picking up a sweet and sour chicken. I broke open a fortune cracker and wrote my number and address on the back of the paper – did you get it? He told me you and Josh were living in a thatched cottage in Devon and you were working at the Met Office in Exeter. But now I hear you're back in the Navy as a reservist and you're getting divorced? Eh? I'd heard you left the Navy ages ago, so I'm utterly confused and believe that the world must finally have gone topsy-turvy bonkers bananas mad, because many things that I'm hearing do not make sense:

1. What's a sailor doing in the desert? Surely this is a misnomer?

2. Unless you've taken up body-building, your physique and personality are not equipped for combat. If you were built like me (an Amazonian Warrior Goddess) it would be different.

3. You don't have the name of a war hero (and I'm an

author, so I know these things). How can someone called Rosie go to war? It's too soft. Surely you should be sitting in a cosy cottage toasting marshmallows, playing that violin of yours to twenty children?

4. As founder member of the Charlie's Angels (Huddersfield Division) I know for certain that you're a bit of a scaredy-cat.

In sum - Rosie Hughes at war? It doesn't make sense.

Despite my best efforts, I didn't get much information out of your Dad. He had to rush off because he had parked on double yellow lines and had lent his dashboard disability sticker to your Aunty Joan – she's got fluid on her knee due to a nasty fall down the steps of the mobile library. But he told me about the forces electronic bluey letter system and pressed your BFPO address (and the mango, bizarrely) into my hands before he disappeared, which I saw as Kismet (the address, not the mango) because I've been desperate to get in touch for ages, but when you didn't phone or write after I gave my number to your dad, I thought it was best to let it go. But now that you've gone to war, all that silliness seems irrelevant, and I just wanted to write and say, 'hello', 'take care' and 'what the fuck, you idiot?!'

But enough about you. My own life has been a series of bad decisions meshed together by good intentions, and you will not be surprised to learn that I still haven't managed to nail it, and by 'it' I mean that thing called love. I've moved back to Midhope and I'm a writer, which despite being my lifelong dream, bores me to death. I joined the operatic society again with the hope of bagging myself a leading man (I never learn), but all of the men are either spoken for or just plain boring, and anyway that casting bitch at MAOS gave the part of Maria in *The Sound of Music* to Jessie Cartwright! So, I told them to fuck right off. I mean to say, Jessie Cartwright? As *Maria*? Please!

It was exactly like that time in lower sixth when they gave the part of Juliet to Cheryl Brown just because she was light enough to stand on the balsa wood balcony. And to rub insult into injury, they've offered me a consolatory part playing a nun, and I don't mean the pretty one. They offered me the part of Bitch Nun, the one with a face like crumpled steel. Honestly, Rosie, Jessie Cartwright has a weak, tinny voice and – mark my words – she will struggle to reach the back row. But I suppose she's impish which fits the stereotypical image of Maria. When will people realise that the real Maria was a buxom, single-minded, man-eater who got chucked out of a nunnery for being a slapper? And I bet she was a total bitch with those kids once she'd got a ring on her finger. And answer me this: who else but me (in West Yorkshire) could play a buxom Austrian ex-nun who shags a sea captain? I nailed that audition. I did my usual Ella Fitzgerald impression and banged out, *Puttin' On The Ritz* (great number for 'filling the stage' with song and dance), followed on nicely by *With*

A Song In My Heart for the emotional pull. (Mrs Butterworth was actually crying when I closed the final line.) Basically, I nailed it, only to hear, 'We'll let you know.'

We'll let you know?!

Apparently, I can't just rock up in Yorkshire after ten years of absence and expect to be a leading lady.

Why? Why can't I?

But they aren't completely daft as they fully expect me to plonk my fat backside on the piano and accompany all the rehearsals – what a cheek! Anyway, I've told them to stick the part of ugly nun – and their piano – up their arses. I'm not remotely suitable for the role and I refuse to play her, it's degrading. Shaun Jones asked me if I'd like to start doing my Ella tribute down the club again (I think he felt sorry for me) but I can't face it. I'm done with singing. Anyway, it doesn't matter as I'm fleeing to Scotland soon.

More anon.

Love, Aggie

P.S. Any hunks over there? If there are, don't forget, he *has* to be tall. Despite my best efforts soaking myself in the Dead Sea for ten hours on retreat last year, I have not shrunk.

P.P.S. On a serious note, I know we haven't been in touch for (what?) fifteen years, but I decided to go for a light (let's pretend nothing ever happened and we were just gossiping over tea and cake) tone to this letter. Do you mind? I know things need to be said to clear the air properly, but can we be in touch while you're away without raking up the past – at least, for now?

Bluey
From: Rosie
To: Aggie

Date: 3 January

Oh, Aggie.

It was just brilliant to get your letter, and it's a crazy coincidence because only yesterday I was in the General's evening briefing, drifting off, thinking of you, wishing we were in touch, and here you are – swear to God! I was thinking about the time we went to the Proms in Leeds on a Sixth Form night out. That woman in the balcony leant forward to wave to her friend and her false teeth fell out and landed in your pint! Hilarious. It could only have happened to you. Did you drink the pint after you fished the teeth out? Probably.

Like you, I've also been wanting to get in touch, but when you didn't reply to the invitation I sent for my wedding a few years ago, I thought, perhaps, you hadn't forgotten (or forgiven) what happened that last summer before we went to university. I confess that Dad did give me your address last year. The fortune cookie made my throat catch. It said, 'A friend asks only for your time, not money' but at that moment, my marriage had just broken down – amongst other things of equal catastrophe – and I suppose I wanted to hide away. Then, a couple of weeks ago, I made up my mind to come and see you before I left for Kuwait, but I bottled it at the last minute and decided it would be best for us to catch up when I get home, when I've got more time.

Like you said, though, let's park all that for the moment. But I would just say this: if you kept away because of what happened with Simon, then I'm truly sorry. He can be a bit of an inconsiderate shit sometimes, but if it's any consolation I honestly don't think he means any harm.

So, why am I in Kuwait with the Army? Temporary insanity is all I can put it down to.

When Josh and I decided to separate, I couldn't bear the thought of selling up my home on Dartmoor. Remember when I used to draw pictures of my dream home? Thatched roof, roses, duck pond, loads of kids? Well, I pretty much nailed it, except for the kids. Josh agreed he'd leave his money in the property for a couple of years and rent in town, he was away at sea most of the time anyway, but if I was staying at the cottage then I would have to pay all the bills. I agreed, but the reality was that I couldn't afford it. To rewind further, I left the Navy in 1999 (after the shortest military career in history). I liked being a Navy Met Officer, but once I married Josh I wanted to settle down and start a family. So, I got a job at the Met Office in Exeter, but joining the reserves was a way of keeping my link to the Navy and it also meant I could afford to keep the house once we decided to split. Then, last November, I was asked if I'd consider deploying to Kuwait, to support the Army as a Met Forecaster. Call it impetuous irrationality, but I said yes (probably because I didn't want to look like a coward). The Met Office released me for six months and before I knew it, I'd picked up my kit, done a bit of training, jumped onto an RAF transport jet and here I am.

Shit look at the time! Must dash. I must prepare a forecast for the 1800 briefing, but I'll write later with more info. Please write as often and as much as you can. I'm miserable and friendless out here. I want to know what you're up to now! You said you're an author? What are you writing? Did you ever finish that steamy novel?

Love, Rosie

P.S. Even though I'm in a target-rich environment, there are no hunks around here – sorry.

P.P.S. Apparently the whole village is in bewilderment as to how you've managed to buy that flash barn conversion overlooking the river. Bloody hell, Aggie! Have your lottery numbers come up or something?

'E' Bluey
From: Mr Hughes, Rosie's Dad
To: Rosie

Date: 3 January

Dear, Babe

How are you settling in? How was the journey?
Mammy wants to know where you are exactly and if
you'll be staying in Kuwait if it kicks off? Are you in a
bunker? Also, she wants to know if you're getting enough
food, especially roughage (I know you've only been there
a day or so, but you know how she worries about your
bowels). Speaking of that kind of thing, we took Fluffy
to the vet this morning because she kept wiping her
backside on Mammy's sheepskin rug. She's had her anal
glands squeezed (£45 quid!) and seems brighter so fingers
crossed the rug will be spared future embarrassment
when Aunty Joan comes over.

I bumped into that big lass you used to knock about
with at school the other day. She's not fat now, but big
enough to see that she still likes her food. She stole my
mango (perfectly ripe and half price too!). I was going
to cut a bit up for Mammy with some avocado, although
why I persevere with avocado God only knows, the
bloody things are either as hard as iron or on the turn
and I never catch them right. Anyway, she's going to write
to you – Agatha, not Mammy. Mammy sends her love

13

in my letters (you know she's not one for writing).

What else to tell you? Bill and Mary over the road are having their windows done. We don't think they've thought it through. Faux wood effect. Nuff said. They're having a big conservatory built, too. He calls it an 'orangery', the daft sod. How can a terrace house cope with an orangery? The new bloke next door to Bill (Tracy and Jack's old place) put in a complaint to the council. He thinks it will block out all the light from his chicken hutch, but Bill is ploughing on with it. We don't mind what he does because, like Mammy says, having a house in the street with an orangery will put the price of ours up and she's fancying a bungalow. But I'll only ever leave this place in a wooden box, so she can think again!

The weather has been raw this week with a vicious wind but at least it's too cold to snow so that's something. Well, I've just heard the letterbox go and I'm waiting for my metal detecting magazine to come so I'll sign off. Mammy is sitting in her chair looking through holiday brochures (she says she fancies a cruise, but I think we all know she could never cope with all the people and the chatter). Maybe we'll treat ourselves to a new caravan at Whitby, although they are such a price these days I doubt we will.

Well, that's all for now. If you feel a bit low over the next few weeks, take out this letter and pretend I'm singing along with Nat King Cole in the car, just like we used to:

Light up your face with gladness, hide every trace of
sadness, although a tear may be ever so near, that's the
time you must keep on trying, smile what the use of crying,
you'll find that life is still worthwhile, if you just smile

And remember - Keep Your Head Down (KYHD)

Love you, babe

MammynDad x

P.S. Did you take my snow shovel to Devon? It had a
smooth handle and the angle of the scoop was perfect.
I can't find another one for love nor money.

'E' Bluey

From: Aggie

To: Rosie

Date: 7 January

Dear, Rosie

Of course I drank my bloody pint! We only had our
bus fare and there was no way I wasn't having a drink.
Admittedly, there was a faint tang of Polygrip and I had
to fish out a bit of popcorn, but other than that, it was
pretty tasty.

Right then, here's a quick update on the past few years.
After university I moved to London and worked as an
editor at Maddison and Black. It was a fab job, loads of
social, loads of shagging and a couple of years later I
even finished my much-discussed first novel (plus

another two). I'll let you into a big secret (but only because you're stuck in the desert and can't spill the beans) ... I ghost-write comedy romance novels for (none other than) celebrity chef, Isabella Gambino (Isabella my arse, she's called Sharon Froggatt). Isabella is a sweetheart and I suppose it's fitting that *I* (a woman who was whipping up a Victoria sponge whilst transiting the birth canal) now write books for the best baker on the planet. Isabella sends me free copies of all her cookbooks, which means I have to run the equivalent of a marathon every week just to keep the diabetic nurse from my door, but here's confession time: after banging out eight books in eight years, I've dried up. My imagination is kaput! My latest work in progress, *My Foolish Heart*, is just not coming together AT ALL. So, I've left my characters languishing in the doldrums, and they hate that.

You'll not be surprised to hear that Mum is frustrated to hell that she can't tell anyone I'm a writer. But truly, it's amazing she's kept schtum all these years. She's still an absolute dragon and I never know from one day to the next if she's talking to me, but on balance, I think she's glad I moved back home (a knee-jerk decision following the breaking of a heart – his, not mine). The problem with writing is that I sit alone for hour after hour lost inside my own imagination, which, as you know, is a bizarre and wild place to be, and what's worse, my imagination is pretending to be someone else's imagination, which adds even more weirdness to the situation.

But at least the lives of my pretend friends are sexy and interesting, which is more than can be said for my crappy old existence at the moment. It's a sad state of affairs when my characters are getting more action in the bedroom than me *breathes deep and heavy sigh*. My latest serious squeeze was a competitive fisherman, David. He got me into bed by saying I was his greatest catch (*please!*). We lived together for a while but it was an average type of relationship. Predictably, I woke up one morning and realised he bored me out of my mind, and even if he didn't bore me out of my mind, there was no competing with his ultimate fantasy – not me dressed in red lycra wielding a whip – but the elusive twenty-pound conga eel (or some kind of big fish or another). So, one day, while sitting in silence at the riverbank burning the skin off my top pallet with scalding coffee, I took my lead from the salmon, told him it was over, fought my way up stream and came home to spawn.

But now, I find that sperm is in scarce supply, which is worrying. There is this one man I met a couple of weeks ago on the Internet who seems rather nice. He's Irish and (thank God) very tall. I've begun to imagine myself playing Maureen O'Hara to his John Wayne in *The Quiet Man*, but without having to live in Ireland or grow roses. Not that I have anything against the Emerald Isle, except it rains a lot and I've promised mum I'll partner her at cribbage next year. She's determined to annihilate the competition – namely Janey Peters – who stole her boyfriend TWENTY YEARS AGO. You've got to hand it to Mum, she knows how to play the long game. I've popped some sweets and magazines into a parcel for you along with one of my books – *But That's Not What I Meant*. You might not have time to read it, what with being on the brink of war and everything, but if you do, feel free to give me a proper review (an honest one).

    Ciao, Bella!
    Aggie

P.S. Yes, I did keep away because of Simon. Your dad mentioned he'd moved to Australia for a while, which must have been a terrible shock. I know how much you all adore him.

From: Wright and Longstaff Solicitors, Exeter
To: Rosanna Hughes

Dated: 3 January 2003
Read: 7 January 2003

Dear Mrs Hughes

Please find enclosed a copy of your Decree Nisi.

We have received an offer of £245,000 for Rose Cottage which Mr Fletcher would like to accept. In accordance with your last instruction we will proceed with the sale. The equity will be split between yourself and Mr Fletcher as per the divorce settlement.

Please find enclosed your updated Last Will and Testament as per your instructions. Please sign where indicated and return one copy to me at your earliest convenience.

Kind regards,
Justin Grant

'E' Bluey
From: Aggie
To: Rosie

Date: 7 January

Me again!
Oh, my good Lord! I've just had phone sex with the Irishman. Gorgeous voice. I was worried he would sound like Gerry Adams, but no, his accent was soft and sexy. I tried to sound less northern and more like a BBC news reader, but as it turns out, panting sounds the same whatever the accent, so I think I pulled it off. The next time we do it, I'm going to wear something sexy and lay on my bed so I can get into the mood a bit more. There's something a little disturbing about having phone sex while

wearing rabbit slippers and watching Midsomer Murders on mute, but I have a hundred per cent success rate at guessing the murderer by the first set of adverts and I'm not prepared to let it slip now. So anyway, don't judge, but I'm meeting Paddy (do you think that is his real name?) in Venice tomorrow for one night – how bloody impulsive is that!? I've got a good feeling about this one.

Ciao, Sweetie, or as the Irish say, 'may the road rise.'

Aggie

P.S. Shit, I hope these letters aren't proof read by the Army.

P.P.S. Guess what? I was going through some old journals yesterday and found that bucket list we wrote together when we finished in upper sixth. It's brilliant, but we weren't nearly as adventurous or sanctimonious enough. I'll write it out for you in another letter – can you believe we actually signed the 'document' IN OUR OWN BLOOD!

Bluey

From: Rosie

To: Aggie

Date: 8 January

Hi, Aggie

Very quick one. Can you do me a big favour, please? A few years ago, I bought Dad a snow shovel from the

Wednesday market and he loved it. It had a black, plastic shovelly bit with a wooden shaft, but the handle was made of cork which he really liked. The thing is, I broke it when Josh and I used it as a sledge on Hound Tor. Can you do me a massive favour and go to the market and see if you can buy another one? If you do manage to get one, please can you rough it up a bit and leave it next to the compost heap (behind the pile of old slates which are behind the greenhouse) and let me know when you've done it. I'll write again tonight.

Love, Rosie

P.S. You mentioned tripping off to Scotland as a throw away remark. What's that about?

Bluey

From: Rosie

To: Aggie

Date: 8 January

Hi, Aggie

Oh my God, the bucket list! Signing in blood was your idea, but it was easier for you because you only had to tear the scab from your elbow (a roller skating incident I think?) but I had to cut my finger with a fruit knife. We must have been mad. I can't wait to see what we put.

Sorry about the abrupt letter re the snow shovel but Dad gets a bit precious about his stuff and I wanted to get the letter into the post straight away. Your letters are sometimes printed off on the day that you type them, which is amazing, but I'm guessing my hand-written ones take a few days to reach you? You asked for some detail of my life in the desert, so here's a potted history of my first week.

We landed in Kuwait City late in the evening on 1 January. After the aircraft taxied in, I ducked down to glance through the window, half-expecting to see the usual airport goings-on, but found myself watching RAF personnel (with their respirator cases attached to their belts) unloading the aircraft. Even though I'm carrying my own respirator case and a pistol, the possibility of being subject to a gas attack suddenly seemed very real. We disembarked the aircraft and were shepherded through a series of tents (the in-theatre arrivals process).

Absolute silence.

No one smiled. I don't think any of the other people on the aircraft (soldiers, mainly) even looked at me. I was issued with NAPs tables (Nerve Agent Poisoning), an atropine pen (in case of chemical attack), some very strong anti-biotics (in case of biological warfare) and ten rounds of ammunition, which I shoved in my ammo pouch. Arrivals procedure complete, I was bundled onto a knackered, cold coach and taken to British Army Headquarters.

I have absolutely no idea how long that journey took. Again, no one spoke on the truck and no one greeted us on arrival at the camp, either. The guys disappeared off and I stood there, alone. It was the middle of the night. I was exhausted and had absolutely no idea where to go or what to do. I put on my head torch and walked down an avenue of tents packed full of soldiers who were sleeping on camp beds or on the sand. One of the tents I passed had a gap between two soldiers big enough to roll out my mat, so I fell to my knees, dropped down my rucksack, got out my sleeping bag and tried to sleep between the two soldiers, but desperate for a pee, I couldn't sleep. It was so bloody cold, too. You would think, being a Met Forecaster, I would have clocked how cold it gets in the desert at night in winter, but I'm clearly an absolute amateur.

At around 6am, everyone got up. I waited for the tent to clear before putting on my Bergen (AKA rucksack) because it's embarrassing. Although I scaled down my kit to practically zero before leaving the UK, picking up my heavy Bergen is a major operation. I have to kneel next to something I can hold on to, hook the straps over my shoulders and then use every bit of strength I have in my legs to stand. Walking is simply a case of forward momentum overcoming gravity. Anyhow, I followed in the direction of the masses and found the portaloos, cleaned up as best I could with wet wipes, went through the whole palaver of putting my rucksack on again, then asked an American where I might get some breakfast and was pointed in the direction of the chow tent. Then, finally, I was pointed in the direction of HQ, where I spent an hour looking for someone who could give me some pointers.

Basically, in terms of delivering a met forecast, I'm on my own.

Regarding the set-up here, it's all a bit Heath Robinson. Everything the American military have is state-of-the-art, but the same cannot be said for us Brits. Our HQ is a marquee-style tent which saw its best in Churchill's day. There are two British armoured brigades in theatre. They have set up camp somewhere else in Kuwait – as have the Paras – and we will also have Royal Marines in theatre, but they are also elsewhere just now. Fox News plays on a big TV on permanent loop in HQ, so I know I'm not telling you anything you don't already know, although I haven't been briefed regarding what I can and cannot include in my letters, so sod it. It's really quite odd watching the news to see the Political machinations as they unfold. I see they are saying that they are trying to find a peaceful outcome. I hope they get one, but war seems like a fait accompli from where I'm standing.

In the middle of the HQ tent is something called the 'bird table' which is roughly an eight by eight trestle table covered in a map showing enemy lines. The table is covered in Perspex and there are stickers on it showing the positions of all the troops. Twice a day, the General appears at the head of the bird table (quiet chap) as does the Chief of Staff. A representative from each army section gathers around the table. A green, old-fashioned telephone handset hangs from a wire above the table. You press a button to speak into it and we all take turns to brief what's going on in our respective departments. This brief goes out to the brigades and to the Paras. We stand around the table in a set order - the met forecast always comes first so I stand shoulder to shoulder with the Chief of Staff, next door-but-one to the General, and watch the operation unfold every day, which means that my voice is the first voice the soldiers hear on the radio every day and will be throughout the whole operation.

Typically, I still haven't escaped from people complaining to me about the weather. Some things never change. I'm bored ninety five percent of the time. The lucky ones are the smokers. The other day I grabbed myself a cuppa and stood with the smokers – just to try to make friends. But I was holding a Polystyrene cup rather than a metal one with a lid that keeps the tea warm, and so I didn't have the right kind of cup that says, 'Experienced Military Woman', so I didn't fit in and had no conversation of worth. It was exactly like being the unpopular girl at the disco. Standing with the smokers I had a flashback to Home Economics and wish with all my heart I had befriended poor Jenny Jackson. The bullies were horrible to that girl and I watched it happen but said nothing. I was a coward and now I've got my comeuppance.

Sorry to be so negative. I'm just lost at sea. In fact, that's the irony. At sea, I wouldn't be the least bit lost. I'd have my bunk, my place of work and my extra duties to stop my mind from wandering. Sea-time was awesome compared to this. I'm also on a downer because my Decree Nisi just arrived in the post – how messed up is that? If I could turn the clock back a couple of years I wouldn't have left Josh and I wouldn't be losing my house. My whole life is shattered, and the person who broke it was me. It's like I've been on a suicide mission to strip my life down to the absolute basics and now I feel naked, homeless and alone. Thank God for your letters and the support of Mum and Dad, I'd be lost without you all.

But ... more importantly, Venice with a total stranger? Are you completely barking mad? Write as soon as you get home.

Love, Rosie

Bluey
From: Rosie Hughes
To: Joshua Fletcher, HMS Drake, Plymouth

Date: 8 January

Hi, Josh
Just thought I'd let you know I made it to Kuwait. Not sure if you still want to know I'm OK, but it seems odd

to have spent all those years together and then suddenly not communicate. I got the Decree Nisi through yesterday and my solicitor told me the news about the offer on the house. It's probably best that the sale goes through while I'm away as I couldn't bear to empty the old place. Can you please put my stuff into storage? Before I left I put my most precious bits and bobs into a blue plastic box. You'll find the box in the little bedroom, it has 'Rosie's Special Stuff' written on the lid. Can you keep that box – and my violin – safe for me and I'll pick them up when I get home? Hope all is good with you?

Rosie

'E' Bluey
From: Mr Hughes
To: Rosie

Date: 9 January

Dear, Babe

Terrible news. The school burnt down last night! Every last bit of it. Shocking. Mammy woke up at 3a.m. to the sound of an exploding LPG tank. The kids have been given the rest of the week off school which has caused havoc for the working mothers. No news on how the thing started, but it's caused a lot of tears and upset and it's distressing for the kids to see it – just a charred pile of rubble – and all their bits and bobs burnt to a cinder. Those nativity costumes have been worn by generations of kids. Terrible.

There's an emergency meeting with the council in the village hall tonight, so I'm sure I'll have more information soon.

Love, Dad x

'E' Bluey
From: Aggie
To: Rosie

Date: 9 January

Hi, Rosie

Just got back from my night in Venice to find out that Midhope Primary has burnt down! The girls are moping around the village in floods of tears while most of the boys are whooping it up (and they wonder why girls out-perform boys). The whole village smells of burnt toast and God only knows how much asbestos we're all inhaling.

I'll write later with the details of Venice but in one word – disaster.

Love, Aggie

Dear Rosie Hughes

'E' Bluey
From: Aggie
To: Rosie

Date: 9 January

Hi, Rosie

I've just got home from a meeting about the school – I didn't know your dad was still a governor? Bless him. I'll not steal his thunder regarding details of the meeting, because I know what you're really aching to hear about is my night in Venice, and what a catastrophic mistake of a lifetime that was.

Paddy was only a bloody jockey – five foot three inches, max! What a liar. It seems the only correct detail on his online profile was that he's Irish, and even then, the accent could have been fake. Who the hell knows with the Internet?

My flight arrived an hour before his into Marco Polo Airport. Clearly, I took the time to sort out my make-up and put on fresh knickers (a lacy thong would have been far too uncomfortable on the plane). I hovered around the arrivals hall feeling sexy, optimistic and very tall. When his flight came through I was so busy scanning the crowd at *my* head height I failed to notice the man standing directly in front of me with his face in my tits and his tongue hanging out.

I'm afraid my expression did not mask my disappointment, cue awkward taxi ride followed by a blazing row in the middle of St Mark's Square about the importance of being earnest (moral virtue, not book) which lasted until we mounted a gondola at the bridge of sighs (bridge of lies, more like). It wasn't a one-way conversation, though. He was sparky, but then he's a Celt, they're like that. He said I was a 'total fecking hypocrite' as I had been equally as economical with the truth as I was clearly not a twenty-seven-year-old model. But as I said, if I *had* put my real age on my internet profile, men my age wouldn't consider dating me because all men are pricks and they only go for women at least seven years their junior (he had the good grace to agree). I turned my back on him under the kissing bridge and instructed Paulo to 'just keep rowing – presto!' (I temporarily forgot the verb to punt, although even if I hadn't, I could not have translated it into Italian. Mum may have improved my language skills by dating a Russian, a Frenchman and a Spaniard, but she never did shag an Italian).

Eventually we cut our losses and decided to go out for a meal together. Over dinner I apologised and explained that my hostile behaviour could be explained (but not excused) by my disappointment. I said we could never have a relationship because:

a. When standing side by side we looked like a comedy duo.

b. He was just too tiny to be able to carry me over

the threshold and I've ALWAYS wanted to be carried over the threshold – not negotiable. His honesty in replying to points one and two (above) was refreshing.

He confessed that the threshold had been the last thing on his mind when he'd asked to meet me. He'd flown to Venice expecting to have the best shag of his life with a woman who had the most magnificent tits and arse he'd ever seen in a photograph (a statement he stood by, which was nice). He'd surmised that if my sexual prowess in the sack matched my performance on the phone, he knew he would be onto a winner and had booked his ticket to Venice immediately (I have now learned that a romantic location in no way guarantees a romantic interlude).

So anyway, we eventually laughed at the scenario and I ordered lobster, which was the same colour of my face having remembered the phone sex. And after a pleasant if slightly strained evening we said our goodbyes at the airport and flew home the next day. I'm so disappointed. I really thought I'd found the elusive one. But, fear not, I'll take a deep breath and, like Paddy, jump straight back into the saddle, so to speak.

With much love.
Aggie
P.S. Sounds like a bloody nightmare out there. Chin up, Buttercup!
P.P.S. Bucket list in next letter, promise.

Melanie Hudson

Bluey
From: Rosie
To: Aggie

Date: 10 January

Hi, Aggie

Oh dear. It sounds like Venice was a bit of a mistake. Shame you didn't get a shag out of the jockey, but perhaps it's for the best. Maybe you need to take a leaf out of your own book? Didn't you say your next title is *My Foolish Heart*? Is your title telling you something?

Life here is much the same. I can't imagine any kind of peaceful resolution coming into play. I bumped into a helicopter pilot I knew in the Navy the other day and he said he feels sick when he looks down from his helicopter and sees the might of the American military (which is only a fraction of their Marine Corps and a bit of their Army) sitting in the desert, waiting to pounce. I wonder how the Iraqi civilians feel, waiting to be attacked? What the fuck are we going to do with all these bombs and bullets anyway? Blow the whole of the Middle East to smithereens?

Write soon
Love, Rosie

Dear Rosie Hughes

'E' Bluey
From: Josh
To: Rosie

Date: 11 January

Hi, Rosie

Thanks for your letter. I've accepted the offer on the house. Not sure on the completion date yet but it'll be a while as the chain has collapsed. I said we would wait for our buyer to sell again as I can't face the rigmarole of putting our place on the market, but it could be months before completion. I'll let you know how it goes. By the way, is it OK if I give Mum the Tiffany lamp I bought you? You never really liked it and she always had her eye on it. Where is it? Did you give it away?

Take care of yourself.
Josh

Bluey
From: Rosie
To: Mr Hughes

Date: 11 January

Dear, Mum and Dad

All remains well on the Eastern Front and don't worry because I'm being well fed. It's the easiest job I've ever had – anyone could do it. I get a print-out of the weather forecast from the Americans and I read it out, job done. The weather never changes in the desert and so I've got lots of time to read books and write letters. I miss you both, but it's honestly not too bad over here. I'm on the General's staff and so I should imagine that, even as the troops move forward, I'll be in absolutely no danger so try not to worry.

Ta ta for now. Give the dog a big hug from me. I've got no idea what happened to the snow shovel. Didn't the handle snap?

Love you loads,
Rosie x
P.S. Did you give my BFPO address to Simon? I haven't heard from him.

Bluey
From: Rosie
To: Josh

Date: 12 January

Josh

I've mulled over your last letter and I'm a bit pissed off
and need to get things off my chest. We've spent what,
ten years together, and all you can say to me when I'm
at the brink of being gassed to death is to ask if your
mother can have my bloody lamp! Re the house, I agree.
Let's wait for the buyers we have at the moment. I want
the house to go to people I like.

Rosie

'E' Bluey
From: Mr Hughes
To: Rosie

Date: 13 January

Dear, Babe

It's all kicking off at home. Even though the embers are
still smouldering, the council have admitted they may

35

not rebuild the school. Meanwhile, the kids continue to be ferried on the bus to Oakworth on a thirty-mile round trip, which is a shame. We're not taking it lying down, though. A petition is being drafted as I type!

To add fuel to the fire, Cecil Robinson wants to buy the school grounds and put houses on it – he's got a bloody nerve that man, but where there's muck there's money! It's causing quite a rift. I bumped into Bill in the shop. He said, 'I'm not building a bloody orangery to have a load of boxes go up in the field behind my house.' Janet heard him moaning (you know what a booming voice he's got) and she bit back (you may remember she used to have a thing going with Cecil). She said he should keep his trap shut because the area needs more affordable housing, and anyway, 'Clamping an orangery onto the arse end of a terrace house in the middle of the Pennines is bloody ridiculous.' He stormed out, but he'll have to storm back in again if he doesn't want a twenty-mile round trip to buy a pint of milk. We're still waiting to discover the cause of the fire, but arson hasn't been ruled out. Terrible.

Nothing else much going on. There's a bit of a barny going on over the road because the man at number 42 keeps parking his campervan on the road outside number 48, but I think that's a storm in a teacup. Mammy and the dog are well. I'll keep looking for the elusive snow shovel. It must be Alzheimer's setting in but I can't find the bloody thing anywhere. I've emailed your address to

Simon. Mammy said to not feel too bad if he takes his time to write; he's constantly on the go and it doesn't mean he doesn't love you.

Love, MumnDad x
P.S. What's your opinion on the school issue? Rebuild or move on?

'E' Bluey
From: Aggie
To: Rosie

Date: 13 January

Dear, Rosie

But I *did* get a shag out of the dwarf! Come on, he's a bloody jockey. How could I refuse an arse that can move *that* fast?

Anyway, Ta Da ... here is the bucket list (we were quite sweet, really):

Umpteen Things We Absolutely Have To Do Before We're Thirty-Five (first draft)

By Aggie and Rosie, Age 15

1. Learn to river dance
2. Climb a mountain (Mount Kenya or Everest base camp)

37

3. Get married and have kids (Rosie only)
4. Watch one sunrise and sunset together every year (not negotiable)
5. Swim with dolphins (if no dolphins, seals will do)
6. Do the thing we are afraid of the most
7. Sleep under the stars
8. Get to grade eight - violin (Rosie) piano (Aggie) and become duetting superstars
9. Send a message in a bottle
10. Read one hundred classic books
11. Master the flick-flack (Rosie only)
12. Meet the Dalai Lama – combine this with going to 'Holi' festival and becoming yogis
13. Ride a horse bareback on the beach
14. Swim under a waterfall (naked)
15. Make a positive difference in one person's life

We got bored by the list at this point and hit the cider.

Come on then: how many have you done? You were always a bendy gymnastic-type, so I reckon you could do a flick-flack if you really tried. What about the violin – surely you carried on with that? God knows why we chose such an arbitrary age as thirty-five to complete the list by. Why so long? Other than getting married I could crack out the whole lot in a month. That said, so far, I've only managed to achieve no's 13 and 15. Although I could probably claim number 1 with a bit of artistic licence, because although I haven't river danced, I did learn tap dancing for a year, so if I do it faster along to some Irish music and keep my arms by my side, I'll have nailed it!

Anyway, another mercy parcel is winging its way out to the Middle East. It includes chocolates and a photo of the two of us posing outside the youth club disco when we were about fourteen. You're wearing wicked Madonna lace gloves but I've got an afro and a snake belt (why the fuck did you let me rebel against fashion all the time?). I've also sent you a recent photo of me. It was done for my agent. I do articles and short stories for magazines in my own name. Let me know what you think of the photo. Do I look too tall? I was going for the 'intelligent but fun' look, but I think you can tell I'm pulling my tummy in. Diet starts tomorrow. I'll confess that I didn't buy the chocolates. Isabella sent them as a thank you for writing her a funny speech for her spot on *This Morning*, but I get a headache if I eat dark chocolate, so I thought I'd send them your way. I wish Isabella would send Milk Tray. Why do people believe the more they spend on a gift, the more significant the gesture?

What else? Oh, Paddy phoned. He wants to get going with the phone sex again (I was a foolish, desperate buffoon to shag him). I said (in my no-nonsense voice), 'No, thank you', but soon discovered that my no nonsense voice just turns him on even more. I explained that I had been swept away in Venice and that the ambience had led me to reveal a wild and exotic side of my personality which, on reflection, would have been best kept under a bushel. Undeterred, he asked if he could join me under the bushel – naked. So, I told him I was taking holy orders (the audition for Maria being the inspiration for that little gem) and hung up. I may have to change my telephone number. Thank God I told him I'm a podiatrist from Hull and didn't let on I write for Isabella.

In other news, my publisher wants me to give Isabella a side-line in erotica. They think her present run of romance has had its day. Do you think the cosmos is rubbing it in that I'm not having regular sex? I'm not sure I'm up to erotica as my enthusiasm for spicing up my (already spicy) sex scenes is waning. I may have to resort to more internet dating for the sake of my career, but if I do, I must remember to only date men who show their teeth on their profile picture. I once met up with a chap who was absolutely stunning, but then he opened his mouth and revealed only *one* tooth – one bloody tooth! A top front incisor. I felt so sorry for him I actually kissed him goodnight ... no tongues, though.

Sod it. You're right. I need a plan for my manhunt. I'll give the Internet a second chance with a new fake name and I should also re-think my fake job. Maybe I'll post a doctored picture of a more streamlined, younger me, and ditch the Nigella brunette look too and go blonde, but I'll keep my tits and arse, obviously.

Ciao, Bella

'E' Bluey
From: The Staff at The Shop, Midhope
To: Rosie

Date: 13 January

Hello, Rosie, love.

Your dad has been giving people in the village your address, so we thought we'd write you a quick letter to say, WELL DONE YOU! We don't see your mum much, but then it's always been your dad who's done their big shop.

Nothing much changes. Tracy Babcock is expecting again (that family allowance must be stacking up) and old Mr Jenkins passed away, bless him. It was a good turn-out at the funeral, but the sandwiches at the club afterwards were a bit disappointing (soggy egg) and Jack Blackmoor got pissed as a newt, daft sod. Mind you, he was like a son to Mr Jenkins, so we'll let him off.

That lass you used to knock around with was in here the other day. It seems like only yesterday the two of you were running in here (it was Mrs Barker's shop then) to buy jubilee lollies for ten pence-apiece. What a little bugger Agatha was. Why did she always insist speaking in French? Far too big for her boots, but that's what happens when your mother disappears off to Paris to work for a Russian Cossack and comes home pregnant with money in the bank. God only knows who the father was, not that it's our business, but with those thighs I don't suppose the apple fell far from the tree. Did you know that the school burnt down? The kids are being ferried to Oakworth, but it's a blooming long way for the little mites every day, and you know how treacherous that road over the tops gets in the winter. Old Mrs Butterworth was in here the other day and she was crying. Her kitchen window overlooks the playground. She loves listening to the kids. But the council say they haven't the money to re-build it and Jed Jenkins wants to build houses (never one to miss out on an opportunity, our Jed).

Anyway, the bread man has just walked in, so I'll sign off. Andrea Jones says, 'Hello.' She works two afternoons a week. I don't think you'll remember her, but she says to say she's the one who used to sit next to you in Geography and fainted a lot. Keep smiling.

Pat (and the girls at the shop)

Bluey
From: Rosie
To: Aggie

Date: 13 January

Oh, Aggie

Thanks for sending the bucket list - I can't believe you kept it all these years. I'll confess that I was overcome with melancholy reading it and felt happy and sad all at the same. Happy, because it reminded me of all the fabulous times we had growing up together – my favourite memories are of us duetting on the piano and violin in your mum's front room (we were bloody good, weren't we!) Your dear old Mum would weep in her chair if we played that old Leroy Anderson melody, *Forgotten Dreams*) – but sad because, compared to you, I feel like I've been living a dull, joyless life for ten years. I'll explain another time, but I've been so preoccupied with wanting to start a family these past few years, I'd forgotten to keep having fun. To answer your question, it was me who stipulated the 'age thirty-five' caveat (there's a surprise). It was the latest age I was prepared to have a baby by (didn't manage that one, did I?).

But here's an idea: can we start the bucket list now? After all, we're both thirty-five in July, so we haven't got much time to crack it out. Admittedly, being stuck in the desert means that my options are limited (can't imagine the Dalai Lama rocking up in the HQ tent and teaching me to river dance), but maybe you could do some of the list for both of us? I'd love that – experience my joy vicariously through your joy – it would help to cheer up my miserable existence *note sad face*.

In other news, I have finally found a friend! Actually, he's very quickly turning into a brother, which is handy, as I haven't heard a peep from my own. He's called Gethyn, he's thirty-seven and he's a doctor in the RAF. He's originally from the Welsh valleys. There's a lovely calmness about him, but he also has a glint in his eye and a dry sense of humour. You'd like him, he's tall and built like a brick shit house. He sings all the time (which is a little annoying) but being Welsh, I suppose he can't help it (singing, not being annoying). But don't get any ideas about me hooking up with him because there is not one iota of attraction between us. However, I'll find out if he's got a girlfriend because if not, he would be perfect for you!

Thanks for the book. I loved it. I've passed it on to Gethyn and asked him to give you an honest review. He's been reading it ALL evening (with a wry smile on his face) so it should be a good one. I think he's impressed with the sex scenes so he'll probably be falling over himself to meet you when we get back. Aren't I clever?

Loads of love, Rosie

P.S. Random question. Do you ever worry you won't get around to having a baby?

P.P.S. Nearly forgot. You've ticked off 13 and 15??? So you've met the Dalai Lama AND bathed under the waterfall naked. I need details NOW (please tell me you did these two things at the same time).

Bluey
From: Gethyn Evans
To: Aggie

Date: 13 January

Dear, Agatha

My name is Gethyn Evans and I'm a doctor serving with the army in the Middle East. Rosie Hughes gave me your book *But That's Not What I Meant* and asked if I would write an honest review. I usually keep my own counsel in such matters (I often find that when people ask for an honest opinion on something they don't really mean it) but Rosie said you were made of sturdy stuff, so I decided to oblige. I am aware you ghost write for Isabella Gambini and please be assured your secret is safe with me. Here is the review:

I enjoyed the book as a pleasant read that passed a couple of hours during, what would have otherwise been, an uneventful afternoon. I don't usually read romantic fiction, not because I allow myself to fall foul of gender predictable norms, but because romantic fiction follows the same formulaic lines of a romantic film and I prefer a read that delves deeper into the human condition - anger, regret, jealousy, fear, betrayal and, of course, love and familial relationships. Yes, your book ticks all the necessary boxes, and there were moments when you were *almost* there, but just when I thought you were getting into your groove, you resorted to humour rather than fleshing out the bones of the matter. Your one-liners were funny, but are you, perhaps, frightened to completely lose yourself in the power of your prose?

I can see that the novel would provide a very good read for its target audience, but have you considered breaking away from formula – is life formulaic? Does a love story always have to have a happy ending to be satisfying and does the happy ending have to show that the couple had, or are definitely about to have, sex? Would Romeo and Juliet have stood the test of time if they had wandered off into the sunset hand in hand? I fear not.

Perhaps the most powerful love story is one which ends unrequited. Take love songs. They rarely end well. You may have noticed that most romantic novels are written by women, while the romantic lyrics in songs, which provide, I believe, a deeper connection to the soul (found, not in the heart but in the gut by the way) are written mostly by men. Take it from a doctor who has treated a great many people suffering from emotional issues, the part of the body that carries the burden of our emotional state is not the heart but the gut, hence the phrases, 'gut-reaction', 'I just knew in my gut', 'butterflies in the stomach', 'I was shitting my pants.'

To surmise, *But That's Not What I Meant* is an enjoyable read that ticked all the boxes that the majority of women in their middle years would expect to be ticked. But I will leave you with this. Goodbyes hurt the most when the story is not yet finished. Isn't this where a story of true love should end? Rosie tells me you're having difficulty with your present manuscript. She also tells me you love to sing. Perhaps you could pour some of that deeper emotion you find in your voice into your next novel and you may find it will start to come together in quite an unexpected way.

I would appreciate your thoughts on my thoughts.

Kind regards,
Gethyn

'E' Bluey
From: Aggie
To: Rosie

Date: 14 January

Hi, Rosie

Unfortunately, I did not swim naked in a midnight triste with the Dalai Lama (his loss!). I was in Wales on a singles canoeing holiday and it was bloody freezing – that Timotei advert has a lot to answer for (my nipples have never fully recovered!). As for the Dalai Lama – OK, it might be an exaggeration to say I *met* him, but I've certainly seen him from a considerable distance and listened to him speak. It was in London a few years ago, when he was giving a motivational speech (inner peace, world peace etc. etc.). It was a life-changing experience. I soaked it all in and can honestly say that I turned into a really lovely person after that (for at least a week, anyway).

Speaking of peace, I see from the news that we're edging closer towards war. I would hate to be in your shoes right now and to think, you volunteered too, you nutter. Regarding the bucket list, I'll give it some thought, but you can't get out of it that easily, Rosie Hughes. War zone or not, life is far too short to be lived vicariously through another. Use your imagination for goodness sake!

In other news, I spent the afternoon at Mum's flat today. It was not a pleasant experience, but I had to put some facetime in just in case I go to Scotland, which, I realise, I haven't told you about yet.

Basically, an old friend from uni (Casey) left Manchester a couple of years ago to run a café and smallholding in Appledart, which is a remote peninsula on the Scottish west coast. Out of the blue, Casey's partner, Shep, was asked to be on standby to step into a reserve place on the British Expeditionary Force in Antarctica – he's a geologist. It's the opportunity of a lifetime. The man who was scheduled to go has failed his medical and is waiting for the results of more tests. If Shep steps into the breach, Casey will go with him – next week! Casey wondered if I might like to go to Appledart and watch over the house for her for six months or even a year. I'm to feed the chickens, make shortbread, recite Burns to customers. Another lady who lives there is going to keep the café open for them and I would generally help out. I wasn't sure at first, but now I think I should jump at the chance, which is why I'm sucking up to Mum (you know she can't stand it when I go away but wants bugger all to do with me when I'm at home). She phoned last week to announce she was having a clear out and to see if there was anything I wanted. This is how the conversation went:

Me: You're having a clear out? Why?
Mum: Bergerac has finished on Sky.

Me: Well, what sort of thing are you getting rid of?

Mum: Everything.

Me: Everything?

Mum: Everything.

Me: Even the ornaments I bought you when I was little?

Mum: Yes.

Me (incredulous): What? All of them? Even the clog?

Mum: Yes, why not? I'm sick of having a mantelpiece covered in crap.

Me: But Mum, I bought you that clog on that school trip to Holland in 1982. I spent all my pocket money on it. And please don't tell me you're getting rid of that blue and white statuette of the flower maid holding the water bowl?

Mum: Which statue? The one with an arm missing or the one with no head?

Me: The one with an arm missing.

Mum: They're both going. Oh, I know you bought them for me darling, but the time has come for me to have ornaments on display that have all their limbs – is that too much to ask?

Me: But they *do* have all their limbs.

Mum: But not necessarily glued on in the right places. I've got a china doll that looks like Hamlet (she starts laughing – actually laughing – at this point), I've got corn-dollies with no heads, pot birds with no beaks and a cracked Old Mother Hubbard cup with no handle. It's embarrassing when people come round (absolutely no one goes round). Anyway, don't be so overly-dramatic.

You'll thank me when I'm dead and you're not lumbered with it all.

And that was that.

It's tragic. I'd have coped better if she'd said she was running off with the pop man (let's face it, it wouldn't be the first time). And what's worse, I stormed round there to rescue my memorabilia and now it's *me* who's got a mantelpiece full of crap and she's right – it looks like a TV set for the Hammer House of Horror. I bet your mum's loft is full of your old stuff – school reports, crap art work and everything. My mother has absolutely nothing of mine. She's an uncaring old trout AND (as I told her) she's even starting to look like one.

Hope all is good with you?

Love, Aggie

Bluey
From: Rosie
To: Aggie

Date: 15 January

Hi, Aggie.

Poor you. But I'm not sure your mum has quite reached 'old trout' status yet. Try to see her good points? Surely she has some?

I know I keep asking for favours, but can you buy me an MP3 player and I'll settle up with you when I get home? Everyone else seems to have remembered to bring music. And can you please put a couple of compilations on a disc for me, like the old-fashioned mixed tapes you used to do for us, and can one of the songs be *Forgotten Dreams*, by Leroy Anderson, and also the English version, *Life in Rosy Hues*. As you know it's a very special song to me, not just because Mum and Dad sang it when I was little (and because we nailed it as a duet masterpiece), but because it was also the 'slow dance' song at my wedding with Josh. Listening to it will be a kind of self-harm, but it'll match the mood I'm in right now.

Also, Mum and I made a pact just before I left. I said I would write to her with the truth of my situation – she knew I'd dumb the whole thing down for Dad. I said I would get letters to her via Mrs Jenkins at the Post Office, but can I send them via you, instead? Perhaps you could find an excuse to drop by and put the letter in her hand out of Dad's sight? Do you still bake? Maybe you could drop round with a cake? I know if you go to Scotland you won't be able to do this, but in the meantime if you could keep an eye on them I'd appreciate it. I'm sure Mum would love to see you. She was upset when you stopped coming round after the Simon thing.

Take care and please don't let your mum upset you. I don't think she means any harm.

Rosie

P.S. Regarding Scotland, you do know it can be even colder than Yorkshire up there, and you hate the cold, right?

'E' Bluey
From: Aggie
To: Rosie

Date: 18 January

Hi, Rosie

Jobs completed as requested. MP3 player dispatched. You'll find mainly upbeat tunes but with a few memories on there from our melancholic teens, and obviously Ella Fitzgerald – to remind you of me, and the snow shovel is in position. I do think listening to *La Vie En Rose* is a mistake, I know I find it difficult to listen without welling up thinking of our duetting days, but if it was my song with my ex-husband, I'd probably end up rocking in a corner (just sayin). Anyhow, your wish is my command, and it's on there as requested. I also downloaded an English translation version, which I think is lovely, although there really is no competing with Edith Piaf, is there?

I went on another date last night (internet, obviously). His card was marked from the off due to his terrible choice of pub. It smelt of stale beer and regret. And

remind me never to go for a meal on a first date again.
He ate like a wild animal and I really didn't like his
hands. It was not the best of nights (am I an unreason-
able cow-bag?). Truth is, I'm not sure about this whole
Internet dating malarkey. Mum is addicted to it and treats
dating websites like other people treat clothing catalogues
– tries something on for size then sends it back (worn).
I know, I'm a big fat hypocrite, but I'm not a mother yet,
she is. And surely there's a moral code that dictates
mothers should behave better than their daughters?

I'd love it if I could meet someone the old-fashioned
way, with eyes across a crowded room, just like in *South
Pacific* when that foreign chap - is he French? - sings,
Some Enchanted Evening. But that kind of thing never
happens to me. When *I* stare around a room hoping to
catch someone's eye I just look like I'm stalking my prey.
They're doing a spot of speed dating at a pub in
Huddersfield next week, so I might give that a go – *that's*
a crowded room after all (and Huddersfield is sufficient
distance from home to avoid the gossips).

Life here is just the same, except for the minor fact
that the village is now at complete loggerheads over the
school issue. Every time I go to the shop or the petrol
station I'm roped into the debate, but I can see both
sides and intend to keep well out of it. Having said that,
there's a meeting tonight in the village hall and I'll have
to go or that bloody Janet in the shop will scowl at me
every time I go in. But on the plus side, we may witness

the lobbing of rotten fruit and the burning of effigies, so it might be a worthwhile trip after all.

Well, must go. This book of mine won't write itself, more's the pity. Still no news on Scotland, but I really do hope I get to go.

Love, Aggie
P.S. Is Gethyn a bit of a cock?
P.P.S. I'm working on the bucket list for you – next one, swimming with dolphins!

Bluey
From: Rosie
To: Mrs Hughes (via Agatha)

Date: 18 January

Hi, Mum

Sorry it's taken me a while to write. I've been waiting for things to settle down a bit. The truth of the matter (and I'm still taking you on your word that you only wanted me to write the truth) is that we've embarked on an express train headed to war, and as the train builds momentum, the desert floor is definitely beginning to rumble with the vibration of western military might, and whatever the politicians are saying at home, I know with absolute certainty that this runaway train is moving too fast to stop now.

It's hard to describe how I feel about all of this without seeming cold because I feel utterly detached. Fox News plays on a constant loop inside the HQ tent, and it all seems so artificial. When the war starts, the guys I work with in HQ will dictate the pace of the operation. But just like the rest of the world, they too will watch the horror on the front line – just three kilometres away – unfold on TV. Try to imagine a tented prison – a prison with no showers, no light relief, no time off for good behaviour; a prison that is far too cold at night and far too hot during the day. And just like a prison, if I step outside I can see no horizon, no people, no life, just a wall of sand and it gets in, on and around everything.

I'll sign off there, but can you please send more wet wipes, sanitary towels (super-plus) and Tampax? I started taking the pill before I came out so I wouldn't get my period, but stupidly left the pills in the side pocket of my big rucksack which I ditched because it was too heavy, so I've missed taking the pill for a couple of days which means I'm bound to get my period in a week or so.

Thanks mum. I'm so sorry to be putting you and Dad through the worry of it all. I realise now how selfish it was of me to come.

Miss you both so much.

Love you, Rosie x

Bluey
From: Rosie
To: Aggie

Date: 18 January

Hi, Ag

Nooooo, Gethyn is not a cock. Not even a bit of a cock. He's lovely. He's just quirky and very intelligent. Why? Did he write to you? What did he say?

Things have changed quite a bit out here. We've left the American camp behind and have hit the Baghdad Highway and are now in the middle of the desert closer to Iraq. I sleep on a camp bed on the sand next to an army truck. It's still very cold at night and my sleeping bag just doesn't cut the mustard. I wear every item of clothing I have (which isn't much) and that just about keeps me warm enough. Please do not imagine me swanning around in Lawrence of Arabia style sand dunes. Imagine a flat landscape like Norfolk but covered in a layer of sand with black stuff (oil presumably?) rising out of it sporadically.

The Army have built a berm around our camp. A berm is a long pile of sand in the shape of a square pushed into a mound that wraps around the perimeter of the camp – a bit like an inverted moat. As we drove north from Kuwait city I noticed that the desert is strewn with abandoned berms – and litter – which is either dumped where it's created or buried by the Army. As far as toilets go, the army dig a deep trench then place a row of porta-loos across it. There's no bottom in the loo so your business goes straight into the trench.

Which brings me onto my biggest fear – losing my pistol. In order to drop my trousers, I have to take my belt off, which holds my holster (men do not have this problem) and I'm frightened to death I might drop the pistol into the trench. Losing your pistol is a serious offence. I think I'd be in less trouble if I shot The Queen.

I've just read the letter back and I've had to laugh at my moaning. I mean, what the hell did I expect conditions to be like? The Hilton? What a naïve fool I was. I have to stop feeling sorry for myself and see the whole process as an exercise in both self-discipline and learning to cope with very little.

That's all for now. Sorry I've nothing much to write about except toilets but I can't write any of the 'war stuff' or I'd be in trouble.

Love, Rosie

P.S. Meant to say, I'm gutted you didn't manage to solve the problem of Maria. But you're right, sod em.

P.P.S. Don't compare your mum with mine. No mum is perfect, although we do expect them to be, don't we? And you have not always been a model daughter either.

Remember when you went through your 'great women
of history' phase and paraded through Midhope dressed
as Boudica for a whole month (Boudica?? Couldn't you
have found someone a little more contemporary, or at
least a woman who shaved her legs and didn't carry a
sword?) – and don't even get me started on your Joan
of Arc antics.

'E' Bluey
From: Aggie
To: Rosie

Date: 19 January

Dear, Rosie Hughes

Fall to your knees this instant and pray for forgiveness
from the immortal one, you poor excuse for a woman,
you! Boudica was – without question – the most impressive warrior of either sex history has ever seen (and I
would kill for that mop of red hair!). You should have
been proud to dress like a warrior queen and have
unchecked body hair for a while - freedom!

So anyway, in other news, being chucked over for the
part of Maria was obviously meant to be. It's decided!
I'm closing the house up for six months and hot-footing
it to Scotland. I catch the train to Mallaig on the 23rd
and then a little man called Hector will meet me at the

pier with his boat and take me to Appledart. My mail will be redirected, so if you've already sent a letter to Yorkshire, don't worry, I'll still get it.

I can't wait to get away. Casey's café is called, *The Café at Road's End*, because it literally is at the end of one of the most remote roads in Britain because Appledart is only accessible by boat, or on foot across the Highlands. Perhaps I'm putting my writing career in jeopardy by going – perhaps it's subconscious–or actually completely conscious – sabotage. My latest novel is due for submission at the end of April, but focus eludes me at the moment, what with Mum popping round every two seconds and the village in uproar about the school and the proposed housing development, it's like a sodding war zone back here, never mind Iraq. I try to keep my letters to you upbeat, but I'm at a low ebb just now. God knows why I shagged that Irish bloke. Talk about desperate. Who flies all the way to Italy to meet a complete stranger? And even worse, who shags a stranger even though she doesn't really fancy him? I'm turning into my mother and it frightens me.

Sometimes I think my life is more unrealistic than my fiction. I'm approaching middle age, single and very lonely, and I can't see how that's going to change. I had some counselling last year, but it was a bit of a waste of time. I spent nearly a thousand pounds to come to a conclusion that I'm a fat old maid who nobody fancies.

But that's not the only reason for fleeing to Scotland. I've begun to despise sitting down in front of the laptop, but I have to keep the Isabella Gambini cash cow coming in to pay the mortgage. I also help Mum out financially, too. In my letters I've been playing the part of eighteen-year-old Aggie Braithwaite. I didn't want you to see the mess I'm in, but if you can fess up about your worries and heartaches, so can I.

My new address is: Skye View Cottage, Aisig, Appledart, Scotland.

My only regret in going is that I won't be able to take care of your mum and dad, as you asked. I'm so sorry, but I'll take them a cake before I go. I should never have kept away – your mum didn't deserve it, after everything she did for me when I was young.

Lots of love, Aggie

P.S. You asked if I want to have a baby. Yes, definitely. But I've often wondered if I would be the same sort of mother as my own, and if that were the case, I'd rather not perpetuate the appalling mamma gene pool. I take it you're asking because it's a subject that is troubling you?

'E' Bluey
From: Mrs Hughes
To: Rosie

Date: 19 January

Hello, Rosie, my love.

Agatha Braithwaite is leaving home again – did you know? She's going on some kind of yoga retreat for a while. I don't know what she's really up to, but from what I remember of Agatha, it won't be yoga. Her mother has come up with some fabrication that she's a ghost writer for a famous chef and she needs to find some space to write her latest best-seller. Do you think her mother is unhinged? She always was a little different, wasn't she? Anyway, I've told Mrs Jenkins you'll send your letters to me via the post office and she'll pop them round.

Dad's getting into a bit of a pickle. This school business is winding him up. I suggested he resign from the Board of Governors years ago and he's beginning to wish he had, but it seemed to fill the void after he finished working, not that he's ever really let go of his working life. Difficult to let go, really, after all those years. I don't think it helps that you're away, and nothing has been the same since Simon left. Look after yourself.

Love you,
Mum. x

Bluey
From: Rosie
To: Agatha

Date: 21 January

Hi, Aggie

Hey! Right now, I have much more in common with Boudica than you do, Agatha 'easy-life' Braithwaite! Remind me who is it that has a loaded pistol strapped to her constantly? And my armpit hair it almost a foot long – I could bloody-well plait it! And don't get me started on my bikini line and leg hair – it's me who is the Amazonian warrior goddess right now!

Anyway, have a safe trip to Appledart. You'll never believe it, but Josh and I went there once and walked the eight miles from our holiday cottage to find your friend's café and had a lovely meal. We watched the sun set over the Isle of Skye. It should have been the most romantic moment of my life, but I ruined it and ended up in a strop. You'll love it there.

Also, for what it's worth, you are not an old maid. You're gorgeous! You're the most lovable, kind person any (very lucky) man could ever know.

Love, Rosie
P.S. Yes, the ticking clock baby issue troubles me, but

more of that another time, perhaps. I'm sorry your life isn't all you would have it be, either – we make a right pair of sops, don't we? And don't worry about not looking after Mum and Dad for me, they'll be fine.

'E' Bluey
From: Aggie
To: Rosie

Date: 23 January

Dear, Rosie

Hurray! I've arrived in Appledart.

Predictably, Mum took umbrage at my decision to leave and is now refusing to interact with me in any way. She said it was yet another ridiculous moonlight flit and, oh, I'm dead to her, but I'm not too concerned. I've been dead to her at least four times before and somehow, I always manage a miraculous resurrection. Casey has already left for Argentina, but I'm too knackered to head to the cottage tonight so I'm staying at the pub. This evening is for eating food I don't have to cook and sleeping in a bed I don't have to make.

I spent the time on the train staring out of the window and thinking about my novel – where I want to go with it. As we left Glasgow, it struck me that I might be able to cobble together a story that ends with a life-affirming train journey. Oh, I know it's been done to death, but who cares, I just need an ending. You know the sort of thing. The rhythmic rocking of the carriage soothes the heroine's troubled mind as she rests her forehead on the cold window and gazes, unfocussed, at the landscape as it passes by. The landscape is a welcome stranger – it harbours no painful connection to the past. When she reaches her destination, the heroine steps off the train, glances around, finds the energy to smile at unfamiliar faces and, with the sudden realisation that all will be well, she takes a deep breath, grabs her bag, and disappears through a cloud of steam into a brighter future. But before leaving the platform, she takes one last look down the line, and with tears in her eyes she watches the train as it disappears into the distance. There can be no going back now, the train has gone; the ending has become the beginning (bla bla bla).

Having pictured myself as the heroine in my own story, I half-expected my own epic train journey (Huddersfield to Mallaig) to lead me to an immediate epiphany and a world of joy. I even booked myself onto the tourist steam train from Fort William to ensure the environment was as fitting as possible. As I walked onto the platform, I visualised myself as Ingrid Bergman in *The Inn of the Sixth Happiness* - kind and ethereal, but with fewer kids. My bubble burst, however, when I realised I was about to board the bloody Hogwarts Express. Dozens – scratch that – hundreds of kids appeared on the platform, all dressed in school gowns and jimmy wigs (homage to Ron Weasley, no doubt) flourishing twigs and shouting, 'expelliarmus'.

I wished they would!

I survived the journey by playing eye spy with the little girl sitting opposite. She was a dour little thing (either that or she was doing a spot of Hermione improv). An hour of mountains and moorland rolled by, and after a final, 'Something beginning with T', the train coughed out its last choo choo and we pulled into Mallaig station just as the rain began to pour. Determined to have my spiritual epiphany one way or another, I said a few expelliarmus' of my own and waited for the kids to disperse before getting off the train. But my old friend Disappointment continued to act as an overly keen travelling companion, and when I stepped onto the platform I noticed a buffer stop and it dawned on me that I would not be left standing in a cloud of steam next to Bernard Cribbins, after all. Mallaig is the end of the line.

You won't be surprised to hear that I've brought more baggage than one woman could possibly need. As I lugged my cases across the road to get to the harbour (of course, it *would* be raining) you popped into my mind and I gave myself a good talking to about travelling light - you survive in Iraq with nothing more than a change of clothes and a packet of baby wipes so why do I need all this stuff? These thoughts stayed with me and I visualised the excess of emotional baggage I'm also dragging in my wake which, in my imagination, was manifested as a great pile of tea chests pushed along by a little Indian boy dressed in traditional dress of the Raj (the boy had a gammy leg too, poor thing). It hit me as my eyes welled with tears (at the thought of the orphaned Indian child) that I really do need to have a break from my imagination for a while, or else I'm probably only one more bad metaphor from parting company with my mental health altogether.

Anyway, an old gentleman dressed in yellow wellies and a woolly jumper (so thick I wondered if he was actually just wearing a whole sheep), snapped me back into the real world by saying, 'Hello, you must be Agatha. I'm Hector. Let's get you on board', (how is it that some wonderful people manage to talk and smile at the same time?). He nodded towards a boat. A handful of tourists were already impersonating a tin of sardines stuffed into the boat's cockpit, hiding out of the rain. I made a right tit of myself embarking. My foot slipped and I'm still rubbing a twanged hamstring having fallen down the last three rungs of the ladder. There was no room for me in the sardine tin, but I didn't really care. My jeans were wet anyway. I perched my bottom on a lobster pot, rubbed my thigh and glanced into the cockpit, but immediately wished I hadn't. A young couple, clearly in love, stole a kiss. The man placed a protective arm around the lady's shoulder and at this point my eyes stung with tears, just as a goffer of a wave hit me side on.

But the wave that drenched me also acted as a slap across the face. The sea washed a lightness of spirit over me that took on an immediate effect, and as the boat edged away from the pier and we began to bounce high then low across the sea, I had an overwhelming sensation that all was going to be well. And it was definitely my overactive imagination, but when I looked back and saw the little Indian boy standing on the pier, gesticulating towards the pile of tea chests I had left behind, I ignored him, which was a little cruel, considering the limp. Instead, I turned to face forwards, looked at the mountains ahead and allowed my body to enjoy the rise and fall of the ocean. It was as if the angels were telling me to travel light this time, and it felt good.

Take care, darling Rosie. Write again soon.

Aggie

P.S. And don't worry, Casey has left her phone line connected, so I'll still be able to send eblueys on the internet, thank goodness.

P.P.S. Re Gethyn, didn't you read his review? I'm still thinking up my reply ...

'E' Bluey
From: Mr Hughes
To: Rosie

Date: 23 January

Dear, Babe

Your friend (the one who played the piano to accompany your violin) came round the other day. Oh, but she did make us laugh. She had Mammy in stiches when I went to the kitchen to put the kettle on. I could even hear them laughing over the noise of the kettle. Agatha told Mammy some cock and bull story about a camping trip she went on a while back. Apparently, she ended up stranded with a load of naturalists in a remote Welsh Valley during a hurricane – do you think she makes half of these stories up? She brought us a lovely cake, though. Triple layer! It's a shame Simon dumped her – she makes a bloody good cake!

Life goes on here as usual. Mammy had one of her appointments yesterday – routine stuff, nothing to worry about. It was good to get her out of the house. She's obsessed with watching the news and I can't stand it. I swear if anything happens to you she will kill Tony Blair. She spent two hours talking about you to the woman sitting next to us in the waiting area. I don't think there was anything that poor woman didn't know about you by the time she left, but at least Mammy chatted to a stranger, which is progress, you'll agree.

We're both hoping you'll come home to Yorkshire for good after this mess in Iraq is cleared up. You'll get a job somewhere round here, I'm sure. You could even go back to university to study something new, you're never too old, and you know me and Mammy will help out financially, where we can. Give it some thought, at least.

Love you, Babe.
KYHD
MumnDad xx

'E' Bluey
From: Agatha
To: Rosie

Date: 1 February

Dear, Rosie

I've completed my first few days in Scotland as an eccentric recluse and can confirm that Appledart is wet, windy and awash with hill walkers. But it doesn't matter, because the majestic hills and aquamarine seas are breath-taking whatever the weather, and the good news is that it stopped raining yesterday (I'm in tune with 'the little things' now, as you can see).

Disappointingly, I'm yet to meet a sexy, kilted Scotsman. In fact, there appear to be no Scotsmen here at all, with or without kilts, or, in fact, any single men within my accepted age bracket (which is widening as each year passes). The inhabitants of Appledart are an eclectic mix of international loners, all of whom (bar one, Ishmael) are over the age of fifty-five. Shaun (the landlord at the pub) owns the only vehicle on the peninsula (except for Hector's 1950's tractor, of course) and uses it to shuttle visitors between Aisig and Morir. He ferried me to the end of the road after my night at the pub.

As for Aisig – you didn't say what a little piece of heaven it really is. I met my neighbours on the first day. Firstly, there is Anya, a white witch in her early sixties who lives in the cottage next door to mine. She's not actually declared herself to be a witch, but the black cat, the well-used pestle and mortar and the deck of Tarot cards kind of gives her away. She's got a pixie cut, a fabulous dirty laugh and a sharp sense of both perspective and humour. I love her already. Then there's Ishmael, a poet, who is a little older than me. I have absolutely no idea how Ishmael found his way to Appledart or where he's from originally. His accent sounds eastern European. I must ask him. Is Ishmael a Jewish name? He's built himself a fab house with floor to ceiling windows overlooking the beach (I thought poets were supposed to be poor?). My cottage, on the other hand, is cosy but damp and dark, and is positioned next to the cafe and sits with its toes in the harbour. Anya likes whiskey, Ishmael does not.

Then there is 'the family' who live near the beach and are originally from Brighton. They provide the bay with a little noise and are *bitch alert* intensely annoying. They've been here since March having watched a few too many TV programmes about escaping to the country. He works from home (something to do with investments) and she flounces around drinking spinach smoothies and making art installations from beach finds. The kids are home-schooled, which means they get kicked out of the house at breakfast and are let back in at teatime (it's an OK life, I suppose). The kids, who have ridiculously posh names I can't remember, run into the café at some point every day, which feels like a tornado passing through. I usually shoo them out after about ten minutes (my tolerance of children has not improved).

The café is perfect (at least, now I've given it a bloody good clean, it is) – I'll be bumping that food hygiene certificate up to five stars, thank you very much! Anya has been keeping the place open, but with a limited fresh seafood option, which is disappointing for some of the visitors. Her stews are awesome, but her cakes are dry – she just doesn't put enough love into them, so as from tomorrow, *I'm* making the cakes! There are a dozen or so customers most days, thanks to Shaun and his Landrover, and even more if there's a walking tour passing through (luckily the type of people who go on walking holidays are also people who don't object to the weather in Scotland in the winter).

To surmise, I love it here, and the good news is there's no mobile phone signal which means that if I ignore their emails, I can hide from my publisher and from Isabella for weeks. But oh, Rosie, for the first time in years I don't feel lonely, even though I'm living so remotely. I suppose, because Anya and Ishmael live alone, and because I go to the café every day, we're all collectively alone, but together.

I've written out the bucket list and stuck it on the fridge (I added, 'drop a dress size, you fat cow – Aggie only') on the bottom of the list.

Anyway, that's my update. Stay safe, lovely lady.

Aggie
P.S. Ishmael is not for me AT ALL (if that's what you're thinking).

'E' Bluey
From: Agatha
To: Rosie

Date: 2 February

Hi, Rosie

I've just got back to the cottage after a stint at the café. The fire and the candles are lit, dinner is reheating on the hob (leftover chorizo and chickpea stew, care of Anya) and I'm going to settle down with a book. Who needs a man, eh? The cottage has a bookshelf full of fab titles, many of them classics, which means I can feel self-right-eous by progressing with the bucket list. Shall I send some out to you?

I've been so busy writing books over the last few years, I've practically stopped reading, and as you'll remember, reading was always my first love (strike that, my first love was and is baking, but reading comes a close second). Also, there's a lovely little piano that is almost in tune, so what with the books and the piano, I can at least start working towards two of my bucket list objectives!

The not so good news is that, despite travelling several hundred miles north to my self-imposed retreat, the writing still isn't flowing. I sit down in front of my laptop and perform my creative ritual every day – light a candle, place my Cornish pixie on the table next to me, and then begin. Only I don't ... begin, that is. It's time to get cracking with that bucket list – maybe it will bring me inspiration. I'm going to start with sending a message in a bottle, and I know exactly which message I'm going to send.

I'm going to sign off now as I want to email Mum. Wish me luck!

Loads of love,
Aggie

From: aggieb@yahoo.com
To: sexymamma@yahoo.com
Date: 2 February
Subject: Don't be mad at me, Mamma

Hi, Mamma

I know you'll be checking your inbox for Internet dating messages, so please don't pretend that you haven't read this. Firstly, I want you to know that I love you, but please try to understand that in coming to Scotland my main priority was to help my friend and yes, I admit, I wanted to get away for a while. But the important point is this: I needed to get away from my life, not from you. I need to understand why I'm no longer able to focus on my writing and, like you have always said, a change is as good as a rest. Do you remember my friend, Rosie – her brother was that boy I dated, Simon (and that isn't in any way a dig at you, I got over that a long time ago). Anyway, Rosie and I wrote a list of random things we wanted to do during our lives, one of them was to send a message in a bottle. I've decided to write my message now, cork it up, and send it out to sea. It will say, 'To whom this may concern: Give love today because tomorrow doesn't exist and yesterday is gone'.

Please pick up the phone when I ring, or maybe you could phone me? My number and address are on the card I left for you on my mantelpiece, next to the clog. Don't go quiet on me again, Mamma. You've done this too many times over the years and each time it hurts more than you can possibly imagine, because it makes no sense. Pick up the phone when I ring, please. I love you.

Agatha x

Bluey
From: Rosie
To: Mrs Hughes (via the Post Office)

Date: 2 February

Hi, Mum

You've probably guessed that I broke Dad's snow shovel. Aggie replaced it before she left for Scotland. Have a look behind the greenhouse. Also, Josh broke Dad's planer when he was sanding down the kitchen door at Rose Cottage, and, come to think of it, we may have nicked his adjustable spanner and wallpaper steamer too. I'll ask Josh to send everything back when he sorts the house out. Regarding Aggie, you're right, she isn't on a yoga retreat. She's gone to Scotland to look after a friend's café. I think a lot of her jolliness is a façade; truth is, she's very lonely. I wonder if she holds on too tight when she falls for a man. Simon said that's what she did with him which is why he left. He said it was a bit claustrophobic. Her mum is furious that she's gone away again and is refusing to communicate. They are almost as bad as each other, with Aggie repeatedly trotting off on a whim, and her mother wanting to keep her close but then acting like a child when she can't.

What's odd about Aggie's trip is that she's gone to Appledart – Appledart! Do you remember, it's where I took Josh for that disastrous holiday when I was pretending everything was OK? It's where I saw that famous psychic and, believe it or not, her prediction is one of the reasons I accepted the posting with the Army – she told me that one day I'd find peace in the desert. Wouldn't it be great, Mum, to stop the fog? To wake up each morning without that feeling of despair. To have a few hours where every single thing I see and do isn't shrouded with the cloak of Angelica's death?

Love you,
Rosie x

'E' Bluey
From: Mr Hughes
To: Rosie

Date: 4 February

Dear, Babe

It's been snowing buckets! But worry not, your friends at the Met Office got it right and so we did a big shop on Friday. We've hunkered down and can sit it out till April if necessary. There is some good news though; a couple of days ago my snow shovel materialised behind the compost heap. Strangest thing: it's got a red blade, not black, and the handle is wooden not cork. Mammy says I'm going mad but I'm sure it's not the same shovel. Anyway, it's a good 'un, wherever it's from. I had the drive cleared quick sticks (mammy was nagging me to get it done so the dog can still get out to have a pee). We've been watching Lovejoy on Sky Gold and are just about to have a splash of whiskey in our tea and then get to bed. This school business isn't looking good. The council want to cut their losses and build an extension at Oakworth Primary. Surely Oakworth is too far away for our poor little mites to travel every day. We're still fighting – the spirit of the Blitz is strong in Midhope. I told that councillor fella at the meeting, I said, 'The school is the heart of our little community, and if that goes, the village

78

will lose its soul'. For once it helps that the council is a slow old beast, so we've a while to wait for a decision. I shouldn't imagine we'll know what's to be done this side of May. Keep your fingers crossed and we'll save the old girl yet!

Love you lots babe and remember, KYHD.
MumnDad x

'E' Bluey
From: Agatha
To: Rosie

Date: 4 February

Hi, Rosie

It's official. I'm never leaving Appledart!

The cottage is lovely, but bloody cold. Some nights I sleep downstairs on the settee, in front of the wood-burner, which is cosy. But despite the cold, Nature is a good friend to me here (we were only on nodding terms in Yorkshire). I will admit, she lulled me into a false sense of security yesterday, but that's some friends for you. The sun, acting as a wrecker's lantern, encouraged me outdoors with an arm full of washing, pegs and a hatless head. Two minutes later, I was back out there in a squall, dragging the washing off the line, pegs flying everywhere, my hair stuck to my head. But on the whole, the cold is *not* keeping me indoors in Scotland, although I will admit that my cheeks and hands are taking the brunt of the breeze. I danced a little jig when I discovered a pot of Vaseline at the back of the bathroom cabinet the other day. Anya has given me a Shetland wool jumper to keep the wind at bay and what with my thermal-lined wellies and ear muffs, I'm good to go.

Why is it, do you think, that we eventually despise the familiar? I never could bear the wind at home. Oh, I know I imagined myself as Cathy searching for Heathcliff on the moors, but I never ventured out if it was *really* windy, and in my adult years, I've been known to stay indoors for a week, concocting bizarre meals from freezer-finds, if a spell of bad weather was passing through. And yet here, the wind - that very same bundle of energy - is a tonic to me and I rush to the beach to greet it every day. I do feel sorry for the chickens, though. They look as miserable as sin. I love all of them, except for one who has the beady-eyed glance of a psychopath. But the rest of my avian friends are all beaks, balls of fluff and twiggy legs. They've inspired me to write a little story called *No Room For Chickens*. Drumming up children's stories is a regular pastime at the moment as it's the only way to quieten down the annoying kids from the 'too good to be true' family. I give their faces a good wipe-down with the dishcloth and then tell them stories, the latest one being about a little boy who wants to smuggle his best friends – the chickens – on holiday with him. They loved it. Worryingly, it's the best story telling I've done in months!

Speaking of feathers, I'm still spitting some of my own. Your mate Gethyn believes me to be the obedient slave of a mediocre story-writing machine. Apparently, I bang out shallow tosh to satisfy the greed of uneducated masses, who wish for nothing more stimulating than a fast read of mindless drivel. He thinks I should write a book that reflects more accurately that complex, yet fascinating enigma often referred to as the 'human condition'. Ask him which human condition would he like me to write about next? Syphilis?

Anyway, must be off, but do kick Gethyn in the shins for me next time he passes your desk – don't worry if you aim higher.

With love, Aggie

P.S. Don't show him this.

P.P.S. Sod it, you can. I don't care.

P.P.P.S No, second thoughts, don't. I'm off to the café. I'm making Isabella's triple layer tropical coconut sponge today. I'll think of my response while I'm baking.

Melanie Hudson

'E' Bluey
From: Aggie
To: Gethyn

Date: 4 February

Dear, Gethyn

Thank you for your review which has taken me some time to digest. You asked for my thoughts on your thoughts. Here they are:

You say my novel is formulaic and lacks a degree of reality. I disagree. If romantic fiction is formulaic then life, too, follows a formula. For centuries humans in the western world have been raised from childhood to expect a stereotypical monogamous relationship. Christian religion, to a certain extent, has played its part in this by promoting marriage, but to be fair to Christianity, being married is surely preferable to living in a harem? On the whole, the lives of my readership follow a formulaic pattern: i.e. they meet a partner, fall in love (romance stage), marry, have children, stay together (or divorce when it gets boring) then die. The course of true love may or may not run smoothly during the 'fall in love' stage, and it's a good job love does not always run smoothly because 'smooth' does not make for an interesting read. It is far more fascinating if the couple concerned have a rough ride before the consummation of their relationship – and yes, by 'consummation', I mean sex. We want our protagonists to have to work for their reward.

Do you know that a reader becomes awash with endorphins when they close the final page of a feel-good book? This is the same physiological reaction we experience during orgasm (I suppose being a doctor you will know this). So, given the choice, wouldn't you prefer to have an orgasm than a headache?

Additionally, although the structure of a romantic novel may be formulaic, the characters and their particular transformation are not. Every story ever told is, at its core, about the transformation of the hero and any story written in the modern day is merely a retelling of past works (I believe Aristotle came up with this particular hypothesis) and with my hand on my heart (or if it makes you happier, my gut) I can assure you that a great deal more thought goes into the creation of a romantic novel than you might think. Having said that, my fiction is a reflection of my own experiences and I do not overthink my stories and the fact that I choose to give my characters happy endings is not just a publishing requirement, but also a matter of personal choice. Isabella's readers are not looking for a book to throw against the wall with utter frustration because half the characters are dead or mutilated by the end of the story – they want a satisfying resolution (Jane Austen got away with it, so why can't I?). In sum, I agree that

Melanie Hudson

in real life, not everyone is blessed with a happy ending, although, unless you are very unlucky, I believe life is a series of endings followed by beginnings interspersed with love, laughter and a little bit of tragedy along the way (the length of the road is, I admit, the one variable we cannot necessarily control).

I will leave my thoughts there. I don't expect you will be reading any of my other books in the near future, but I am glad to have provided a little light entertainment on what, as you say, would otherwise have been for you a dreary afternoon.

Regards,
Agatha

P.S. Although the gut is the place in the body where emotions are stored, a Valentine card with a picture of a twisted gut on the front (perhaps with an arrow through it and little a cherub vomiting while mopping up human faeces) would not, I suspect, sell well. So, for the sake of aesthetics, can I ask you to acquiesce and accept the heart as the universal image of love?

P.P.S. I cannot abide Romeo and Juliet.

84

'E' Bluey
From: Mrs Hughes
To: Rosie

Date: 4 February

Dear, Rosie

How are you holding up, my little love?

It's been a difficult week here. Dad had a bit of a run-in at the shop on Wednesday. Old Mr Butterworth was buying his paper like he does every morning, and Dad had popped down for a box of biscuits because the vicar was coming around for tea (he wanted to do a pastoral visit because you're away with the Army and Dad hadn't the heart to say no).

Anyway, it's a sorry tale, but the abridged version from Dad is that he overheard Mr Butterworth telling Janet about how he'd written to the Prime Minister to complain about the war – and that apparently, we're no better than the Nazis. Dad was standing behind the bread trolley and out of eyesight but I'm sure Mr Butterworth would never had said anything if he'd known Dad was there. Dad lost his temper and said (amongst other things according to Janet who told the vicar), 'No one calls my daughter a Nazi, you silly old fool,' which isn't like Dad. Mr Butterworth got upset and had to sit down. He said he hadn't meant to offend anyone but was entitled to his opinion. They had a blazing row during which time Dad told him he was being disloyal to the troops and then Dad had to have a sit down too. Janet called for the doctor and somehow the vicar called into the shop on his way to our house and they all had a cup of tea.

Dad went off metal detecting for the rest of the day – in the snow, he *is* a silly old fool – and I sat with the vicar talking about the school. The reason I'm telling you all this is because Mr Butterworth has asked the vicar for your address. He wants to write to you. Maybe you could pop a note back to him in the post, he is ninety-two, after all, and he was in a POW camp.

    Love you,
    Mum x

'E' Bluey
From: Aggie
To: Rosie

Date: 4 February

Dear, Rosie

Summation of week two:
    Number of words written: zero
    Number of cakes made: ten
    Number of cakes eaten: ten

Number of hours spent beachcombing with Anya's cat (who follows me around and freaks me out): about forty

Fuck-a-doodle-do!

I tried to buckle down to a spot of (Sunday night homework) crisis writing on Wednesday but spent three hours staring out of the window watching a boat with a red sail jib towards Skye. Eventually the sailors gave up, but credit to them, they gave it their best shot. It struck me that I'm in exactly the same situation – luffed up. No matter how much a person bangs away at something, if the wind isn't with you, it's best to drop your sails, go home and try again another day. So, in harmony with the sailors, I closed my laptop down, put my wellies on and went back to the beach, once again leaving my poor characters bobbing around in limbo. As I closed the laptop lid I could actually see the heroine looking up at me saying, 'Where the fuck do you think you're going?' (she's not what you might call, erudite). Some characters are so bloody needy, it's suffocating.

But the good news is that I still love my little cottage, although I'm rarely in it. What with walking to Morir and back a few times a week for rations (Anya gets me to cleanse her crystals in the river while I'm there) and helping out at the café every day, I haven't got the time to feel guilty. Speaking of Anya, I hadn't appreciated just how busy (and famous) she is. Get this: Anya (purveyor of dirty laughs and rude jokes) is also an internationally-renowned fortune teller (so I was right, she is a witch!). Who'd have thought it? Tourists flock on pilgrimage to see her (when I say flock, this is Appledart, so I mean she gets about five punters per week) but at fifty quid a pop it's not a bad little earner. Can you imagine how lost you would have to be to come all the way to Appledart just to cross someone's palm with silver? I've asked her to read my cards – she won't. Friends are taboo, but she says I have a bright yellow aura around me, so that's nice (at least, I hope that's nice?).

We've had a couple of days of fine weather. Anya's two horses, Jekyll and Hyde, live in one of the fields next to my cottage. Jekyll is a Shetland pony and Hyde is a girt-big shire horse. Jekyll is the boss, which is brilliant. It's a rare day the sides of my jeans aren't smeared with horse dribble. They get into a shitty mood if I don't have a little something sweet for them in my pocket whenever I wander past. My lemon drizzle goes down a treat, but it's hilarious because I swear Hyde pulls that face when the sour of the lemon hits that spot behind the back of his jaw!

Well, cakes to make so ta ta for now.

Love, Aggie

P.S. Don't think I'm not keeping track of events in Kuwait. We don't get newspapers here, but I do listen to the radio every day. I haven't heard from you in a while. Hope you're ok.

P.P.S. Oh, and I'm going swimming with dolphins tomorrow, just for you (yes, in *this* weather!).

Handwritten Letter
From: Mr Butterworth
To: Rosie
Date: 4 February

Dear, Rosanna

I hope this letter finds you well and that you are bearing up during your spell away with the Army.

I wanted to write a short note to say that we are thinking of you. Your father and I had an altercation in the shop and I would not have you believe that Mrs Butterworth and I are not fully supportive. However, I cannot say that I am in agreement with the Prime Minister's stance in Iraq and have written to Downing Street to state my objection to the deployment of our troops. I pray Mr Blair listens to reason and the situation does not escalate to war. I know the reality of conflict. But as horrific as our situation in 1942 was, at least we knew we were fighting the Hun. I feel it is easier for a soldier to put his life on the line when the enemy is clearly defined, but I'm not convinced this is the case in Iraq. I hope I am proven wrong, but at ninety-two, I will probably not live long enough to find out. Despite my objections, please do know that we are proud of you – all of you.

Take good care.
Edward and Margery Butterworth

Bluey
From: Gethyn
To: Agatha

Date: 5 February

Dear, Agatha

Thank you for your reply which gave me great food for thought. I'm concerned I may have crossed a line. If so, I apologise. I'm in the habit of writing papers on medicinal matters and have become used to issuing blunt and, perhaps, detached opinions. I am enjoying our discussion, though, and was wondering if we could continue with our correspondence? War is a funny old business and the distraction is refreshing.

In your reply you said that your writing is a reflection of your own experiences. If so, one of the books you sent to Rosie is called *Millionaire's Muse*, does this mean you have at some point been the muse of an eccentric millionaire? If yes, did you really pose naked in front of the Eifel Tower, or was that artistic licence?

Yours, Gethyn.
P.S. You are quite wild with your use of quotation marks. Is this an occupational hazard?

Dear Rosie Hughes

'E' Bluey
From: Mr Hughes
To: Rosie

Date: 5 February

Dear, Babe

We had the Jehovah's Witnesses round today. They'd heard you've gone to war and took it as an angle to get in. Mammy felt sorry for them and let them get a toe in the door. I couldn't stomach it so went out with the metal detector. I went to Bickersthwaite – I swear there's a Roman hoard buried there somewhere. As usual I didn't notice at the time slipping away and my feet went numb in the snow and I've picked up a bit of a chill. Mammy says it's gone onto my chest and wants to book me into the doctors, but there's no point. You have to know two weeks in advance that you're going to be ill in order to get an appointment when you need one, and you've got to be practically dead to get antibiotics now-a-days, so I'll give it a miss.

The dog went for a shampoo and set yesterday afternoon. Looks a treat and smells sweet too - although the first thing she did when she got back was to scrape out the soil for a new nest for herself in the snow under the hedge between us and next door, scruffy little bugger. Her nails had grown quite a bit so they gave them a trim. Can't think how they could have grown considering the amount of digging she does.

Oh, I found a lovely silver bangle at Bickersthwiate. It was under a big old English oak at the edge of a field. It's Victorian. Wonder who it belonged to? I'll post it out to you, it's yours now. Luvyababe. KYHD

Mumndad xxx.
P.S. Meant to tell you, when I'm dead my best spade goes to you. Mammy thought it should go to Simon, but he'd just let it go to rust. It's got a lovely handle on it. You'll have another garden again one day, my love, and you'll dig up your veggies with my spade and you'll lean on it and take a moment and remember your old man who spent hours and hours walking the fields, looking for an elusive pot of gold with that very spade in his hand.

'E' Bluey
From: Agatha
To: Rosie

Date: 5 February

Dear, Rosie
Well, that's another thing on the list ticked off – swimming with dolphins. Although I didn't exactly see any dolphins, but I'm sure they were with me in spirit (we did caveat that seals were 'as good as' dolphins, didn't we? And I did see a seal pop his little head up about

half a mile away, although it could have been flotsam as I didn't have my glasses on).

To explain; Shep and Casey put out some lobster pots last year, but they must have forgotten about them in their rush to leave Appledart. The pots were annoying some of the Mallaig fisherman (don't ask) and needed fetching in. But two of them had got caught up in a buoy, which meant someone needed to dive in and untangle everything. That 'someone' was yours truly (Anya is frightened of lobsters and Ishmael can't stand the feel of a wetsuit on his skin - it takes all sorts). I looked like a bloody whale, but at least that's something else ticked off the list, and believe it or not, I kind of enjoyed it, although Ishmael (who rowed me out to the pots) was not impressed when I accidentally (on purpose) soaked him through. I felt fresh. I felt invigorated. I felt alive (and I'll NEVER do it again!).

And so, life, basically, is good. I'd forgotten the joy of meeting people and I bloody love it. The café is such a relaxing place to be, with the wood-burner going and the music on, and what with baking cakes and nattering to the tourists, I haven't the time to ponder. Visitors tend to fall into the café – exhausted but happy – and the ones who have a 'bottomless coffee' tell me all kinds of things, too (stuff you would normal confess to a priest rather than talk about to a random stranger). Anya says it's my golden aura (I've progressed from yellow to gold) that lulls them in. But the recipe to success when it comes to loosening lips is my lethal combination of rounded hips, a big bosom and tempting cake. People simply can't help but tell me their secrets.

But oh, Rosie, I've heard some upsetting stories, and it's a rare day I'm not crying with a customer by mid-morning and laughing hysterically with the same person by mid-afternoon. I could fill a book with all the stories – several books, in fact. But I've adopted the café owner's Hippocratic Oath. And anyway, real life is far too crazy and full of bizarre coincidences to be believable in fiction, so my lips are sealed. I think I've edged Anya out of the café a little bit, but she doesn't mind. Anya is one of those calm beings who maintains a steady oneness with the universe. I'm sure the tides flow to *her* bidding, not the moon's (although her magic muffins may be helping the rest of us to be taken under her spell). She always has a couple hidden under the counter for visitors who are in extra need of kind-heartedness, and I can't help but polish off the crumbs!

The less positive news is that I finally found the courage to open my inbox. Isabella Gambini emailed twice this week, and my publisher three times. Thank goodness there's no mobile phone signal here. Neither of them says it, but both have hinted towards a question mark hanging over my mental health. I haven't emailed back. How can I? There is absolutely no point asking for an extension to the deadline because I've come to the conclusion that I'm all written out. In the past two weeks I've begun to remember what it's like to spend a decent part of the day conversing with friends – ones who aren't imaginary, and I like it. I have nothing to give to Isabella right now and especially not erotica. Also, if I was already suffering from a crisis of confidence, Gethyn's email was the death nail. The thought of writing one more love story makes me feel utterly depressed. But I do wish I didn't have their emails hanging over me, and I wish I had the moral courage to write back. But seriously, who will ever find me here? I could hide away forever, or until the money runs out, which, if I don't keep writing, will be very soon the way my mother spends it. Hope you're safe.

Lots of love,
Aggie

Bluey
From: Rosie
To: Aggie

Date: 6 February

Hi, Aggie
Sorry I haven't written this week. HQ has moved location, but it's all the same shit, same sand, same people.
Sea swimming in February? Are you sure you really are the Agatha Braithwaite I once knew? Truly, though,

I'm so jealous. What I would give to feel so free. But I am feeling joy knowing that our list is pushing you on, so keep going and remember – your joy is my joy.

We had a sandstorm yesterday (thank God I forecasted it). I stepped out of HQ during the thick of the storm in the hope of finding the portaloo, which was a big mistake. I only stepped away from the tent for a moment but became completely disorientated in the blowing sand. It was so frightening, and I did the worst thing possible: desperate for a pee, I kept walking away from the security of the tent. By absolute luck, or perhaps sixth sense, I literally bumped into a portaloo and managed to prise the door open against the wind and hide inside till the worst of the storm passed. Gethyn bought me an Arabian scarf when he went to an American camp in Kuwait City a couple of weeks ago. Thank God I was wearing it. Despite wrapping it around my head a few times, I had to pour water from my bottle into my eyes which were red and streaming, just to be able to see. The moral of this little story I suppose is this – it's one thing forecasting bad weather, but another thing entirely to know how to operate in it.

But back to something more normal, I'm sorry Gethyn annoyed you – it's probably my fault. I told him you were desperate for an honest review and that the male perspective would be refreshing. Sorry if I've made things worse. He's a good bloke – honestly.

Love, Rosie

P.S. You'll say, 'Get lost, no way,' but I've met Anya, too. She read my cards when Josh and I were in Appledart. She's proven to be incredibly accurate so far, unfortunately.

From: aggieb@yahoo.com
To: sexymamma@yahoo.com
Subject: Seriously, Mamma. Don't do this again.

Date: 6 February

Hi, Mamma

I've phoned several times, but you never pick up – why? I know you're OK because I phoned the post office and they said you've been in. I know you're upset, but just email me and tell me why you've gone quiet. I can feel your hostility from here and it's putting a bad smell on my time in Appledart and I really don't want that to happen – not this time. I'm sorry if my going away upset you but I'm having a lovely time. Please be happy for me. I love you unconditionally. Can't you do the same for me?

I'll phone again tonight.

Love you,
Agatha x

'E' Bluey
From: Aggie
To: Rosie

Date: 6 February

Helloooo from sunny Appledart!

Actually, it's been sleeting all week and I've been in a depressed haze regarding my writing crisis. But it doesn't matter because Anya tells me that she's sent angelic beams of divine light to shine down on me, which is handy.

I found a self-help book on Anya's bathroom window-sill called *Be Careful What You Wish For*, and I'm certain it's going to turn my life around. The gist of the book is this: the universe will provide me with everything I want/need/desire, all I have to do is ask for it - who knew life was so easy? If the author, *Summer Santiago* (hmm) is correct in her assumptions, to find the man of my dreams all I have to do is write down his character on a piece of paper and, hey presto, he'll appear by my side. No time scale was placed on the manifestation of my wishes because Anya says angels refuse to work to deadlines.

But there is a bit of a catch. When I write down my wishes, preferably on recycled paper, it has to be on the night of a full moon (there's a surprise) and I have to bathe the paper in moonlight for at least an hour before burning the arse out of it. I suppose the plan is scuppered if it's cloudy. Do you think using Vesta matches dilutes the magical effect of the moon? Should I use flint? I'll admit to being a tad sceptical regarding Summer's hypothesis. After all, I write things down for a living and none of the men in my books have materialised. But, nothing ventured nothing gained, I suppose. I'm going to have a productive afternoon writing down all the character traits of my dream man, warts and all. Oh, shit, if the universe is listening right now, I'm just kidding about the warts (jeez, you have to be so careful with this stuff). I'm not going to be unrealistic, though. I'll ask for a run-of-the mill, loving and kind man (who just happens to have great abs and a villa in Florence).

We're going to light a fire on the beach tonight and perform the ritual then. It's not quite a full moon, but Anya says the universe doesn't care if the moon is full, that's just for health and safety purposes so you can see where you're going in the dark. With any luck, my soul mate will wander into the café tomorrow and our eyes will cross over my pert meringues and that will be that, job done. Ishmael is coming along to the beach tonight, but he's going to do a spot of night fishing and watch us from a distance (he's a bit too inhibited to dance around a fire and chant) but I think he's worried we might set ourselves ablaze so needs to keep an eye out and a bucket of sand handy – a bit daft as we'll be surrounded by sand and next to the sea, but it's nice for someone to care. Ta ta for now.

Love, Aggie

'E' Bluey
From: Aggie
To: Rosie

Date: 7 February

Hi, Rosie

Me again. Well, it's 1a.m. and I am far too hyped-up on caffeine to sleep.

So ... I wrote down a list of everything I wanted my dream-man to be. This was a harder afternoon's work than you might imagine. At first, I tried to steer away from the romantic hero type and dreamt up a normal man – he was called Jason. Unfortunately, by the end of the afternoon, Jason was drowning under a sea of potato peelings in the compost bin. He was so bloody boring I fell asleep on the counter just imagining him. I decided to seek expert advice from Ishmael, who was fixing his fishing nets on the beach, and after having argued it down to the bone, Ishmael said I should just wait and see who I naturally fall in love with – hopefully, a nice, faithful, run-of-the-mill fella, and to forget magic.

Pah!

I told him that I don't bloody-well want a run-of-the-mill fella and if this is my one chance to manifest my hero, then, fuck it. I'm going to conjure up the best damn stud monkey I can dream of!

By 7p.m. I was still sat in the café with my pen wedged

between my teeth and staring at a scrappy piece of paper sitting on the counter (I crossed out fewer errors on my O level maths paper) and at 9p.m. Anya dragged me out of the café (her halo had slipped a bit) saying she'd got the fire to its peak and I would just have to go with what I'd got. So, we went outside and bathed *the man with no name* (ooh, book title?) in the exotic power of the moon for half an hour. Summer Santiago said to bathe him for a full hour, but there's only so much dancing and chanting two women can do, especially wearing wellies, ear muffs and Argyle jumpers. Eventually we rolled him into a thin taper and set him alight, but then, suddenly, when the taper had burned half-through, I panicked, blew it out, ran back to the café, put him on the draining board and stared at the words, *must have good girth*. Anya gave up at this point and went home to watch Morse on Sky.

The reason I panicked is this: I suddenly thought, 'What if it all comes true?' What if Mr Perfect really does pitch up? The book isn't called, *Be Careful What You Wish For*, for nothing, and if there's one thing I'm aware of when it comes to dreaming up characters, it's that the hero should be adorable, but flawed, and my dream man had absolutely no flaws. I realised, hopefully in the nick of time, that I didn't want the universe to give me Mr Perfect Pants after all (hmm, another book title) because I'd have to pretend to be *Mrs* Perfect Pants, and I'm not sure I can pull that off. For example, can

Mrs Perfect Pants accidentally fart in her husband's company and look up to the sky and say, 'Did you just hear thunder?' Can she have bat wings, or one eye pointing marginally in the wrong direction (why why why didn't mum get me an eye patch when I was little?) and a penchant for fantasising about Monty Don while watching telly and sucking out the insides of a Ferrero Roche?

No, she cannot.

And after twenty years of living with the human embodiment of Barbie's Ken, I would look up to the sky and say to the universe, 'Seriously! What were you thinking sending me *this* perfect piece of shite?' And the universe would shrug and say, 'We told you to be careful what you wished for, you twat.'

Anyway, I made sure the flame was completely out by stamping on it, which has left a terrible black mark on Casey's tiles. But now I'm worried because I did perform a mini-ceremony, and what if that ceremony generated enough magic to have him pitch up, but not enough magic to have him manifest exactly as requested, which would mean that I'd be lumbered, not with Mr Perfect Pants, but a *mutant* version of Mr Perfect Pants ...

This way lies madness

Ciao, gorgeous
Aggie

Bluey
From: Rosie
To: Aggie

Date: 8 February

Hi, Aggie

You are a complete nutter, but I love you. Has Mr
Perfect Pants shown up yet?

I'm sorry you're having a crisis of confidence with
your writing. I know it's probably no consolation, but I
loved *But That's Not What I Meant* – I couldn't put it
down. Also – and you're going to faint when I tell you
this - but Gethyn got his mum to send him copies of *all*
your books. Yes, all of them! I know, bonkers. I think he
feels guilty because of the review. You should see his face
when he's reading your stuff – tickled to death is the
best way to describe it.

Anyway, Gethyn and I had a good hour thinking about
the bucket list last night (he wants in) and decided that
we can at least try to bang some out while we're here.
These are the ones we think we can manage:

1. River-dance – Gethyn reckons we should save this
for our last day here but believes it's truly doable – can't
see it myself.

2. Watch one sunrise and sunset together.

3. Do a flick-flack or at least do a flip on a trampoline
(Gethyn has a plan for my training schedule).

4. Do one thing we are both afraid of (not difficult out here. It's a frightening place every single day).

5. Sleep under the stars (nailed it already).

6. Send a message in a bottle (hmmm? I only see sand).

Nothing much else to tell you. Preparing for war is pretty boring which means I have lots of time to think, which is exactly what I wished for when I decided to come here, but it seems that having an abundance of time to think is terrible as it serves to clog-up the mind even more. There's talk that, once the war starts, HQ would most probably be taken out by either a terrorist or a chemical attack. Well, that's certainly something to look forward to! Please keep the news from Appledart coming in.

Love, Rosie

'E' Bluey
From: Andrea Evans, Midhope on the Moor
To: Rosie

Date: 8 February

Dear, Rosie.

You probably won't remember me, but it's Andrea Jones. I sat next to you in geography class in the fifth form. I work at the shop now. I know Janet has written but I wanted to write too and say how much I admire you for going away with the Army and for what you've achieved in your life (your dad is very proud of you and we hear everything about you in the shop).

Not much to tell you about my life. I didn't get a proper job after school. I married Kev Evans and had a family. We bought one of the new houses they built on the rec. We've got four kids so I'm pretty much run-ragged. We split up a couple of years ago. He's living with Abbie Peterson now, but he has the kids at some point every week, he's good like that.

You got it right, I think, having a career first. I've done nothing with my life. I always wanted to be a nurse, but Kev said I was too shy and soft and should stay at home with the kids. Anyway, it's too late now and even if it wasn't, how could I train for a new job when I've got my kids to look after? I'm not surprised you've done well. You were always so pretty and clever. I remember your mum always bought you lovely shoes.

Anyway, I just wanted to say that I'll never forget how nice you were to me in school. Not many people wanted to sit next to me because of my alopecia, but you always did, which was kind. Are you still in touch with Agatha Braithwaite? She comes in the shop quite a bit now she's moved back to Midhope. She's gone off somewhere again (like she does). Nobody really knows where she's gone. There was talk of Scotland but then someone else said she's in prison for fraud. Her mother looks dreadful.

Janet can't stand Aggie, but I can. She always makes me laugh! Look after yourself.

Love, Andrea

'E' Bluey
From: Aggie
To: Gethyn

Date: 8 February

Dear, Gethyn
    In answer to your questions:
    1. I wasn't offended by your review, I simply disagreed with your hypothesis.
    2. Yes, I was a muse – to an artist. He had cataracts and needed to 'feel' my form rather than just look at it. He was rich in cash but not in spirit. He was not particularly eccentric, either, that was artistic licence. He was, however, fairly romantic (money helps with classic romantic gestures as poor men cannot afford to be romantic) but I didn't like his kisses (imagine a conga eel feeding on a melon and you're there) so that was that.
    3. Quotation marks are hardly a hazard (although I was almost decapitated by a giant exclamation mark once). Surely the use of quotation marks is better than writing, 'ooh er, missus' each time a double entendre is suggested?
    Regarding any future correspondence, I have never

been regarded as a distraction before and I'm not sure I'm happy with this terminology. Writing letters eats in to my busy schedule and I have no wish to be abandoned once you are no longer in need of distraction. If you can confirm that our correspondence is something you take seriously as opposed to using me as a temporary form of entertainment, I shall correspond.

Regards,
Agatha

'E' Bluey
From: Aggie
To: Rosie

Date: 9 February

Hi, Rosie.

It's late afternoon and I'm sitting in my cottage looking across to Skye. I love this time of the day - the still time - when the birds are thinking about settling down after a last flurry of excitement, when it's not quite dark but not light either. The sea is a lovely translucent evening blue – that colour which is a perfect mix of blue and pink – and the lights in the tiny villages on Skye are just beginning to twinkle. Anya says twilight is nature's way of putting mammals and birds (and everything else that scamps about on the planet) in a calm place before bedtime – like Horlicks or Camomile tea. But most humans have stopped noticing how everything, even the sea, takes a little time out at twilight, which is a shame. Have you noticed that we rush around at the most calming times of the day? If we were more in tune, rush hour would become meander hour; wouldn't that be lovely?

But I'm melancholic because twilight is a special time for me. I can't help but think of Mum and those lovely years when I was little. She used to stroke my hair and sing me a bedtime song; I insisted on the same song every night:

Just a song a twilight, when the lights are low,
And the flickering shadows, softly come and go,
Tho' the heart be weary, sad the day and long,
Still to us at twilight, comes Love's old song.

Maybe I should grab my coat and enjoy the last dregs of twilight – go roaming in the gloaming, as 'twere.

Love, Ag

Bluey
From: Gethyn
To: Aggie

Date: 9 February

Dear, Agatha

But you *were* a distraction – a welcome one. I should have been attending a meeting with the Chief of Staff, but I became so engrossed in your letter I missed the beginning of the meeting.

Back to our discussion. I agree, the same stories are indeed told over and over again (nothing is new under the sun) and they can be as individual as they are timeless. But I've been giving some thought to the formulaic element of the romantic novel and feel that it is, on the whole, a story arc that acts as a disservice to women.

To explain: the classic idea that a stereotypical romantic male – the hero – will ride up on his charger (after a great number of obstacles have been scaled) and rescue the damsel in distress, only serves to perpetuate the idea of the white knight. I do not believe men can live up to this stereotyping. Are romantic novels setting men up to fail? And weren't white knights, in actuality, dark characters? Men do not have the same mental processes or hormonal fluctuations as women, we do like to please and are capable of falling in love, however.

So, what happens when we meet a woman we really like? We pursue her (men like to pursue) but in our pursuit we know women have a set idea of what constitutes romance and we endeavour to meet this need and expectation, even though it is all just a temporary act to satisfy the ego of the woman in the eyes of her peers. Inevitably, the man becomes settled into the relationship and the artificially heightened romance phase (which was an unnatural process to him in the first place) falls away. Funnily enough, the woman becomes disenchanted when his true persona comes to the fore. Ah, and that's another point, I am not comfortable with the use of the phrase, 'happy ending' – use of inverted commas allowed in this case, I feel. Rather than saying that a book or a film has a happy ending, shouldn't we all agree to say that there is a pre-requisite in contemporary romantic fiction for the main protagonists in the story to achieve an acceptable outcome by the end of the book, whereby the reader believes that such an outcome will lead to the continued happiness and contentment of the hero beyond the remit of the story?

Regarding your writing style, if art reflects life, then you, Agatha, are the hero in your own story, and if all stories are the same (an ongoing journey of transformation) shouldn't you also keep pushing yourself further to enable your own personal growth?

Yours,
Gethyn

P.S. I disagree that poor men cannot be romantic. Perhaps the crux of the whole issue is that we differ in what constitutes as romance.

P.P.S. You were happy to be a muse to a millionaire but not happy to be a distraction to me.

P.P.P.S. You said you were almost decapitated by a giant exclamation mark. Can you expand on this?

P.P.P.P.S. Harems can be hugely successful blueprint for living harmoniously, but that is a discussion for another time, perhaps.

P.P.P.P.P.S. Something about you has led me to be unacceptably frivolous with postscript. I hope you write again soon.

Bluey

From: Rosie
To: Aggie

Date: 10 February

Hi, Aggie

It's midday and I'm sitting on a sandbag in the sunshine drinking tea, and for once, I have great news.

We finally have a tent of our own!

Gethyn managed to procure (OK, steal) a tent for us to sleep in. He's refusing to say where it came from, but it's American and Gethyn is very good at cards.

Honestly though, Ag, what an absolute relief it is to have a home of our own. I don't have to sleep next to a lorry and fold my bed up every morning and can leave my kit in one place. I still go to the wash tent to get water from the bowser for a wash, but at least I can have a quick 'baby wipe' clean-up in private now, although, to be fair to the guys out here, I often think that they are more embarrassed than the handful of women who also use the wash tent. This time away with the Army seems to be teaching me how to become indifferent to being a woman. Although, most of the men here definitely see me as a woman first, then as a northerner (so sick of having my accent mimicked), and then as a met forecaster – 'here she is, Little Miss Sunshine, the weather girl'. My life here is more challenging physically than if I was a man, but luckily my navy days taught me how to be resilient. I'm fed, watered, I don't have to shoot anyone (hopefully) and as long as I stay determined to cope with it all, I'm sorted.

In other news, it's really hotting-up out here, and I would know as I have to read the temperature out to the troops every day. The operational tempo is hotting-up too, which has led to the army digging out trenches around the HQ for us to jump into if the war should suddenly start, but they just look like empty mass-graves to me.

What news from Appledart? Has your soulmate manifested (or has anyone pitched up who you might even just snog?). I think it was a good idea to help out at the café. A handsome backpacker is bound to pitch up at some point, or a mysterious foreigner, perhaps? Hope so.

Write soon.
Love, Rosie

'E' Bluey
From: Aggie
To: Rosie

Date: 14 February

Hi, Rosie

Happy Valentine's Day!

That's fab news about the tent. I suppose I shall have to cut Gethyn some slack as he came up with the goods (although it pains me to say it). Did he tell you we're continuing with our correspondence? I'm writing because he is one of our chaps 'at the front' and so deserves my gratitude, although I'm yet to be convinced he isn't a bit of a cock.

The fire ritual on the beach worked (kind of). Within a day of the ceremony I did indeed have a date. His name was Sven, a Marine Biologist from Sweden (honest to God that was his name and profession, even *I* wouldn't create someone so clichéd) and he was staying at the pub on a two-day diving break.

He sauntered (like a cheeky, adorable Adonis) into the café, with the rain dripping off his chiselled jaw and his trousers sticking to his bulging thighs, and I swear a great shaft of sunlight entered the café, making his dazzling blue eyes sparkle and his teeth glint whiter than an advert for toothpaste. I was cool for at least the first ten minutes but flirted my arse off after that. Anya's nose kept twitching, so I should have known better than to accept his offer to join him in the pub for dinner, but of course, I just couldn't say no.

Did I tell you I travel to the only other village on horseback now? I ride Hyde and Jekyll comes along on a halter lead – he can't stand being left alone. At 7p.m., I pinned my courage to the sticking place, Ishmael saddled me up, slapped Hyde on the behind (which is ever so risque for Ishmael) and I set off with a torch and a sense of purpose, on the five-mile journey in the dark to the pub.

Let's face it, there's desperate, and then there's me.

I arrived in one piece (although I did take a faint smell of a stable yard into the pub with me) and we had a lovely dinner – all very Scottish West Coast, oysters, scallops, skinny fries – and the conversation was fun. But my God, the man loved himself. The pub was packed with tourists, most of whom I'd met in the café during the previous few days and after several glasses of Sauvignon Blanc, Sven went to the toilet and I realised that there were only five words on everyone's mind – 'will she or won't she?' I looked around and realised that absolutely everyone in there, including Sven, and let's face it, including me, expected our evening to end in Sven's bedroom. I felt like a tart – and I don't mean Bakewell.

I thought, 'What would Boudica do?'

So, when he came back from the loo, I took control, kissed him hard on the lips, thanked him for a lovely evening, jumped on Hyde and left. Sven was too cool (or stunned) to care.

Anya was waiting for me at my house when I got home. She'd lit the fire and the candles were burning – what that woman doesn't know isn't worth knowing. She asked no questions but insisted we had a nightcap. We played cards and I eventually fell asleep on the settee. I woke up this morning with a cashmere blanket over me and the fire stoked up – that's the benefit of sisterhood for you. My days of hooking up with transient men are over, but if my resolve weakens (and I can't believe I passed on a ripped body like Sven's) I have learned one thing: if Anya's nose starts twitching, I must stop flirting.

Lots of love, Aggie

Bluey
From: Rosie
To: Aggie

Date: 15 February

Hi, Aggie

A few observations: life in the desert is SHIT. I stink! The proper collective noun for the Army is 'Wankers'. They might win this war, but the Iraqis will never give in, not really. I will probably snuff it in a chemical attack. The bogs are shit, but at least I can now sit to poo as my arse is no longer cleaner than the toilet seat, although I do have to be careful not to zip a few flies into my pants when I pull my trousers up. Gethyn is miserable too. He's having a morality crisis as he knows that if he wasn't in the RAF, he'd be marching on Downing Street brandishing an anti-war banner.

Cheer me up, Aggie! Did Mr Perfect Pants show up? Perhaps I should have a go at writing down my own wishes while I'm in the desert. A full moon over the desert is an awesome sight so I reckon it must be four times more powerful (in terms of magic) than the itsy bitsy thing we get at home. I'll give a go on the next full moon, but with that kind of power, I really had better be careful what I wish for, eh?

I got your letter about your mum's behaviour and I wish I could phone you. Am I surprised she's behaved this way? No, not at all. Her behaviour always struck me as irrational. She's a child, Aggie, and just like a child I genuinely don't believe she has any concept that her behaviour is bizarre, but she seems to be unable to cope with rationalising emotion. True, she's also a passive-aggressive nightmare, but you aren't going to change that. You aren't going to change her. My 'pocket psychology handbook' suggests she's frightened you'll leave permanently and so she pushes you away before you do. I was going to suggest that you ask Anya for some spiritual healing, but if there is one thing I'm realising while I'm over here it's this – the only real healer on this planet is Time.

Gethyn and I had a chat the other day about something that's been bothering me. He said I should visualise the problem I have by placing it in a hot air balloon. Then I had to visualise myself desperately clinging on to the balloon from underneath. He said, as long as I hold on, I'll be pulled in the wrong direction, and no matter how much I try or for how long, eventually I won't be able to cling on anymore, and I'll fall from a great height and get hurt. He said the best thing is to just let go while your feet are still on the ground – and whenever the pain comes back, accept it, but visualise the balloon and keep letting it go. But you know, even though we might be dragged into the guts of hell, there are some balloons that are welded to us and are impossible to let go of. I'm hopeful that one day, the thing will have simply drifted off while I was looking in another direction, and I won't even have noticed.

Also, while I'm on a roll (sorry) I hope you don't mind me saying this, but I think you should stop looking for a fella for a while and focus on something more important. Ignoring Isabella is insane. I'm afraid I'm going to give you some tough love now, but ignoring emails, phone calls or texts from her isn't fair – and it's exactly what your mother does to you. Even if Isabella and the publisher are getting on your wick, ignoring them is rude, Agatha Isadora Braithwaite, and it displays a lack of courage. Write to Isabella with the absolute truth, rather than run away from the problem, and this will fix the issue immediately. You aren't suddenly going to produce a finished novel in the next couple of weeks, so tell them, then play the piano and sing, or go to that café of yours and have a bloody good laugh or cry or dance or anything, really.

Do you remember that time when I brought Mum to the park to talk sense into you rather than leave you to smoke pot on the roundabout with Shane Jackson? That was a turning point in your life. If I'd left you to your own devices, you would never have been as successful as you are now, and I'm not going to sit back and watch you throw the towel in again. You need a break from writing stories for a bit, that's all. Helping at the café is perfect, but don't get side-tracked. I know you're lonely, but please do yourself a favour and put finding a man to one side for a little while. Try to be happy single (I know I'm being a bloody great big hypocrite but it's much easier to sort other people's problems out, rather than your own) but if we can both learn to be truly happy alone – without husbands or babies and mothers – then we will only ever know happiness when, hopefully, we're blessed with finding these people, and we'll be better prepared for whatever life holds in store in the future (that's the theory, anyway).

Love, Rosie

Dear Rosie Hughes

From: aggieb@yahoo.com
To: igambini@hotmail.com
Subject: The Worst Ghost Writer Ever!

Date: 19 February

Hello, Isabella

I'm so very sorry to have been incommunicado lately. Are you terribly cross with me? The thing is, my very close friend who lives in an (almost) inaccessible part of Scotland, has had a family catastrophe and pleaded with me to rush to Scotland on a mercy mission to help keep her little café open so that her business doesn't fold. What could I do but drop everything and rush to her side? Internet access has taken a while to arrange and the phone lines are hit and miss but, fingers and toes crossed, this email will be delivered successfully.

As far as the latest manuscript goes, I will confess that *My Foolish Heart* is not coming along particularly well, and I'm afraid I will not make the deadline. I know this will not be the news you were hoping for, but I wanted to escape for a while in the hope that the creative juices would start to flow again. The café isn't busy at this time of year, so I'll get cracking over the next couple of weeks and have the first draft with you by the end of April – can you get this squared away with everyone?

But more importantly, how are you? How are Saffron and Anise-Star? Did Anise get her new pony?

With much love, Aggie.

P.S. I'm truly sorry to have let you down, especially after all you have done for me. I completely understand if you choose to find another writer.

Bluey
From: Rosie
To: Aggie

Date: 19 February

Hi, Ag

I sent you a letter of tough-love a few days ago and I really shouldn't have. I'm so sorry. Your email to me about your date with Sven must have crossed in the post and now I feel like such an arse. Your letters are fantastic, and I know you're only trying to keep me amused. Please, please pay no attention to anything I said.

But anyway, I have some upbeat news from the shithole for once. Gethyn and I had a brilliant time this morning: believe it or not there is great fun to be had in the simple act of digging a trench. The Sergeant Major threw a couple of spades in our direction and said we had to dig a trench directly outside of our tent in case the war suddenly kicks off and the scud alarm sounds when we're asleep. Obedient as ever, we got digging. Now when I say trench, you're better off imagining a mouse scratching than a trench, but you have no idea how hard

120

digging a trench actually is, even in sand. We dug to about a foot deep, then gave up, laughing. We aren't worried. When the shit hits the fan we'll not be in our tent anyway, we'll be in the HQ tent supporting the guys on the frontline, so we think the depth of the trench is pretty much immaterial, but it gave us some exercise for a few hours, which I'm guessing was the whole point. If we do have to use it and are hit by a scud, the trench will double up as a coffin, so it's perfect.

So, in the Army's eyes, Gethyn and I are even more effing useless pieces of poo than they suspected, but as Gethyn said, we're not useless, just pragmatic free-thinkers who refuse to follow the crowd. There is a deep, ingrained level of prejudice in the British armed forces and it goes like this: The Army resent/hate the RAF and tolerate the Navy. The Navy tolerate the Army and look down on the RAF. The RAF resent no-one because it's an emotion savoured by those who are discontent with their lot and the RAF are, on the whole, a comfortable, contented clan who spend a great deal of their time hunkered down in hotels (according to the Army). Everyone respects the Royal Marines.

Because we're relaxed, non-conformists (well, Gethyn is and I'm taking my lead from him) I'm categorised as nothing more than a civilian and, to be honest, they aren't wrong. Although, you would have been proud of me the other day. A young army captain shouted, 'Hey, Weather Girl' across the desert to catch my attention. Now, I don't mind being hollered at, but I won't be regarded as a 'girl'. This might sound a bit precious on my behalf, but when you're on the brink of war and are one of only a handful of women surviving in a hostile environment, it's vital not to be seen as a modern day Private Benjamin. I turned around, walked towards him, smiled and said, 'Call me that again and I'll cut you balls off, dickhead' and then walked away.

I know! ME!! I said that!

I genuinely have no idea what came over me, but I did get my period the next day.

Love, Rosie

P.S. Guess what? Gethyn is in a relationship. Has been for years, apparently. She's from Surrey – dead posh (he doesn't seem too enthusiastic though).

'E' Bluey
From: Josh
To: Rosie

Date: 19 February

Rosie

Of course my letter was impersonal. You walked out on me over a year ago. You asked for a divorce. I've barely had two words from you in all of that time – what do you expect? Regarding the 'gassed to death' comment, you said in your first letter that you were perfectly safe on the General's staff and I believed you. Why tell me you're safe if you aren't? Stop testing me.

Josh

From: igambini@hotmail.com
To: aggieb@yahoo.com
Subject: Re: The Worst Writer Ever!

Date: 19 February

Dear, Aggie

You are not the worst writer ever and you haven't let me down. I'm just relieved to have heard from you. And I'm not on the lookout for another writer, you ninny. My voice is your voice, and it's a voice worth waiting for so I'll arrange for an extension to the deadline. You've always delivered everything we've ever asked for, so don't worry.

The girls are fine but Anise didn't get the pony. She's going through a phase of despising me, so the pony had to be put on hold. They are both going to Switzerland to stay with their father over Easter. I hate it when they're away. I'm hoping Anise misses me this time, but I won't hold my breath. The winter seems endless, I'll be glad when it's spring. Where are you, exactly? Where is the café? Keep in touch.

Yours affectionately, Isabella

From: aggieb@yahoo.com
To: igambini@hotmail.com
Subject: Re: Re: The Worst Ghost Writer Ever!

Date: 19 February

Dear, Isabella

Thank you. Thank you. Thank you. I'm so relieved. You're a wonderful, wonderful friend. The café is in Appledart on the west coast of Scotland. It's heaven but I must dash as I have the day's cakes to bake. Isn't it odd that I'm saying this to you – it's usually the other way around! Maybe you should try your hand at writing now that I'm baking, but don't be too good at it or I'll find myself out of a job. With much love.

   Aggie

'E' Bluey
From: Aggie
To: Gethyn

Date: 19 February

Sir,

   Two things:

   1. Your postscript, '*Perhaps the crux of the whole issue is that you and I differ in what constitutes as romance*'

was clearly an attempt to rile me, the implication being that I have a materialistic view of romance while you are driven by a deeper ideology.

2. Trust me, in real life, a genuinely poor man has more pressing things on his mind than romance, and if the silly fool hasn't, he should have.

3. I do not wish to discuss the socio/economic benefits of a harem with you and never will. I have two women heroes, the first is Boudica (obviously) and the second, Scheherazade (the storyteller in *One Thousand and One Nights*) – who probably knew a thing or two about so-called harems. Scheherazade (in case you don't know) was a very clever woman who devoured books on literature and history in her youth. Anyway, the King of the land (A Tosser) married a new virgin queen every day and also each day beheaded the previous day's queen (his first wife was unfaithful, and he decided to punish all women for her transgression). Scheherazade's own father was the man who took the virgins to the King each night and this 'troubled' him. When he ran out of virgins he told his daughter the story and, of her own free will, the next night, she entered the king's bedchamber because she had a plan to save her father and her womenfolk. Cleverly, Scheherazade decided to outwit the King by telling him a new story every night. She would leave the story on a cliff-hanger, and the King, hanging on her every word, kept her alive until the next night so she could finish the story. This telling of interconnected,

clever stories (the stories become a magic carpet) continued for one thousand and one nights, by which time, exhausted, the poor woman ran out of ideas (I know how she felt).

But if you think about it, there were two weapons in the bedchamber each night – the king's sword and Scheherazade's words. The words, of course, won over in the end. The King fell in love with Scheherazade, the murdering of Muslim women ended and she became his permanent queen. In sum, Scheherazade did not agree with the subjugation of women, and nor do I.

4. I've often wondered what the view is like from *the moral high ground*. Perhaps you could enlighten me? Does spending a great deal of time at such a level lead to a lightness of head? This could explain a great deal.

5. With regards to your question about the exclamation mark, I once supported Isabella at a book signing on Oxford Street. A giant punctuation mark was hanging from the ceiling directly above her head. It became loose and began to fall. I noticed and pushed her out of the way, which was every bit as dramatic as it sounds. Unfortunately, I was not nimble enough to dodge the bullet myself, and sustained a deep gash to the skull and lost consciousness for a few minutes (ok, seconds). As my editor forced me to kill off use of the exclamation mark early on in my career, one might regard it as karmic revenge.

I've sent you another book: *For What it's Worth* (which is both the title and the sentiment).

Regards,
Agatha

Bluey
From: Rosie
To: Aggie

Date: 21 February

Hi, Aggie

We've moved – we're always moving. The tent has been packed away and I'm sleeping with a few others in the open desert again next to a truck with a stretch of tarpaulin draped across us as we sleep. It's still freezing at night but the heat will kick in soon and then I suppose I'll complain about that, too. Last Friday I managed to scam a trip into Kuwait City with Gethyn. He has a civilian friend from med school who works there. We met up with him and stayed in his apartment. It was the most amazing night of my life. Guess what? I had a bath – an actual bath, Aggie - AND a gin and tonic (life does not get better than that). I'm now back with the Army in the desert and have moments of absolute abject terror when I think about what may happen soon. In a way though, I wish the war would just kick off. After all, if

I'm going to die, I'd rather be clean and still have the aftertaste of a good strong G&T in my mouth as I draw my last breath.

Love, Rosie

Bluey
From: Rosie
To: Mrs Hughes (via the Post Office)

Date: 21 February
Oh, Mum, how did I end up in this mess?

Why didn't I just stay put in my marriage and in my lovely home in Devon? I wish my future held more certainty, but from where I stand at the moment, I'm looking ahead to a wide-open abyss with no structure and no real purpose.

I've done what you suggested and stopped writing to Angelica in my journal, but it doesn't help. No matter what I do or where I go, she's always there. I know it sounds odd, but I keep getting the scent of tomatoes – not the tomatoes you buy at the supermarket, but the real tomatoes in Dad's greenhouse. Do you remember the day I lost Angelica? I was holding her in my arms. Her skin was so perfect, this immaculate child, but she was so cold. Then Dad came and took her from me. He smelt of tomatoes that day.

Anyway, I'm just sitting and watching as HQ is

being packed up around me. Off we go, nomads in the desert. I had my anthrax jab yesterday, God my arm hurts. I would give anything to be home right now. I'm a whinging, whinging, woman and I'm not good enough to wear this uniform. Don't worry about my ramblings too much. I'm only letting off steam. Living out here is a paradox. You cannot help but live each day as it comes and yet I find that I have too much time on my hands to be able to live in the moment. I'd give anything to be at home with you and Dad right now, sat in front of the fire with the dog on my knee - watching kids' telly, drinking tea and eating marmalade on toast, asking Dad to nip to the shop for a video and some French Fancies, like he used to. Maybe if Josh and I got back together and somehow, miraculously, we had another baby, the sadness would go away. Did this work for you? Did I ever really replace Anna? I know you've never wanted to talk about her, but maybe it's time.

Love you.
Rosie x

Bluey
From: Gethyn
To: Aggie

Date: 21 February

Agatha

Your book arrived today. Thank you. Would you like me to review it?

Gethyn

'E' Bluey
From: Aggie
To: Gethyn

Date: 21 February

Dear, Gethyn

And another thing:

I now regret sending you another novel as I don't share your conviction that I could write anything worthy of your praise and I have no intention of changing my ways. I blame book clubs for this literary snobbery. The members of such clubs never dare to stand up to their book club leader – often dictatorial types. I swear most book club members trot along and have a nice chat about a literary book, but then go home and secretly devour a bit of Jilly Cooper. My own village book club gathering is a sombre affair, other than in December, when I host the meeting and ensure everyone leaves inebriated on rum punch.

Rosie informs me that you don't agree with the war and that you believe invading Iraq is morally wrong. If you don't agree with the war, why are you there? Could it be that, in order to carry out the requirements of your job, you've had to compromise on your own personal belief system? In your opinion I have let myself down by writing formulaic fiction in order to keep the money flowing in, but isn't what you're doing exactly the same thing? The difference between your situation and mine is that, to my knowledge, no one has died from reading my fiction, although Isabella did inform me that she received a letter from a lady who almost decapitated her husband when she threw one of my books at him while he danced the tango with a 'young trollop' on the cruise liner *Oceana*. I was glad to have been of help.

Agatha

'E' Bluey
From: Aggie
To: Rosie

Date: 21 February

Hi, Rosie

I can't even begin to imagine what you're going through right now but do remember that we're all with you in spirit. Don't worry about the tough love speech. I needed it. And you were right about Mum, but this merry-go-round of emotional instability can't go on. I have a hole in my heart in the shape of a mother, and it's been that way for as long as I can remember. When she's being nice to me, the hole starts to heal a little, but then, when she turns cold again, the wound opens up and it becomes angry and exposed, and with every concurrent spell of neglect and disassociation, the soft tissue becomes hardened, and my heart is less likely to bond together in the future. So, for the sake of my heart, before it hardens over completely, it's time to let go and not think about the fact that she will never be the one to say, 'I'm sorry' or even better, 'I love you'.

With much love, Ag
P.S. I followed your advice and wrote to Isabella – all is well. Thank you, my lovely friend.

'E' Bluey
From: Aggie
To: Gethyn

Date: 21 February

Hi, Gethyn

I sent you a letter earlier that contained some harsh words. I'm so sorry. I didn't mean any of it – I get carried away and, like a rabid dog, I don't know when to loosen my jaw from its grip. Maybe you push buttons in me that touch the sore spots?

Best wishes,
Aggie

From: aggieb@yahoo.com
To: sexymamma@hotmail.com
Subject: Last time trying

Date: 21 February

Dear, Mamma

This is my last email. I can't keep banging my head against the goldfish bowl. Every time I let my guard down and show you love, you close the door. I know you didn't want me to leave Midhope, but it's not forever, and even if it were, aren't children allowed to spread their own wings? When I came back to Midhope I never said it was forever (OK, I did) but things change – *I* need to change.

I'm not sure when I'll be home. I may sell up and start again somewhere new. My door will always be open - walk straight in and put the kettle on when you want to come back. There will always be Blue Ribbon biscuits in the tin.

I love you. Agatha x

Bluey
From: Rosie
To: Aggie

Date: 22 February

Hi, Aggie

It can't be long now. We practised the drill for a scud attack yesterday and unfortunately, I was shouted at because my hair was tied in a bun, which meant the straps of my respirator at the back weren't tight enough which prevented my face from bonding a firm seal. I felt like such an amateur, and you know how I hate to look like a girl. So, my hair has had to go. Gethyn cut it off. He borrowed the cartographer's scissors. I now have a very short bob cut. He did good job. At least, I think he did a good job, but with no mirror I haven't a clue what I look like, but it doesn't matter. Gethyn says I must

134

remember that, in working with the Army, I don't have to morph into being a man, and that I'm allowed to look presentable and cling on to some form of femininity. But, do you know, once the hair was gone, I felt so incredibly light and free, just like Jo in *Little Women*. I'm glad it's gone.

But if my hair weighed me down, my rucksack has weighed me down even more. What a f..king nightmare. When I left the UK, I didn't think I'd be able to whittle down my essential items any further, but now I carry only my pistol and respirator case and a small day sack holding a few pairs of pants, a change of uniform, head torch, blank letters, pens, a note pad, a packet of baby wipes and my journal, which means I can move around more easily without looking like a complete girl.

After the 'big hair cut' we sat in our tent with my golden hair abandoned at my feet and had a really good laugh. I've been Rapunzel for far too long, with all that long blonde hair weighing me down. Years and years of sadness were locked up inside the atoms in that hair, and it felt good to let it go. I might not have been bonded to that respirator before we cut off my hair, but my bond with Gethyn will be steadfast for the rest of my life. Guess what he did to get me laughing? He put *Stayin Alive* on his MP3 player, turned the volume up to max, and we danced around on the sand in our little tent, which we've been able to put up again at this particular location. Then – in tribute to you – we jived around to, *Let's Face*

The Music And Dance (I'd already told Gethyn how well you can belt it out!). It was brilliant. We've decided to always do this whenever one of us is having a rough day. It's a shame he's seeing someone because he would have been perfect for you. I'll see if I can get to the bottom of his relationship – maybe it's on the rocks? Let's hope so!

Write soon with news of the café, I'm desperate to hear all your news. Big hugs,

Love, Rosie

Bluey
From: Rosie
To: Mr Hughes

Date: 22 February

Hi, Mum and Dad

Not much to tell you other than that I'm safe and well. My friend Gethyn and I spent the morning filling sandbags, which killed a few hours. After filling about twenty bags, we stopped for a cuppa and fashioned a sandbag into the shape of a football to have a kick about. Before we knew it, a handful of Americans joined in and we'd got ourselves a game of soccer – it was like the Western Front all over again, only with Americans, not Nazis.

But on the whole, my life is extreme boredom

interspersed with weather forecasts. Is this how older people feel? I manage to while away half an hour cleaning my pistol every day, although Gethyn often does this for me as he finds it cathartic, and then there are always a few magazines kicking around. Talking to Gethyn fills the rest of the gaps, but it's a peculiar life. One army captain provided an entertaining hour by setting up a sweepstake for the start date of the war. Gethyn has gone for the 19 March and I've gone for the 21 March. I could win about $200 if I'm right so fingers crossed. Not much else to tell you.

Love to you all, Rosie x

'E' Bluey
From: Mrs Hughes
To: Rosie

Date: 22 February

Dear, Rosie
   Sweetheart, I don't talk to you about Anna because there isn't anything to say. I also can't tell you what to do about Josh, my love, but what I would say is this: having another child would not act as a miracle cure to your sadness. I think the way ahead can be summed up in only one word – acceptance. Start writing a new story for yourself, and please make it a happy one.

Do you know why Dad and I called you Rosanna? Well it absolutely was not to keep Anna's name alive in yours, but because we loved the sentiment of the song, *La Vie En Rose*, and it's what we wanted for you - a life in rosy hues. We thought that by naming you Rosie Hughes you would automatically be blessed with happiness – if you think about it, it's your destiny, your right. So, when you come home, re-write your life in a way that brings you joy and be good to yourself. I think you're going through a process that has needed to happen for some time and you will be in pain, on and off, until you come out of it at the other side. Perhaps spending this time away is exactly what you needed to see a clearer path ahead. You're grieving, Rosie, and the process will take time. Eventually, you will come out the other side and feel an overwhelming sense of freedom – of renewal and when that comes, you'll be free of it all. This is how I feel about Anna.

Regarding my depression (yes, I know it's the black dog that floats above the surface that we never discuss), I want you to know that I am not depressed because of losing a child. I suffer from clinical depression and bouts of anxiety attacks because I'm made that way. Sometimes I worry that the same black dog hovers around you, too. All I can really say is that I'm thankful every day for the patience and love of your father and that I have renewed hope, lately, of seeing a brighter future. Regarding Josh, if you feel that your marriage can be saved and his love is worth fighting for, then fight for it, but be careful what you wish for, my love, and be sure your feelings aren't being influenced by your present situation in Kuwait. Perhaps it would be best for you and Josh to delay the house sale until you get home - then decide.

About Aggie. I should have told you before, but she came to see me not long after you both left for university. She had come home for the weekend and wanted to talk to me privately about Simon and I can tell you that the reason she distanced herself from your friendship was because she found out that you'd paid Simon to take her on that first date – he told her himself as means of 'putting her off'. Simon may be my son, but he's an inconsiderate so-and-so sometimes. She was devastated and felt like a fool who had been played and, in a way, she was. Also, you did drop her completely when you started seeing that boy from Huddersfield, which meant she didn't have her home to go to anymore – her home, after all, was our house. And on the rare occasion she did come round during that summer, Simon had moved onto that other girl, so it must have been really hurtful for Aggie. I'm not blaming you, my love, I'm just pointing out that it was a difficult time and perhaps if Aggie was guilty of anything, it was being too trusting, rather than too needy.

Lots of love. Stay safe.

Mum x

Melanie Hudson

Bluey
From: Rosie
To: Josh

Date: 23 February

Josh

You're right. I'm a bit lost right now, and I shouldn't have taken it out on you. I'm sorry. I'm far from perfect. Your mum can have the lamp. When you go to the house you'll find the lamp in my box of special things.

Rosie

Printed Letter
From: Nathan Browne's Secretary, Brown's Culinary Almanac
To: Mr Shepherd, The Café at Road's End, Appledart

Date: 20 February

Dear Mr Shepherd

We are writing to inform you that we are considering including The Café at Road's End in *Browne's Café Guide* 2004 edition. Due to the unique positioning of your café, Nathan has decided to visit personally as he intends to holiday on Skye afterward. You will understand an element of surprise is necessary to provide an accurate

140

review and so the exact date of the visit will not be given, but I can tell you that it will be at some point before 15 April. . If all goes well, The Café at Road's End will find a place in our 2004 guide. If not, take consolation in the fact that competition is fierce and it is a great accolade to be considered.

  Kind regards,
  Rebecca Geary

Bluey
From: Rosie
To: Aggie

Date: 24 February

Hi, Aggie
  Do you mind if we quickly talk about Simon? I want to say something and then it's said and hopefully I will be forgiven. I got a letter from Mum yesterday and she said that Simon told you that I'd paid him to go out with you. This absolutely is NOT true. There is no way I would ever do that. I now understand why you were so upset. Good God, Aggie, why did you never say anything? In fact, don't answer that question, it will take me down a road I don't want to go down. Just please believe me when I say that I'm absolutely not guilty of this. Simon was, and I'm afraid still is, a child.

It's now four hours later. I had to stop writing because someone approached me and asked me for a quiet chat and so today was not awesome after all – there's always something. I can't believe it, but I was taken to one side by a chap who told me to try to be a little bit more masculine. He actually told me not to smile so much, or to be jolly when giving my brief. He said I'm coming across as a little bit too girlie. I wanted to slap his stupid face. Surely it doesn't follow that the deeper your voice and the more aggressive your stance while talking, the greater your ability to do your job. I can't stand all that wide-legged, masculine posturing shit. But then, bizarrely, he stroked my arm twice while he continued talking. What the fuck? I feel like shit. Have I been sexually harassed or was he just being nice? Am I too jolly in public? If so, I'm a bigger actor than any of them - if only they knew how suicidal I've felt these last couple of years. Dad told me, no matter what, keep smiling. That's all I'm trying to do for Christ's sake.

Oh, and the Secretary of State for Defence pitched up today. Gethyn and I watched to see if he was fed the same food in the mess tent as the rest of us (we lived in hope) but he got posh sandwiches and a proper cup of tea. I would kill for a proper cup of tea.

Love, Rosie

P.S. How's the bucket list going? You'll be pleased to know I'm working on my flick-flack (I'm getting some

142

dodgy glances) but my reckoning you are yet to: climb a mountain, see a sunset, sleep under the stars, send a message in a bottle and ride a horse on the beach (but it seems to me you're in the perfect place to nail that lot in a day – job done!).

'E' Bluey
From: Aggie
To: Rosie

Date: 27 February

Dear, Rosie

Re the bucket list; yes, you're right. I probably could bang out quite a few by teatime. Is that a good thing? Perhaps we should have been more adventurous in our dreams?

Re Simon, I know you didn't mean any harm, but unfortunately, he was a very convincing suitor (actor) and I fell head over heels in love with him. Little did I know it was all a game. One day I was the apple of his eye and the next, shit under his shoe. I tried to cling on initially because his sudden change in behaviour was bizarre and made no sense. I suppose I got clingy in the naïve hope he would change his mind, so (now I realise) to get rid of me and stop me going to your house he said he'd only knocked about with me because you paid him to. I felt like I'd been used, especially as I lost my virginity to him, which is such a big bloody deal. It was like you'd all had a joke at my expense and the worst thing was, like I said, I had genuinely fallen in love with him, which is why – although I know it was years later – I didn't come to the wedding. Also, we were very young, and if I'm honest, I didn't cope well with you having a boyfriend and I was crazy jealous. True, you dumped me that summer (and I bet you can't even remember the name of the lad you went out with!) but I would have done exactly the same thing if I had met someone first.

There is something else, too, and if I told you, you would understand why I kept away, but please don't ask because I won't say, and it's not because I don't treasure your friendship, but some things should remain hidden to protect the innocent, even between best friends.

But more importantly, yes, you have been harassed! If it happens again tell him he's making you feel uncomfortable and if that doesn't work, shoot him! Failing murder, I think it's time for you to channel your inner Boudica – the ultimate Briton (and I'm being perfectly serious). You've always scoffed at my worship of her, but it really grips my shit that she isn't revered properly in our country. She lost everything to the damn Romans when her husband died – she was flogged, and her daughters were raped. But did she cave in? No, she bloody well did not. Her own people were happy to follow a

144

woman into battle and she almost won, too. Then rather than allow herself to be taken into slavery, she killed herself. Obviously this is a massively abridged version of her story – but what a story! And it's all true, too. So, I say again. Channel your inner Boudica. Don't subjugate men – work with them, lead them if necessary - but never ever be subservient!

Also, I'll send some classic 'empowering' books out to you from Casey's bookshelf – you can start on that list. I know they aren't my books to give away, but she won't mind - good books should gather momentum, not dust. I've just thumbed through the shelves and pulled a few down; there's *Emma* (always good for a spot of self-assessment), *The Enchanted April* (a masterclass in character), *The Railway Children* (resilience in the face of catastrophe), *Anne of Green Gables* (anyone who can spell chrysanthemum is a hero in my book), but unfortunately, there's no *Vagina Monologues*. If you only read one book, though, read *Women Who Run with The Wolves* (I just knew Casey would have it). She also has a thing for Jackie Collins, thank God. Do you want *The Stud*, *The Bitch* or *The Sinners*? I'll pop in *The Stud* (you're very welcome!).

My news is mixed. On the plus side, I plucked up the courage to do the thing I'm afraid of the most. I wrote to Mum and said, 'goodbye' (admittedly it was in the hope of getting any kind of reaction) – but no reply. Then, last night, I looked to literature for my own guidance, and pulled *Alice Through the Looking Glass* from Casey's bookshelf for my bedtime reading. In it, Time says to Alice, 'Everyone parts with everything eventually, my dear' and I realised that I have to let Mum 'be' not let her go and accept that some relationships are simply impossible to break/forget/blow up.

Gethyn has done me a favour too (but DO NOT tell him this). He said the white knight character doesn't exist: he's right and so are you. What the hell am I doing exerting all this mental energy on finding a man? I've spent so long writing romantic stories, I've started to obsess on expecting the same story for my own life. I'll admit that I can't help being a romantic person, but I'm going to direct my efforts on something tangible. I'm going to build this business up so bloody well, Casey and Shep will be quids-in by the time they get home, and I know exactly how to do it. Here's how:

Over the past few years I have done a million and one-night classes: I'm a masseuse (Swedish), I've conquered Spanish (*usted me puede decir el camino a la estacion de tren, por favor?*). I can tango like an Argentine hooker and can even paint a passable water colour inside an hour. I can knit (the nativity scene was my shining moment, although baby Jesus looked a bit ropey). I can make crumbly soap, can decoupage my arse off and make flowers in felt. Admittedly, I went to each night class with the purpose of meeting a man but the problem was, all the other women also went along with the singular purpose of meeting a man, which was a win-win situation for the one relatively attractive male who pitched up. BUT! It's time to put all this talent to some use, and I've decided to start some 'themed' café sessions, including 'piano request night' – I'll let you know how it goes.

But, oh my God, big big news! Nathan Browne (as in, *the* Nathan Browne from *Browne's Good Food Guides*) is coming to the café at some point over the next month. This is a big deal. If our little café gets a page in Browne's guide, Casey and Shep will be completely sorted. And what's even more amazing is that Nathan Browne himself is coming – yes, Nathan Browne, here, at this café, eating my cupcakes! We've been told to expect him 'at some point' before 15 April which means I'll have to sharpen up my act because Nathan expects originality. Anya does the savoury stuff at the moment, but I think her menu is a little bit *too* original, if you know what I mean (unless he doesn't mind getting stoned). I'm soooo excited.

Love, Aggie

P.S. I haven't had a reply from Gethyn this week and I'm concerned I may have crossed a line. Is he cross with me?

P.P.S. Eh? The Bee Gees? I thought you said he was thirty-seven, not fifty-seven!

Bluey
From: Rosie
To: Agatha

Date: 27 February

Hi, Aggie

Just in case you ever need to know, I can tell you that it's really quite difficult for an eight stone woman to run onto a rotors-running helicopter in the desert while carrying a backpack – not much more to say on that subject, but on the plus side, it's quite exciting, really.

Army HQ is a funny old beast to watch. So hierarchical. It's becoming clear that, for the army officers around me, this time is crucial in terms of their career prospects. The posturing in front of the Chief of Staff is fascinating. The Brigades do this too, on the telebrief – you can hear it in their delivery. But do they want to impress the General or are they trying to prove that their particular field of specialisation has a necessary role in modern warfare? The Paras are desperate for a defining purpose here. The only people who don't seem to peacock about are the Royal Marines - I don't suppose they need to. Come the dreaded day, I'm sure all this posturing will fade. I've changed my mind about my gender status. I'm very grateful to be a woman – what a blessed relief to live in this world and not have to prove myself as a man.

Love, Rosie

Bluey
From: Rosie
To: Aggie

Date: 27 February

Hi, Aggie

Yes, Gethyn *is* a little quiet lately. We've not danced to the Bee Gees for a while. He's finding great difficulty in being here. But anyway, whatever you put in your letter to him, I wouldn't worry. He's a strapping Welsh bloke, so I can't imagine you could have upset him too much.

By the way, thanks a million for the MP3 player. It was really good of you to find the time to buy it and download all the music – even though you must have been busy packing to go away. The music selection is fab and I'm loving the flash back to your mother's record player collection. It was always ABBA, David Cassidy, Joni Mitchell or the Carpenters, depending on what mood she was in, wasn't it?

Oh, speaking of mothers, can you get a Mother's Day card for me next month, please? I know this is really insensitive of me bearing in mind the situation with your mum. Maybe you could send one to your own mum, too? I know, I know. She's still a cow-bag, but sometimes, isn't it just easier to keep playing the game?

And finally, why don't you ask Isabella Gambini to design a menu for the café?

149

Love, Rosie

P.S. Quick question, just throwing it out there; do you think I'd be nuts if I asked Josh to give our marriage another go? This could be my, 'do one thing you are afraid of' from the bucket list.

'E' Bluey
From: Mr Hughes
To: Rosie

Date: 27 February

Dear, Babe

Sand bags? Why do you need sandbags if you're working in a bunker in Kuwait?

Well, today is the first day it's felt like spring might be on its way. There was something in the way the birds were singing and the way the sunlight caught on the kitchen window that gave me the definite feeling that we've turned the corner. Mammy say's it's a good day for metal detecting (in other words, she wants me out of the house). There's one particular field just past Holmfirth that's been laid to pasture for years. The farmer has ploughed it so I'm off to speak to him this afternoon and see if he's happy for me to go on before he sows it. Oh, I know I've been looking for the elusive pot of gold for years, but this time I really do get a definite feeling that there's something big to be found in this one.

Mammy thinks I'm daft, obviously, but she won't be thinking I'm such a crackpot when I dig up a Roman hoard and we're gallivanting off in our new caravan!

With regards to the school, the council will vote in May, but it's not looking promising. I've been doing all I can to push to keep the old girl open, but I've a feeling that those holding the purse strings at the town hall are simply going through to motions. One group of mothers have turned to vigilante tactics and are threatening to picket the school bus, but another set of mums agree that the school is too small and under-funded and are happy to pack their kids onto the bus at eight o clock in the morning and forget about them until tea-time. Whatever they believe, once the school is gone, it's gone and most of us reckon the village will lose its soul if it goes. Time will tell, I suppose.

Love ya babe,
MumnDad x

Bluey
From: Rosie
To: Mrs Hughes (via the Post Office)

Date: 27 February

Hi, Mum
Thanks for your advice about Josh and letting go of

Angelica. And thanks for being honest about your illness. Yes, I gave Simon *so* he could take Aggie out for a drink, not *to* take her out on a date. I did it because she was lonely, and I felt guilty because I wasn't hanging around with her so much anymore. It was wrong, but I hope you believe that it was done with the right intentions. I didn't think either of them would take it any further. I just thought it would be nice for Aggie to have someone take her out for a drink or to the pictures – I never expected him to come-on to her. I've written to Aggie to apologise, though I have bent the truth a bit to save her feelings.

Anyway, guess what. The other day, I cut off my hair and had a long chat with a doctor friend of mine. What I realised during that chat is that I've always felt that I live in my dead sister's shadow. Dad won't let me open up to you, but it's hit me since I've been away that I've been buttoned up within your grief as well as my own. But because we never talk about Anna, I felt you never let your heart open to me in the way you would have opened up to her. There are times when I have resented my dead sister, because I thought you held a part of you back, for her. I thought I could see it in your eyes. I told Dad all this years ago, but he said I was being daft and not to bother you with it. I also told him I've never liked my name because I didn't think it was entirely mine. I thought you only called me Rosanna so that Anna would live on – in me. If Anna hadn't died I would have been called something else entirely, or maybe I wouldn't even be here.

But since reading your letter I realise that I've created all this trauma within my own mind. Why do we do this to ourselves? Punish ourselves with fearful stories? Why didn't I just talk to you? Dad was right, the whole thing was daft. When I accepted my posting to Iraq, I didn't care if I lived or died. But with the war almost on me and the scuds about to fly, I realise that, if I'm going to fight for this life, I have to have let Angelica die, so that I might live. Why, why, why have I clung on to all this for so long?

Please forgive me for blaming you for my own short-comings, Mum, and when I get home, let's find a way to allow our eyes to dance when we're together – and always.

With all the love in the world, Rosie x

Bluey
From: Gethyn
To: Aggie

Date: 27 February

Dear, Agatha
Don't worry. You're right. I'm a hypocrite. Disregard

my ridiculous ramblings about fiction, I was probably quite irritating in my opinions.

Kind regards,
Gethyn

From: igambini@hotmail.com
To: aggieb@yahoo.com
Subject: Running Away

Date: 27 February

Dear, Aggie,

Oh Lord, I know this must sound quite random, but do you have a room to spare? If so, may I come and stay with you for a little while? I've reached an absolute block with my latest cook book and can't think of anything new or inspirational to add and I'm not sure I even care. Can I run away to Appledart to be with you? Maybe I might find inspiration in the café?

Please do say if this request is taking our friendship too far. I was talking to a close friend about you and she says there's some kind of infamous fortune teller who lives near you. Maybe I'll pay her a visit while I'm there?

With love,
Isabella

Bluey
From: Rosie
To: Aggie

Date: 28 February

Dear, Aggie

This has been such a great day! Gethyn nicked a Land Rover and, out of the blue, we escaped to a US Army base and guess what? There was a trampoline for sale in the BX – a bloody trampoline! We spent two hours trying to do somersaults in the shop and nobody stopped us. We managed it, too!! It was worth getting a bollocking afterwards because it was such an amazing day – I washed my hair; I used a clean toilet; I had ice cream AND a Coke. It's the little moments that are the best!

Ta ta for now.
Love, Rosie

'E' Bluey
From: Agatha
To: Rosie

Date: 2 March

Hi, Rosie

Gethyn has written back. It was short and polite. I'm

such a cock sometimes. Did he tell you what I wrote? I'm so ashamed. I'll have to think up an excuse to write back to him show that I'm not a bitch. I'll throw a few funnies in and send him a cake or something, that'll draw his friendship back.

Regarding asking Josh to try again, you haven't really said what happened and so I'm worried about offering an opinion. This is the sort of question that requires a whole day (if not two) on the subject. You know the sort of thing; tea, cake and two women walking arm in arm on the beach, *The Wind Beneath My Wings* playing in the background.

Alternatively, and without my guiding arm and scrumptious bakes to fall back on, you could just flip a coin on it. Heads you get back together, tails you don't. If you are disappointed when it lands on tails, you'll know what to do. Simple.

How's the bucket list going? My piano playing is coming on well, but I think I'll head up a mountain next!

Love, Ag

From: aggieb@yahoo.com
To: igambini@hotmail.com
Subject: Re: Running Away

Date: 2 March

Hi, Isabella

Of course you can come! I would love it. In fact, I feel divine providence at work because you may just be able to help in a way you would never have imagined, but more of that when you get here.

Come as soon as you can.

Love, Ag

From: igambini@hotmail.com
To: aggieb@yahoo.com
Subject: Re: Re: Running Away

Date: 2 March

Hi, Aggie

That's fantastic. Thank you so much. I'll come this week. How do I get there? What should I bring?

With love,
Isabella

From: aggieb@yahoo.com
To: igambini@hotmail.com
Subject: Re: Re: Re: Running Away

Date: 2 March

Wow! This week? Well, why the hell not?

Bring walking boots, wellies, warm clothes, gloves and the best coat you can find – nothing fashionable but something that required the sacrifice of a thousand geese should suffice. Take the train to Fort William, then change for Mallaig. Let me know what time your train gets in and I'll arrange for Hector to pick you up in his little boat. Must dash, got to bake.

Aggie

Bluey
From: Rosie
To: Aggie

Date: 4 March

Hi, Ag

I flipped a coin like you suggested (actually, I didn't have a coin, so I threw a dollar note into the air) and it landed on the front, which meant 'no' I shouldn't get back with Josh. And you were right, I was disappointed. So, I threw it in the air again and it bloody-well landed on 'no', again. I just kept throwing the thing in the air until it landed the right side up. So it seems I genuinely do want to give it another go with Josh, but does he want to get back with me? That's the question. What to do, what to do?

Love, Rosie

P.S. Thanks for the books. I started on *Emma* (I take it that it was a 'not-so-subtle' hint at the pitfalls associated with meddling in a friend's love life?)

'E' Bluey
From: Aggie
To: Gethyn

Date: 4 March

Dear, Gethyn

You're not a hypocrite. You're on the brink of war and I should be a grateful citizen and not a ranting old cow.

As an apology, I have sent you a signed copy of Isabella Gambini's latest cook book entitled, *'Just Desserts'*. I persuaded Isabella to create recipes that use only ethical, organic foodstuffs. The reason for sending the book is because the forward was researched and written by me. Maybe we should discuss other things and steer clear of romance, as perhaps this is a subject upon we are unlikely ever to agree.

Regarding the writing, I'm super-sensitive at the moment because I'm suffering from a spot of writer's block (or maybe I'm just exhausted with it all) so when a friend asked me to run her café in Scotland, I jumped at the chance. Again, Rosie will explain, but in a nutshell, I'm writing to you from an oasis of calm in a world of conflict. I'm living in my friend's cottage which is one of a handful of fisherman's cottages positioned around a cute and ancient little pier. Beyond the harbour is a golden beach which is just idyllic, whatever the weather. The Isle of Skye sits five miles out to sea and on a clear day like today, I can almost reach out and touch it. My neighbours include a psychic and a poet and the café is in a converted byre which, like the peninsula, is perfect. The byre has a red tin roof, whitewashed walls and the windows overlook the pier and beach. It's called, The Café at Road's End, and I love it.

Basically, I've found a timeless paradise of pure escapism. But although the scenery is straight off a tin of Highland shortbread, I am yet to hear a Scottish accent, and I wonder if Appledart is actually my very own Brigadoon – a place that appears through the mist once in a while - where the inhabitants are not real at all, but guardian angels. It's like I've been able to step out of the real world and into a fictional abyss for a little while. Isn't it strange how you allow your life to carry along on the treadmill for an absolute age, and then suddenly, boom! An amazing adventure calls out to you and it's simply impossible not to go.

Yours, Agatha

From: igambini@hotmail.com
To: aggieb@yahoo.com
Subject: Re: Re: Re: Re: Running Away

Date: 4 March

Hi, Aggie
I'm all booked! I'm flying to Inverness tomorrow, staying there overnight and I arrive at Mallaig at 1p.m. the following day. One question. What do you mean, boat? Should I be nervous? I can't swim.

With love,
Isabella

Melanie Hudson

From: aggieb@yahoo.com
To: igambini@hotmail.com
Subject: Re: Re: Re: Re: Re: Running Away

Date: 4 March

Hi, Isabella.
The boat is a must. I never said the journey to The Café at Road's End was easy, but it's worth it - honest.

Love, Ag
P.S. You can ride a horse, right?

Bluey
From: Rosie
To: Aggie

Date: 6 March

Hi, Aggie
My day today:
- Got out of dusty camp bed and dressed in front of twenty hairy-arsed soldiers.
- Washed with baby wipes as men had taken all hot water from boiler to shave (fair enough, I should have got there earlier).
- Had breakfast – I've succumbed to a wrinkly sausage in the morning.

162

- Went to work, sneered at the Army.
- Met up with Gethyn now and again for a cuppa.
- Gave inconsequential periodic met briefs.
- Ate lunch (US Marine Corps bag meal – nice).
- Ate dinner (stew – camel?).
- Brushed teeth.

But oh, all the books have arrived (not sure how we're going to cart them around but we'll find a way). Do you realise you sent a cook book to a fifteen-stone food addict who's living off war rations? Hilarious, but so cruel, especially as he is *always* hungry. I've been watching him flick through the recipes and it's like watching a well-behaved Labrador drooling at a cooked chicken sitting on the kitchen table.

Thanks a million, though.

Love, Rosie x

Bluey
From: Rosie
To: Mrs Hughes (via the Post Office)

Date: 6 March

Hi, Mum
It's 10p.m. and I'm sitting in the back of a truck writing this from the light of my head torch. We're moving to

another location in the desert at about 12.30a.m. I'm so tired. I think it's Thursday but if someone told me it was Friday I wouldn't argue. I wish I was out walking on Dartmoor on a rainy day, with my walking boots on and experiencing that tight, fresh feeling on my face. I feel like a prisoner. I *am* a prisoner.

When we're on the move I have to sleep in a designated billet alongside the truck and there is this one man who watches me. He watches me wash, change out of my uniform, even brush my teeth. Perhaps my discomfort is not about a lecherous man who gets under my skin, but about my relationship with myself. Maybe that's what I have to discover, but how can I learn to be a woman if, in this particular world, I need to be a man?

I'm over-thinking it again.

Love you. Rosie x

'E' Bluey
From: Aggie
To: Rosie

Date: 10 March

Hi, Rosie
  Oh, fuck, re the cook book! I'll send rations, too. How about a hamper?

I've been listening to the news. Nightmare for you!

In other, less significant, news you will never in a million years believe it, but Isabella Gambini is coming to stay with me - and to think you said I should ask her for help. Crazy! I'm beginning to think Summer Santiago (*Be Careful What You Wish For*) might be right. Things seem to be coming together at last (except for Mum, of course, but it would take more than a miracle to sort that woman's head out).

Oh God, Rosie. Keep safe!

Love, Ag

P.S. And as for *Emma* – am I really that transparent?

Bluey

From: Rosie

To: Mrs Hughes (via the Post Office)

Date: 10 March

Hi, Mum

I need your help pretty quickly. I have no idea why, but every time I go to the toilet, as soon as I release my belt my bladder empties of its own free will. I just about get my trousers down, but I pee all over my pants. Maybe it's stress, or maybe my dreadful caesarean scar is playing havoc with my bladder? Please can you go to a cheap shop (Matalan?) and buy me loads of pants and send them straight away? I haven't the time to keep washing out and it would be unthinkable to stink of pee.

Love, Rosie x

Bluey
From: Gethyn
To: Aggie

Date: 16 March

Dear, Agatha
  I bloody love you!
  Thanks a million for the hamper. I've tried my hardest to share everything, but I've been a bit of a glutton, especially with the cake. I hope you don't mind, but I traded the quails eggs for a packet of Chocolate Digestives with a Royal Artillery Major (I think he had a more select upbringing than mine). The wicker basket has also found a use. We fashioned it into a highly productive rodent trap and are catching one or two rats per day! You're one in a million.
  Not much time today, but I'll respond soon with some thoughts on Isabella's cook book. I'll try to be less obtuse than last time, promise.
  G.

Bluey
From: Rosie
To: Aggie

Date: 16 March

Hi, Aggie

A Harrod's hamper? How absolutely awesome. Thank you. Gethyn has really cheered up.

Opening the hamper was such a surreal experience and a fabulous taste of home (even if it was, as Gethyn reminded me, a taste of stereotypical England sold from a shop owned by an Arab). There was even a tiny ornament of Big Ben. I keep it with me tucked into the bottom of my respirator sack and smile every time I see it. We've hidden the booze. We're going to drink it when the war is over, whenever that is.

Life is still plodding on – same old, same old. Maybe by the time this letter reaches you I would imagine it will have begun. Shit, Ag, this is really happening. What has life come to when you've scaled your life down to such a bare minimum that the most important possessions you own are a gun and an atropine pen? I've discovered the secret to sound mental health out here is to find absolutely anything to do to keep busy. Spending time with my own thoughts is the enemy. Oh, and I don't despise the Army anymore. Overnight I morphed into becoming one of them (it's easier than resisting). We (HQ staff) handed over our body armour today. Not all the guys on the frontline have it and they need it more than we do, but I hope we're not attacked, because ten bullets and no body armour is unlikely to keep death from my door. Sorry if this sounds a little glib, but I've reached a level of acceptance that my fate is no longer in my hands. Having said that, we were ordered to start taking NAPs (nerve agent poisoning) tablets today in case of chemical attack, but Gethyn and I have had a chat about it and we're not going to take them. We're playing the odds game.

We've been told that if anything happens to our loved ones at home during the early stages of the war we will not be informed, which leads me on to one last favour. Can you promise me something? If I don't make it back, can you please watch over Mum and Dad for me? Bake Dad lots of cakes, buy him a drop of whiskey now and again and take Mum for trips out to the garden centre, especially at Christmas – she loves that. She suffers from depression (you probably guessed) and what with Simon in Australia, they're pretty much alone and Dad doesn't have the happiest of lives when she's on a downer. When the fighting starts, we may not be able to correspond for a while, but whatever you do, keep writing to me and I'll write back when I can. Speaking of Simon, you'll not be surprised that I haven't had one single letter from him. But that's my brother for you.

Much love and the best of luck with the café. Maybe I'll find my way back there one day, once this lot is over.

With a tsunami of love.
Rosie

Bluey
From: Rosie
To: Andrea Jones

Date: 16 March

Hi, Andrea

Thanks so much for your letter. It meant a great deal to me to receive it. The best thing I can say about life at the moment is that I have food to eat and water to drink and as one of my colleagues said, some people on the planet don't even have that. It's true, no matter what your situation, there will always be someone who can be in a shittier pickle than you. Right now though, there won't be many, and those without food and water probably won't be wondering if they are about to get bombed or gassed, but then again maybe they are – when you're in a shitty situation, the crap tends to gather momentum.

It was lovely of you to say that I'm an inspiration, but in all honesty, if I could choose between my life and yours, I would choose yours. You're a mother and that surely is the most important job of all. Having said that, maybe the time for you to follow your own personal dreams is coming to the fore. Perhaps you could look at ways in which you could follow your dream to train as a nurse – you were always the one to take the mice and hamsters home from the classroom in the holidays. I bet you would be fab.

Follow your heart, Andrea. You never know where it might lead (perhaps best not to listen to me, though. Look where I ended up!).

Take care and thanks again for writing.

All the best, Rosie.

Bluey
From: Rosie
To: Aggie

Date: 17 March

Dear, Aggie
We've moved again. Can't remember when I last slept.
My day today:
1600 - Took down 12 X 12 tent with Gethyn.
1710 - Realised tent would not fit in bag. Refolded tent.
1725 - Couldn't find tent pegs. Felt like civilian.
       Realised had left two poles out. Repacked tent
       with poles.
1800 - Finally finished with bloody tent.

1805 - Found friendly army bloke to help carry tent to truck.

1805 - Stood in desert waiting for Army to pack up all of HQ. Mammoth task they don't want help with from amateurs.

2130 - Got thrown into truck without Gethyn by a Warrant Officer and landed on food supplies (tins).

2135 - Set off through desert in very long, lights-out convoy to destination unknown (very slow and very bumpy).

0100 - All vehicles stopped. Told we must wait in present location for five hours (amazed to have been given any info).

0110 - Pitying US Marine gave me a camp bed as I had bedded down directly on the desert floor.

0111 - Fell asleep.

0300 - Woke up with hyperthermia. Couldn't be arsed to do anything about it as even small functions seemed beyond possible. Remembered that I'm not a baby and need to stay warm. Put on extra clothes. Fell back to sleep.

0600 - Got woken up by army bloke. Looked up to see lines of men peeing against trucks (realised it's not just dogs that need something to pee against). Wondered where on earth I was going to pee? Pee'd round back of truck. Couple of blokes saw me. None of us cared.

0700 - Got to new location, re-built HQ. Much respect to Royal Signals guys and gals for doing majority of work.

1000 - Had biological/chemical attack exercise. Far too close to enemy now. Feel that the day has very nearly arrived.

I wish I had my violin. But never mind. How was your day?

Love, Rosie

Bluey
From: Rosie
To: Mrs Hughes (via the Post Office)

Date: 19 March

Dear, Mum.

I'm sitting in the HQ tent watching Bush's address to the nation on TV. It's so surreal. I stood outside in the dark earlier and looked across at the glow of a couple of Iraqi oil fields in the distance. It's a very important commodity – oil – isn't it? Hope Dad is bearing up OK. Big hug for the dog. Sorry for the short letter. Don't know what to write.

Love, Rosie x

Bluey
From: Gethyn
To: Aggie

Date: 19 March

Hi, Aggie

Well, the hour to go over the top is almost upon us. I considered declaring myself as a conscientious objector but have singularly failed to act with moral fortitude and have followed the masses instead. Is this how all wars gather momentum, with individuals who no longer think or act as anything other than a collective? Saddam Hussein has done many terrible things, and he's clearly an imbalanced sociopath. Maybe he's ill (I've heard rumours), but surely what we're about to do is not rational either? If I thought this war was a genuine humanitarian mission I would feel better, but I'm sure it's a smoke screen. But for what?

I re-read your Scheherazade letter and it struck such a note. Here I am, in Arabia. And collectively with my colleagues, like Scheherazade's father, we are carrying out the bidding of the King, despite our objections. But there is no story-teller to save us, to weave me a magic carpet. Words have not been mightier than the sword.

Have you ever read Kipling's *Law of the Jungle*? Despite everything history can teach us, it seems the men who run countries and armies are not as clever as Scheherazade

173

– they have not the intellect to learn from stories or to weave words into peace – and so the law of the jungle remains ignored. As a result, I cannot see how our aggression in Iraq will not lead, in time, to an almighty backlash, possibly giving rise to Sheer Khan. But as you told me, every story needs a villain, and there may well prove to be a twist in this tale yet, and the illusion someday be revealed.

Whatever the case, the war starts tomorrow or the day after that. I will throw my soul to the devil and try to survive the storm.

Take care, Ag.
Gethyn

Bluey
From: Rosie
To: Mr and Mrs Hughes

Date: 19 March

Dear, Mum and Dad
Some people have written letters to their loved ones, only to be opened if they don't make it home. This kind of letter writing is not for me, but the notion got me thinking. Why do we always wait until it's too late to tell the people who are dearest to us how we feel? I'm absolutely not going to die, but if I had written a letter, this is probably what it would have said:

Dear Rosie Hughes

To my lovely Mum and Dad – thank you.

Thank you for always having a full fridge and a topped-up biscuit tin. Thanks for handing me the remote control and saying, 'Watch what you want, love.' Thanks for putting the gas fire on in June when I'm cold, and thanks for keeping my bedroom exactly how I left it. Thanks for buying me my first car and slipping me a tenner when I went out with to the pub. Thanks for putting me through university, even though you couldn't afford it, and thanks for all the times you went without the things you wanted, just to make sure I didn't go without. Thanks for all those magical Christmasses, and for holding my hair out of my face when I threw up. Basically, thanks for unswervingly providing a home where the weight of adulthood floated away from my shoulders as soon as I stepped through the back door. I love you with all my heart. Please try not to worry.

Your loving daughter,
Rosie x

PART TWO

'E' Bluey
From: Aggie
To: Rosie

Date: 20 March
    Oh Jesus, Rosie. It's started. I hope you're ok. Stay safe, lovely lady. Not sure what to write, nothing seems relevant. Oodles of love. Ag x

'E' Bluey
From: Mr Hughes
To: Rosie

Date: 20 March

Dear, Babe
    Well, it's started then, my love. For God's sake, keep your head down and no heroics. Write as often as you can.

All our love.
MumnDad xx

'E' Bluey
From: Josh
To: Rosie

Date: 21 March

Hi, Rosie

I'm sorry, too. Fuck the lamp. I see scuds are hitting Kuwait. It should be me out there, not you. Take great care.

Josh x

Bluey
From: Gethyn
To: Aggie

Date: 22 March

Dear, Agatha

It's 3a.m. and for the first time in a couple of days I have time to myself to sit still for a few moments.

I haven't written many letters since I arrived in Kuwait, but of the few I do write, for some reason, I feel that I can be the most honest with you. As the death toll rises and the war gears up, so my job has also ramped up and my attitude to the event has turned from varying shades of grey to black and white. In very basic terms, I'm the guy who provides a detached overview for battlefield first aid. It's much harder than I expected it to be. The death toll is comparatively low, but each singular death is still a person's life snuffed out. And there are those who are injured to care for, too. I've had to make some hasty decisions and all I can hope is that I've done well.

I wonder if anyone is keeping track of the Iraqi dead and injured. The children? The animals? All just a few miles away from where I sit as I write this letter, but I'm on the safer side of the line. The other side must be a frightening place to be. The arsenal at our disposal via the Americans is immense. It's so immense, in fact, that the Iraqis haven't bothered launching their aircraft to fight back – there's no point.

I wish the Iraqi's had had the sense not to fight back at all – they can't possibly win. I wish they had said, 'OK, America. Do what you will, but we won't lose more lives than we have to.' But how can a nation just lie down and not fight back? On those terrible first two nights, when the British Marines began the assault on the Al Faw peninsula, I managed to lay down for a couple of hours between scud attacks and I could feel the force of the war reverberate through the desert. It's very difficult to explain, but I swear the

Earth knew what was happening, and I think it wept a little.

I'm so proud of Rosie. I can't believe she was put into this situation so completely unprepared. Since the war started she has found an inner strength from some deep recess within her soul that fires her on. I hope she knows how valuable her role here has been. I've tried to tell her, but it seems to fall on deaf ears. Having a woman around, and not just any woman, but a woman with a warm smile, whose voice on the radio to the troops every day is calming and gentle, has been a blessing. Some men have dealt with Rosie's presence here better than others. Perhaps the very few who have felt the need to subjugate her, do so out of fear – fear that they will prove to have less moral courage than the little blonde lady who speaks of nothing but sunshine, every single day. Her nickname, in fact, is Little Miss Sunshine (and she hates it) and it's meant with nothing but love, but perhaps they don't look deeply enough into her eyes. If they did, they would notice the sadness that lies beneath.

My eyes are stinging so I'll sign off, but please do write soon. I'm ashamed I encouraged you to veer away from the lighter side of your writing. Humour and a little joy is surely the best medicine a person can have during dark times. I keep one of your books in my respirator sack, and when my sadness consumes me, I take it out and read a few pages. The lightness of your spirit is the best antidote to war I could have found. I said in my last letter that I was lost without my very own Scheherazade to save me, but of course, I now realise that Scheherazade and her stories have been with me all along. And for this, I will be forever in your debt. Thank you.

G

Letter
From: Headmistress of Midhope Primary School
To: Rosie

Date: 23 March

Dear, Rosanna

I don't know if this letter will reach you now the war has started, but my name is Angela Cartwright and hopefully you will remember me as I'm the Headmistress at Midhope Primary School.

The reason I am writing is to tell about an eleven-year-old boy who would like to write to you. On the day the war started we held a special assembly for collective worship and prayed for all the victims of war – it's such a worrying time for the children and so confusing, too. I had heard from Janet at the shop that you are caught up in the conflict and so I mentioned in assembly that a lady originally from our village was serving in Iraq.

After the assembly, a boy in year six, Oliver, asked if he could write to you. I phoned your parents to ask for your address. Your Dad felt you wouldn't mind if Oliver corresponded, so I allowed Oliver to use my laptop during lunch to pen a letter and I helped him with his spelling etc.

You must be exceptionally busy, but if you could find the time to reply to Oliver I would appreciate it. He's a soulful child but also wilful and disruptive. His name is particularly appropriate as he is presently in foster care having suffered from a disturbed childhood. The fact that he has asked to write to you has taken us all by surprise. He's a very bright boy and could do well in life but does have some learning disabilities, including difficulty in handwriting which is why I'm allowing him to use my laptop to write to you and helping him with his typing. Unfortunately, he will almost certainly move on again in a few months, as I believe his present foster mother is shortly to cease to provide care. If you reply, it would be best if you send your return letter to me at the school address (mail is being forwarded to our temporary billet) and I will pass it on to Oliver. Take care of yourself, Rosanna, and remember that we're all very proud of you.

Very best wishes, Angela

Here is Oliver's letter:

Dear, Rosie

Mrs Cartwright told us about the war and we were told to pray for you and all the soldiers. We had a really long assembly today. My bum hurt but we did pray for you and so all the children think God will now make it so you don't die.

I asked to write to you because I want to know about the war. Have you got a gun? Is it hot out there? Why are we at war? Is there a lot of sand? What about lizards? Is Saddam Hussein going to send bombs to England? Have you shot anyone? Are you scared? Will you get a medal? Did you know our school burnt down? We have to get the bus to Oakworth now. Some of the mums and dads don't let the small kids get the bus and they drive them to school. I get the bus.

Yours faithfully, Oliver

Bluey
From: Rosie
To: Aggie

Date: 23 March

Hi, Aggie

It's 11 p.m. and there is a quiet but busy throng going on around me in the HQ tent so I thought I'd take a moment to write, although I'm not sure when you'll get this.

We went to war a few hours earlier than expected. Despite feigning bravery, I was frightened to death, but it's strange how quickly you can teach yourself to stay calm. One missile landed far too close for comfort, but the Patriot system seems to be neutralising most of them before they land. The front-line troops are doing incredibly well but it's horrendous when you hear them crying out for support on the radio, especially if there are no aircraft immediately available to run in and help out (most jets seem to be going to Baghdad).

Scud attacks have been steady since the war started, but don't worry because they are an inaccurate weapon and the good news is there's no sign of gas yet. Because I haven't much work to do, I feel like a fly on the wall watching the nightmare unfold. I would honestly donate a major organ just to be busier right now. Despite working for the General, we at HQ only discovered that the war had started at the same time as the rest of the world – when Fox News showed footage of the first US missiles being fired into Iraq. I'm not sure how I thought I'd hear news of the start, maybe I thought the General would come out and fire a starting pistol? Almost immediately the first US missile was launched against Baghdad, the scud alarm went off and we were ordered to jump into trenches. We were already kitted up in our chemical suits and I wish I'd taken more notice of the defecation and canister changing drills now. Surprisingly though, when the alarm sounded for the first time, I felt an immense sense of resigned inevitability wash over me. We piled into the trench like sardines and I now regret my complacency regarding the digging of trench – how naïve I was and what a bloody fool.

I'll never forget that first time in the trench. The soldier to my right was shaking violently – it was impossible to know the age or gender of the soldier because the body was covered in an NBC suit, over-boots, latex gloves and a respirator. I took the person's left gloved hand in my right one and we kept our hands held tight, hidden under my leg. We sat there for about ten minutes and waited for the all-clear. When he took off his respirator, I saw that the poor lad couldn't have been a day older than twenty. The scud attacks have been merciless, and we've jumped into trenches many times today and it's a day tinged with nothing but sadness and news of losses, but we've got through it. We gather around the bird table several times per day and each brigade, including the Marines and the Paras, brief the General via radio link and listen to how the brigades and marines are advancing. I have to admit, it's fascinating. This is the blackest period of my life, and yet since the war began I feel utterly invigorated. Is it wrong to feel so alive?

Love, Rosie

Bluey
From: Rosie
To: Mr and Mrs Hughes

Date: 23 March

Hi, Mum and Dad
   Just a quick note to say that I'm safe and not to worry.
I'll phone as soon as I can. Love you.

   Yours, Rosie xx

'E' Bluey
From: Aggie
To: Rosie

Date: 24 March

Hi, Rosie
   I haven't had any letters from you for a little while
so I'm just going to keep on writing in the hope that
my E Blueys are still being printed off for you.
Anything I can think of to write in this letter seems
rather banal considering your situation, and I'm not
really sure what to write other than news from the
home front, so I'll do that and hope it keeps your
spirits up.
   The main news to report is that Isabella is here and

is bunked up with me at the cottage. I wasn't sure if we would get along. You must admit, it's a bit weird having a celebrity chef rock up on your doorstep, but it seems that celebrities have exactly the same habits and insecurities as the rest of us, so I told her, 'Mi casa es tu casa', and she was happy to crack on. My only house rule is that I'm prepared to share absolutely everything except my Bic razor. She readily agreed to my condition, so I've put her in charge of the chickens. She loves the café and I can tell she's trying not to take over, but I don't mind. OK, I do a bit. Anya would call it karma.

Isabella couldn't have come to a better place for a little peace from the rigors of celebrity status, but you should see the faces of our customers when they walk through the door to be greeted by the lady off the telly! Anya and Ishmael are possibly the last two people on the planet to care about her celebrity status, and 'the noisy family' are far too hippy-happy-clappy to notice a famous chef moving into their manor. I'll admit, though, in the darkest recesses of my soul, I'm hoping word *will* get out that Isabella is here. I dream of doubling our customer throughput from ten to twenty customers per day. But as our numbers depend entirely upon how many people Hector can squeeze into his little boat, we will always be exclusive.

Despite our little shenanigans, I don't want you to think that we're not keeping up to date with the war.

Isabella and I sat on the beach last evening, watched the sunset and said a prayer. At first, we said a prayer for you and Gethyn, but then I remembered I had sent you *The Railway Children*. In the film version, Dinah Sheridan (the mother) reminds Jenny Agutter (Bobby) to remember not just her father in her prayers, but *all* prisoners and captives (or something like that). And so, in a similar vein, we said a prayer for *all* those who are affected by war, on whatever side, in whatever battle. Despite our prayers, however, we've decided to listen to the news just once every day – I'm afraid it's just too stressful to listen any more than that. But our thoughts are with you, always.

Stay safe, beautiful lady.

Love, Ag

P.S. A lady called Stella Valentine came in yesterday – isn't that just the best name ever! I'm going to nick it for a book – or even better, a pseudonym.

Bluey
From: Rosie
To: Aggie

Date: 26 March

Hi, Aggie

I'm following your lead by taking a moment to enjoy

a little peace and quiet at twilight, sitting at the map table and drinking a cup of tea, writing letters.

Night times seem busier in terms of the operational tempo than during the day, which means the scud alarm goes off regularly in the early hours. The bird table briefings have increased in number and intensified, and we all hold our breath in the hope that more UK losses won't be reported, but each day and, especially, each night, we hear the inevitable news – more losses. Do you think it's too late to find God? If not, where should I look and, given the circumstances, shouldn't God find me first?

The tempo has ramped up for Gethyn, and I haven't seen him much since the war started. He sits by the radio in the US Marine tent waiting to dispatch assets and has gone into operational doctor mode. He is suddenly the most serious, single-minded operator I've ever known. Shit, scud alarm's just gone off. Must go.

I'm back. It landed a mile or so away. Anyway, must have a look at the weather and phone round the brigades, see what they need from me.

Take care, love Rosie

Melanie Hudson

Bluey
From: Rosie
To: Mrs Hughes (via the Post Office)

Date: 27 March

Hi, Mum

I'm sat on the sand outside our sleeping tent taking in some sun for twenty minutes. To the right of me a bunch of US Marines are playing the card game, Uno. This seems to be the wrong game, somehow. Shouldn't Americans be playing poker and drinking whiskey?

We're on the move again tonight, edging ever closer to the border. I see the importance of my job now. The weather really matters in a war. I gave the air liaison staff a separate briefing a couple of days ago and the reality of war hit home all the more. I had to wait to brief them and listened as they got caught up in securing air support for the Commandos who were in trouble with an Iraqi tank brigade. Three American F18s, four AV8Bs and two A10s later, the marines were out of trouble. I don't want to even begin to imagine the twisted carnage that that kind of fire-power left behind.

Thanks for sending the knickers and baby wipes, by the way, and all the sweets and magazines, too. It's all keeping me going. Thanks a million, Mum.

Love you,
Rosie x

Bluey
From: Rosie
To: Oliver, via Mrs Cartwright

Date: 27 March

Dear, Oliver

Thank you so much for your letter. It's lovely to know people at home are thinking of us. I've got plenty of time to write to you because when I'm not working on a weather forecast there isn't anything much else to do, except eat and sleep, so we all write lots of letters. I'll try to answer your questions:

It's mid-afternoon here in Iraq and you are right, it is hot in the desert during the day. We try to stay in the shelter of the tents as much as possible and keep physical activity down to a minimum so that we don't suffer from heatstroke. It's a nice temperature at night now that it's early spring, although it wasn't when I arrived. In January and February, it was freezing at night but by July it will be so hot it will be very difficult to sleep, and working outside during the day will be almost impossible. Helicopters may have to stop flying during the day as it will be far too hot.

Yes, I have a gun. It's a pistol. I haven't fired my pistol during the war and I hope I never will. In fact, I only fired it a few times in my life. I'm not a real soldier, I'm a weather forecaster. I'm here because I'm in the Royal

Navy Reserve Forces and I was asked to come and work with the army headquarters staff.

Sand gets everywhere, and it is all that you can feel and see and taste. I wear a scarf around my head and face to keep the sand away from my mouth and nose and hair.

You are not going to be bombed. Saddam Hussein cannot bomb the UK. British children are safe.

I'm neither sad nor happy to be here. I'm nothing, if you can understand that. I'm very sad about the war, though. I was lonely until I found a friend. He's called Gethyn and I would be lost without him.

I will get a medal.

I can't tell you for certain why we're at war. I'm not sure even the General knows. All I can say is that our Prime Minister sent us here and we have to trust that he would only choose to do so if he had a very good reason.

That's my questions answered, perhaps you could answer some questions for me: How did you feel when the school burnt down? Do you mind travelling by bus to your temporary school? Do you think they should rebuild the school in Midhope? My dad wants it to be rebuilt. He's asked for my opinion, but I would like your advice on this.

Thanks again for writing and for praying for me. I hope you write again. Ask any questions you like.

Best wishes,
Rosie

'E' Bluey
From: Mr and Mrs Hughes
To: Rosie

Date: 27 March

Dear, Babe

The village is enjoying a bit of a ceasefire at the moment. Although maybe I'm not hearing any news because everybody I bump into is walking on eggshells around me because they know you're away with the army. Mind you, it'll only take one misplaced comment in the shop or the petrol station and they'll all be at loggerheads again. Mammy and the dog are both doing well. Mammy said to tell you that we're not planning to open up the caravan at Easter like we normally do – Whitby can wait until we know you're safe. We want to be at home during the fighting just in case you manage to phone, and the signal on my mobile is dodgy at the coast.

Aunty Joan sends her love. Her knee is doing much better now, but she's a long way off going back to line dancing at the Legion. The jammy bugger has managed to wangle a disability sticker for her car. They'll hand them out to anybody with a bit of a limp these days!

Did you get the silver bangle I sent? Did I mention it's Victorian? I'm still trying to get access onto the field at Holmfirth. I'll find that pot of gold yet love and then you'll never have to do this bloody awful job again.

Love ya babe.
MumnDad x

Bluey
From: Rosie
To: Aggie

Date: 27 March

Dear, Aggie
 I'm now officially in Iraq. Crossing the border was bizarre. Some Iraqis waved (mainly children) which felt odd considering the hard-fought battles the forward line of troops have faced, but there are pockets of resistance everywhere and no-one is safe. We threw food and water down from the trucks to the children so maybe that's my first attempt at ending world hunger? (I'm not sure the circumstances count!) I'm excessively tired having only had four hours sleep in the last forty-eight and I'm frightened again and suddenly constantly on edge. Sorry, but that's all the energy I have to write tonight.

Love, Rosie

'E' Bluey
From: Aggie
To: Gethyn

Date: 28 March

Hi, Gethyn

What a hateful situation you find yourself in. My ranting to you about the vagaries of romantic fiction seem inconsequential now and I feel guilty that my life has not been disadvantaged in any real way by the war. Perhaps if we had to endure food rationing or had doodlebugs landing in our laps we might have a greater realisation of what is going on. I can't help but feel that as a nation we are far too comfortably-off to be at war – shouldn't I be unable to bake due to a shortage of butter? Ishmael tells me that events in Iraq unfold on our TV screens twenty-four hours a day, but the cottage I'm living in doesn't have a TV, so I'm not able to be a war voyeur, thank God.

I popped round to see Rosie's parents before I came to Appledart. I took a Victoria sponge (you can't go wrong with a Victoria sponge). They were both pale, behind the smiles. I was given the obligatory cup of tea, but it's clear they will both be holding their breath for a while, so it's not surprising they are pale – after all, it's impossible to be ruddy of cheek if you are short of breath. Rosie's Mum had the same kind of distance in her eyes I remember from childhood. But listen to me! I need to buck up and send you some first-class sarcasm.

Yours aye, Aggie

P.S. To show solidarity for your plight, for the rest of the war I'll wear a rough tweed skirt and draw a line up the back of both my legs each day with eyeliner as fake stockings. Enduring cold legs in the Highlands is the least I can do for the war effort.

'E' Bluey
From: Aggie
To: Rosie

Date: 29 March

Hi, Rosie.

How's the war going? Can you believe you're in a situation where I'm even asking you this?

The news from here is that I'm now playing agony aunt to Isabella. Her initial euphoria has worn off and the realisation of her situation has hit her. I hadn't realised she was in such an emotional mess. She keeps crying and it's driving me nuts. Yesterday, I wrapped her up in ten layers of warm clothing, made up a picnic – a flask of coffee, cheese and chili-jam sandwiches and a couple of slices of lemon drizzle (one of *my* recipes- ha!) – walked her along the beach and, once I'd heard the whole sorry story, she fell into my arms and wailed like a banshee. Then she ate more cake (I think she was a little curious as to how I got the sponge especially zingy) and eventually she sighed a massive sigh and smiled.

'Well, Isabella,' I said, 'if you will insist on acting like a doormat, what can a man do but walk all over you? And you need to stop crying too, or you'll have to have some serious work done on your face before your next stint on the telly,' that seemed to sort her out!

She's had a shitty couple of years, bless her. Of course, a man is involved. One of her daughters is causing her all kinds of grief, too. But not to worry, because I sense Anya is working on Isabella surreptitiously. She's been talking to her (generally) about emotional ownership and taking control of one's own thoughts and actions, in other words, 'get a grip missus'. Ishmael keeps out of it all and disappears off as soon as the topic of conversation turns to men.

But - oh my God – Isabella can bake! It's like watching an alchemist. Even Anya is impressed. I've noticed that Isabella tastes everything – every ingredient - as she adds it, but then never eats much of anything once she's baked it. Surely this is self-harm? Her savoury snacks are little morsels of heaven, which is a nightmare. I'm already the size of a house, but with Isabella baking up a storm, I'm going to be the size of two houses by the time I leave here.

That's all for now. Send some warm sunshine our way.

Take care. Thinking of you always.
  Ag

Bluey
From: Rosie
To: Mrs Hughes (via the Post Office)

Date: 28 March

Hi, Mum

I thought I'd better let you know that I'm now in Iraq. But again, try not to worry, I'm about three kilometres back from the front line. I've adopted a 'them and us' mentality now that the bullets are flying. After all, if I was to walk out of this tent and wander into Iraq, I would be captured or shot, so whatever my thoughts might have been about the futility of the war before it started, those thoughts are irrelevant now. Survival is the key. We've stopped wearing a chemical protection kit in HQ and we operate on a risk basis because it looks like Saddam has neither the will nor the means to gas us. When the scud alarm sounds we no longer jump straight into trenches but wait to see where the computer predicts the scud is going to land. If close by, we hit the trenches (it's rarely close by). I'm being completely honest with you in the hope it will show you not to worry. Yes I'm in a war zone, but under the onslaught of American hardware, I doubt the Iraqis would have the energy or ability to attack our Head Quarters, so all is fine. Say hello to Aunty Joan, and a big hug for the dog and Dad.

Love you, Rosie x

'E' Bluey
From: Aggie
To: Gethyn

Date: 29 March

Dear, Gethyn
   Thought I'd write again as soon as I could, just to show you're in my thoughts. How are you? I know it's an obvious thing to say, but I do very much hope that you are safe.
   The latest from me is that I seem to I have found my niche. Running the café is fabulous and I seem to have more energy than I've had in years. All my victims (did I say victims, I meant customers) have to walk quite a way to get here (hence the metaphorical concept of reaching 'the end of the road') and have mammoth appetites.
   I always point their noses in the direction of the

savoury specials board and the cakes on the counter while I'm helping to peel off their waterproof clothing, and we make sure the aroma as they walk in is a mixture of home baking and peat fires – perfect! The weather has been particularly cruel this week and so visitor numbers have been down. Only the rock-hard, stalwart walkers, or those poor souls who are in dire need of Anya, are prepared to cope with the icy winds whistling over from Skye. But I do love to see their ruddy faces light up as they fall through the door.

Working here has been a real eye-opener regarding human behaviour. You would think the customers would rush to the roaring fire on entering, but they don't, they edge their way towards it, like they're cautious that it might breathe out a dragon's breath. But once enveloped within the heat, that first wave of comfort is tangible. The next wave of comfort is the tea pot, and the wave after that (the biggest goffer of all) is Anya's stew. Dessert is literally the 'icing on the cake' (I'm mixing my metaphors now, but you know what I mean), and as the last little crumb is dabbed off the plate with a moist fingertip, it's like the crashing sea of their emotional angst has finally rested on the shore – calm and sated. By the time my customers walk out of the door, their souls have been cleansed by a tsunami of warmth, carbohydrates and sugar - it's lovely. The occasional gluten/sugar free lost soul appears, but we cater for that so they are sated (but never in quite the same way, I think). Anya pops in and out, but likes to maintain a mysterious air about her (it doesn't pay for a fortune teller to overhear details of her client's lives in the cafe – that would be cheating).

Isabella is on the mend – did I tell you she's staying with me? If not, get the details from Rosie. She's taken to walking the beach every morning with Anya's cat (what that cat doesn't know isn't worth knowing). I keep an eye on her from the window to make sure she isn't sitting on a rock – rocking (a melancholic habit I banned on her first day). As Anya and Isabella are often absent, I'm the café's host, and I don't mind in the least. You would never in all your life believe the things people talk about over coffee and cake, and what else can I do but eavesdrop? Many visitors make their way to the end of the road alone, kind of on mini-pilgrimages, which makes for interesting conversations, because if they want to talk, I'm all ears. Bizarrely, my pineapple upside down cake in particular seems to loosen the tongue of the lone traveller – what's *that* all about? Is pineapple a lip-loosener? Tell GCHQ! Anya believes all this listening is good for my spiritual development. I've always been a first-rate eavesdropper, but in conversation, I'm usually the natterer. But here in Appledart, perhaps because of the stillness of the hamlet and the easy-going nature of my lifestyle, I don't need to chatter anymore; I don't feel the need to monopolise every conversation simply to entertain, and I pass my days with my elbow resting on the counter and my right cheek resting on my hand, just listening – I know, you don't need to say a word: I'm experiencing my own transformational growth (but as I told you, life is formulaic).

The big news (and Rosie may have told you this already) is that Nathan Browne (as in, *the* Nathan Browne who publishes *Browne's Culinary Almanac* etc.) is making his own journey to the end of the road in the very near future. I emailed Casey and suggested we put him off, but she says he may never come back if we don't let him in now. I sought guidance from Anya, but unfortunately, the Tarot and the angels proved fruitless, and Anya simply sighed and said, 'There are greater energies at work here'. So I've decided to relax, let it all happen and make sure the café is as awesome as possible by the time he arrives.

What else? Oh, I now regularly ride a horse. The reason is a practical one. I need to streamline the café's outgoings because at the moment we pay the landlord at the pub to deliver our fresh produce. Casey didn't have this cost to bear because her partner, Shep took his little boat across to Mallaig to buy provisions once a week, but we don't have that luxury because although I'm not adverse to cranking up the boat, I have never mastered the art of parallel parking. And if I can't park a car, what chance do I have of parking a boat? Horses are easy to park. All they need is a slap on the arse and a sugar cube and they're happy (aren't we all?). Ishmael saddles up

Jekyll (with additional saddle bags) and I ride to Morir and back a few times a week. I love it. Travelling on horseback is fitting for the place.

So, to surmise, I'm now a Wild Highlander (it suits my hair) and although I sound a tad conceited, it seems I was born to ride – it's so easy - and other than smelling like a stable yard, it's a lovely trip out. My little jaunt eats into my writing time, but isn't fresh air exactly what I needed?

Write soon,
Aggie

Bluey
From: Rosie
To: Mr Butterworth

Date: 29 March

Dear, Mr Butterworth
Thank you for your letter, it was kind of you to write.
I work in the army headquarters and I can say with absolute certainty that my experience of war *can not* even begin to compare to yours. There is a lot of pressure (not so much for me, but for my colleagues) but no direct combat.
We're in Iraq now. Crossing the border was a surreal experience. We travelled by truck in one big convoy and

crossed the desert at night. We made camp in the early hours and slept for a short time by the trucks while soldiers kept watch around us. After a couple of hours of sleep we made tracks and crossed the border early the next morning. Crossing the border was an uneventful evolution and not at all what I expected. We drove onto the deserted Bagdad highway and headed north, and before we knew it, we were in Iraq – no gun battle, no hassle, nothing. The only Iraqis we came across were children who ran along the sides of the trucks. We threw sweets and water onto the road for them.

When I first arrived in theatre I felt like a fish out of water. What was a Royal Naval officer doing on the battlefield? But now I realise I'm an equal out here. I'm one of Her Majesties Forces. No one forced me to sign on the dotted line, and as the days have passed I've come to accept my life here and respect my colleagues (they irritated me at first, but I think that was about my own insecurities rather than their behaviour).

I do understand your concerns regarding the justification for the war, but right now, I'm here and I have a job to do. The marines had a hard time on the Al Faw Peninsula, but they have done incredibly well, and I'm beyond proud of them - I'm proud of all of us. We were sent to the desert ill-equipped and, in my opinion, unprepared for a war no one at home wanted, but we've made it happen. All I know is, for now, I have to remain focussed and wear my uniform with pride.

Take care of yourself, Mr Butterworth, and say hello to Mrs Butterworth for me. When I get home, I would love to pop round and 'exchange notes'.

Best wishes,
Rosie Hughes

Bluey
From: Gethyn
To: Aggie

Date: 30 March

Dear, Aggie

It's 2a.m. and I've just walked back into the HQ tent after stepping outside for a moment to get some air. There's no moon tonight. Just for a second, I was able to sit, take in the stars and pretend that war wasn't raging around me, that it didn't exist. I've never meditated before, and I don't believe I intended to tonight, but it was like I had lifted out of my own body, and just for a moment, I wanted to wander into the desert, drift away and never look back. But I knew if I started walking, even after a few paces, without the moon's guiding light, I would never find my way back to the safety of the tents. I stepped back inside, picked up a blank Bluey and wondered who I'd like most to write to at this moment of peace, and it was you.

I wonder if Bush and Blair know how frightening war really is? A jet passed over HQ earlier today. I thought it was an Iraqi jet and I can tell you, just for a moment, until I realised it was one of our own, I was petrified – my emotions were certainly in my gut at that moment! There's something beyond frightening about being on the receiving end of an attack from the air. If I was an Iraqi woman, holding a child in my arms and waiting to see where the bombs were going to fall, I don't believe I could cope with such an ordeal and I hope, more than anything I have ever hoped in my life, that this war is for good reason, because if it isn't (and we are yet to find the promised WMD) then in years to come I'm not sure I'll be able to rationalise in my mind what we're doing here, or maybe I'm being overly-sentimental. Maybe the horrible truth is, when I get home, I'll be so busy with my easy western life-style, that other than the occasional pang of guilt – the occasional flashback - I will have forgotten all about it.

But enough of my melancholy. You said your writing isn't going well. Surely more happy endings are in the pipeline? As your newest and biggest fan, I do hope so.

G

P.S. If you can get your hands on a violin do you think you could send it out for Rosie.

Bluey
From: Rosie
To: Aggie

Date: 31 March

Oh, Aggie.

Why is the value of something – someone – so much greater when you don't have it, than when you do? I spent the last year absolutely sure that separating from Josh was the right thing for my future (and for his) but now I miss him like hell and can't ever imagine being with another man. Shit, I've messed up. I've not mentioned this before – and please don't be upset that I haven't told you - but one of the reasons our marriage broke down was because my baby, Angelica, died. After three previous failed IVF attempts, I finally got pregnant; but the pregnancy was a disaster. I developed pre-eclampsia at thirty weeks and was hospitalised because my blood pressure sky-rocketed. My whole body blew up with fluid retention. The hospital staff hoped to keep me stable for as long as possible, but at thirty-six weeks, my body packed in and I developed eclampsia and started to fit. They rushed me to theatre and delivered the baby. Tragically, she died three hours after delivery. Josh was with her, but I was in intensive care fighting for my own life. I was pumped with magnesium and Lord knows what else and had a blood transfusion.

I never held her while she was alive, which haunts me to this day. When I was stable enough to hear the news, they told me she had gone and rested her in my arms. The only name we could think of was Angelica. When you wrote about feeling a gaping hole in your heart in the shape of your mum, I realised it was the perfect way to describe how I feel about my baby. I don't want to let go of the balloon she rests in, but maybe here in Iraq, finally, I will.

Anyway, I don't want to think about that right now. I'm alive and that's more than can be said for the poor people who we repatriated today. What's worrying though (and I haven't even admitted this to Gethyn) is I seem to have lost my capacity to display emotion and I've been this way for some time. Standing in line earlier today with my colleagues, paying our silent respects to five soldiers laying in coffins covered in union jacks, I didn't shed a tear. One young soldier standing further down the line collapsed, but I felt numb. Am I a monster? Sod it, I don't want to write about that either.

Love, Rosie x

Bluey
From: Gethyn
To: Aggie

Date: 31 March

Hi, Aggie

It's the witching hour again and I can't sleep. We move further into Badlands every now and again, but I'm not worried as this brave young warrior called Rosie says she'll protect me (she's suddenly turned into Lara Croft and I honestly think she could kick a bit of Iraqi arse, too). She wanted to chirp me up, so she read me your *Be Careful What You Wish For* letter, the one where you attempted to conjure up your dream man in the moonlight (please don't be cross with her, if you knew the circumstances, you wouldn't be). As ever, your letter forced a smile to cross my lips, but it also got me thinking about you (I know what you're thinking, 'Oh God, here he goes again with the lecturing bollocks').

In one of my earlier letters, I said the heart was not the correct imagery for love. On reflection, I was wrong. To explain:

The thing about the heart is that it does not have to think about beating, it just does it, from the first beat until the very last. Since I wrote my first letter to you, I've come to realise that, like the very first heartbeat, love is not something a person can manufacture artificially, it starts in a single moment. And once it has begun, true love will not stop until the heart dies. So, you were right, the heart is the correct symbol for love, after all.

And so, in my random round-a-bout way, the thing I wanted to say to you is this: please believe me when I say you do not need to conjure up a man or read any self-help books. Everything you'll ever need to know about life is already inside of you – inside your heart. I confess, all of your books have been sent out to me, and three of your novels in particular touched me deeply. *When I Let You Go, But That's Not What I Meant* (hilarious) and *Here You Come Again* were all fabulous books, and I realise to my horror and embarrassment that you absolutely did not require a pompous lecture from yours truly about the merits of the romantic novel. However, despite all of the above, perhaps one day in the future, just for me, you could try your hand at a different kind of love story – perhaps one that doesn't focus on the white knight?

Anyway, I'll sign off there, but please don't worry about being single in a world of couples, because I promise you this, Agatha Braithwaite, your soul mate will appear by your side one day, and it will almost certainly happen on the day you least expect him to pitch up.

G

Bluey
From: Rosie
To: Aggie

Date: 1 April

Dear, Aggie

I'm so desperately tired tonight, I'm not sure how much sense this will make. I can hear the shelling of Basra. It's become normal. The scud attacks that plagued us last week are less frequent as we are now too close to the enemy for them to range on us. Special Forces are on the hunt in the western desert for scuds and WMD. They won't find the WMD. That's not what this is about, not really. The biggest threat to British troops now is from local suicide attackers – I suppose there's not much else can they do. The Army don't annoy me anymore. Has this fish found water? I seem to be coping better than some of the staff – is this because they're taking naps tablets, or is it because I have a true friend and I am able to laugh and dance with him, even on the worst days? I arrived full of self-pity and spent the first few weeks here moaning, as you well know (sorry). But having been stripped naked of all preconceptions and previous persona, I feel like I've been able to get as close to a new beginning as possible. I don't need a baby to live anymore, I've given birth to myself. I am enough, in me, myself.

Dad is right, if you just keep smiling, life is easier, whatever it throws your way. I think my smiles (even though at times they have been forced) are becoming contagious. I've noticed others smiling back at me – finally – and their shoulders seem to relax a little. Just maybe I have had a purpose here, after all.

With love,
Rosie

'E' Bluey
From: Aggie
To: Gethyn

Date: 6 April

Dear, Gethyn
I'm so very touched the person you chose to write to at the moment you felt lost in the desert was me and I'm genuinely honoured to know that my books have given you light relief during a difficult time.

I've not managed to write one word this week. Maybe the title – *My Foolish Heart* - is wrong. I was listening to a 70's CD this morning and had the idea that all my future titles should be taken as inspiration from Bee Gee songs. For example, *How Deep Is Your Love,* could be an erotic novel about a gigolo deep sea diver with an 'impressive instrument' who entices women into his under-water world – OK, it's terrible.

Anyhoo, I'm a little miffed with Rosie for sharing my letter with you *sniffs, irritated*. Some bits of information are strictly for girls' eyes only. On balance, though, I'm glad she did read it to you, because your words have given me the confidence to keep going. However, I'm afraid I do not share your optimism regarding the materialisation of my soul mate. But if Mr Right does pitch up, I hope he gives me a little prior notice, or at least enough time to jump out of my PJs, put a comb through my hair and ditch my fuzzy slippers!

I was awake last night at the witching hour too. I tried to write, but nothing came. I'm a quarter way through my latest novel and despite your words of encouragement, although the *will* is there, the *way* is not. Some people believe that writing is inspired, in the truest, biblical sense of the word, and that any creative process is channelled via another source. If this is the case, the deep well containing my source of inspiration has dried up, and I'm not even sure I want the water to start flowing again. I love my new life of interaction, and the thought of sitting alone, writing, hour after hour, fills me with absolute dread. Truth is, I had become too lonely to be alone anymore. Keep smiling, lovely man.

Aggie

'E' Bluey
From: Aggie
To: Rosie

Date: 8 April

Oh, Rosie

I'm so sorry about the loss of your baby. I wish I could wave a magic wand and take all the pain away. I'm not going to try to give you words of wisdom, because you will have heard them all before, but I am sorry. It's perhaps easier for me than for you to be childless because I've never yearned to have a child, it's just something that I thought I'd get around to, one day, if I met the right partner. I suppose to sum up, I won't sweat it if I'm never a mum, but if I fall in love, and if we decide we would like to start a family, then yes, I'll go for it. Anyway, if you ever want to talk about it, or scream at someone, or just go out one night and get totally wrecked – I'm there for you.

My mother, the old cowbag, still hasn't been in touch. I haven't contacted her this week and I won't again. No doubt I'll see her when I get home (not that I'm sure I want Midhope to be my home any more). I have a few decisions to make, but not right now. Now is the time for providing a little TLC to the café pilgrims – and I bloody love it!

Life here continues with its renewed twists and turns. I decided to let Isabella settle in a bit before dropping the Nathan Browne bombshell on her, which is an appropriate word to use as she did look fairly shell-shocked after I broke the news. She blushed bright red and had to grab onto the counter to steady herself. AND, for the first time in her life, not only did Isabella Gambini proceed to overly beat her meringue, she forgot to add eggs to her cake mix, too. Hmm, something's fishy here, me thinks. Do you think they had an affair? Oh – wait! Even better! Could Nathan be the *real* father of her first child? So exciting. I'll wheedle it out of her soon, and if not, I'll just get Anya to slip something 'special' into her gin and then we'll discover the truth!

Love, Aggie
P.S. Are you sure Gethyn is in a relationship?

'E' Bluey
From: Oliver
To: Rosie

Date: 7 April

Dear, Rosie

I'm glad you have a friend. School was ok today because we did maths, but tomorrow is The Huge Write and I don't like holding a pen too long and even if my work goes on the wall, I don't have anyone who would want to come and see it and because I write slowly, I sometimes have to miss playtime to finish my writing. I love writing letters to you because I say what I want to say and Miss types. Here are my answers to your questions:

I don't have a best friend because I've moved from school to school too much. The other kids in school are ok but they made their best friends by Year Three, so I don't have one as I didn't go to school much then and even if I had gone to school and got a friend I would have moved away from him by now, so it would be a waste of time. I didn't cry when the school burnt down. I don't know if I feel lonely, but it might be nice to have a friend. My last foster mum said there's no point wishing for what you can't have – she was talking about a dog because I wanted a dog. I like fishing. I don't mind the bus now, but I will mind it in the summer because I'll have less time for fishing in the evenings. I like all sweets. Didn't you want your best friend in Iraq to be a girl?

Oliver

Bluey
From: Gethyn
To: Aggie

Date: 7 April

Hi, Aggie
Don't force the writing, forget about it. You'll know

when the time is right to start again. I'm glad you're enjoying life at the café. It sounds wonderful. I'd love to be there right now and can imagine myself drinking tea from a giant mug (do you have giant mugs? I hope so), eating one of your cakes and staring out of the window at the changing landscape of the sea while blithering on to you about everything and nothing. I don't know how much Rosie has told you about my life (probably nothing, why would she?) but over the past couple of weeks - for once - I've found myself talking over a few bits and bobs, and this has helped. I think we both used the war as an excuse to get away, which is beyond ridiculous.

But back to Appledart. I'm trying to imagine what your friends look like. I imagine Anya is someone in her sixties who wears hippy clothing and has long white hair – is that correct? And how old is Ishmael, you didn't say? Do you spend much time with him? What colour are the horses? Are there any seals? Have you had much snow? So many questions, but I have to say, Agatha, for an author you haven't imparted much information. Please remember, I'm living in a black and white world at the moment and it's your job to paint me the colours of home.

G

'E' Bluey
From: Aggie
To: Gethyn

Date: 11 April

Hello, you.

Don't you think it's odd that we've become friends
(I hope you *do* regard me as a friend now?). I don't
suppose either of us would have believed we would
have become such confidantes so quickly. We must be
kindred spirits.

In answer to your questions regarding my neighbours,
here is a little detail: Anya is beautiful, both in spirit
and in looks. She has very short spiky hair dyed bright
red (it was purple when I arrived and will be a different
colour altogether next month). She's in her sixties – I
think. She never discusses any men in her life, but she
gives off an aura of a woman who has known great
passion. She moves like a cat. She is centred, calm and
at one with her soul. She has never suggested any kind
of need to have a relationship and I get the impression
that she's so utterly at peace with herself she doesn't go
out of her way looking for one.

And Ishmael? Well, he's striking-looking. He's quirky,
too; abstract, kind, a little bit on the spectrum, perhaps?
I haven't asked his age but I would guess forty. It's
difficult to say because Appledart seems to give its

inhabitants a timelessness about their looks. It's as if everyone who lives here becomes fixed – tree-like - remaining constant with time. Wrinkles exist within their landscape – steady and sure and content. I do sometimes wonder if Ishmael and Anya have something going on (he tiptoes to her house late at night). How wonderful if that were true – an older woman with a younger man? What a refreshing change and what an absolute goddess!

The family-of-noise are blonde, white-teethed, healthy, completely self-contained and, although they're REALLY annoying, are actually growing on me. Then there's the Aussie, Shaun, who runs the pub (five miles away). He's never lost for company as he has a constant stream of guests arriving to stay at the hotel thanks to Hector's boat. The only people who enter into his life are transient – and he's happy that way. He's burly and hasn't got a clue about small talk, but he is practical, which is a great asset for the rest of us. The three of us - Ishmael, Anya and me - spend one evening a week at the pub, usually on the night the fiddler comes across from Mallaig. We sing, and I play the piano and it's all just fabulous (I know, aren't we the twee ones?).

As for Appledart, it's a mountainous peninsula only accessible by boat or on foot. The hills that rise directly from the water's edge are steep and marvellously atmospheric. A couple of handfuls of cottages are divided between the only two hamlets - Aisig and Morir. Both have pretty little harbours. Morir faces out into a sheltered inlet of water and has a calm quality, but Aisig (where I live) is much more open to the elements. Looking up from my laptop and out of the front window, I can see the Isle of Skye, and the Cullin Mountains beyond, which are snow-capped and will remain so until late spring. Because of the Gulf Stream we don't get too much snow, but it's cold. We endure quite a lot of rain, which turns to ice on the track, which is why Jekyll and Hyde are invaluable.

The best days are the days of clear blue skies when the air is so crisp it could be cut with a knife. But whatever the weather, as soon as I step outside my front door I feel soaked through in the freshness of it all. My cheeks have never been so ruddy, and I have never slept so well. I have a wood-burning stove at home in Yorkshire, but it only serves as a luxurious appendage to the central heating system. In Aisig, my wood-burner is my only source of heat and it is the heart of the house. However, like a child, the stove requires constant attention, but I love it despite its neediness. We burn peat and the smell is delicious. My bedroom is always freezing cold, but I stoke up the wood-burner at night and when I dash downstairs in my pyjamas and slippers in the morning, the embers are still glowing and I'm toasty and warm in seconds. The cottage is an eclectic mix of bargain-hunt treasures, herbs, spices, old magazines, dust, Afghan rugs and house plants. I love it. It smells of earthiness and incense.

Before I came to Appledart I was lonely, but now I'm here, I'm happy. My only fear is that the portal to Brigadoon will close soon, and I'll have to slip out of my pretend reality and return to my real one.

Stay safe, my friend.
Aggie
P.S. I'm working on the violin.

'E' Bluey
From: Mr & Mrs Hughes
To: Rosie

Date: 8th April

Dear, Babe
   Are you still safe in Kuwait? I see scuds have been hitting the city. Wouldn't you be safer in the desert? Mammy wants to know if you're getting enough sleep? We're watching the news as much as we can. Terrible business. I'll kill Tony bloody Blair if I ever get my hands on him. Simon phoned last night to see if we'd heard from you. Mammy was so pleased he phoned, she even agreed to take a little run out to the garden centre afterwards. Don't think badly of him if he hasn't written. He's just so busy. But, credit to him; I haven't seen Mammy

smile much since you went away and his phone call made her chuckle (he can wind her round his little finger, that one).

For God's sake, KYHD.
Love you.
MumnDad xx

Bluey
From: Rosie
To: Aggie

Date: 9 April

Dear, Aggie

I think Gethyn is still in a relationship, but I'm not sure how solid it is (you know what men are like, they never get down to the proper detail).

I had such a shitty day today. At the evening briefing when the Chief of Staff asked the Brigades (via the communications link) if they had any points, some bloody colonel piped up and asked why the sand storm we had experienced that morning hadn't been forecast. He said, 'If the Met girl isn't up to the job, get someone else in'. He then went on to say that the wind direction I had given at the beginning of my brief was different to the one given by the NBC (nuclear, biological and chemical) guy and this was unacceptable. I wasn't given the opportunity to explain which left me standing in the brief like a humiliated, inept, naughty school girl. The Chief of Staff said he would 'speak to me in private' which I suppose was the professional thing to do, but that brief goes out to the whole of the army, and I would have loved to fight back and say:

'Fuck you, you numb-nut, arse-wiping cock-face, tosser. I get the met forecast from the Yanks, so have a dig at them! AND, by the way, if there *is* a sandstorm and a chemical attack at the same time, the wind direction will be so variable it won't matter – you'll be completely fucked. And another thing, if there's a chemical attack, put your fucking respirator on rather than try to remember the wind direction which probably will have changed since the morning briefing!' Can you imagine the look on everyone's faces if I had said all that and just let rip!

Also, why did he assume the NBC officer (a MAN) was right and I (a WOMAN) was wrong? Whatever the answer, he's fucked over my reputation good and proper. Gethyn said I should put it in context and see that the man was clearly operating under extreme pressure, was stressed out, desperate to look after his troops and may be under the effect of NAPs tablets, and that I shouldn't take it personally. Luckily, Gethyn had a compass on him, so now, before each brief, to get an accurate wind direction, I step out into the desert and look for an oil refinery, follow the fumes and get the wind direction from that

– clearly, if that arse-wiping colonel had any sense, he would do exactly the same thing! Why oh why didn't the army bring a fucking met unit with them, or at least give me some basic kit – like a fucking hand-held anemometer?

Please save all my letters. When I'm back at the Met Office I must remember to read them to remind me that nothing that happens at work can ever be as frustrating as this. Rant over.

Love, Rosie

Bluey
From: Rosie
To: Aggie

Date: 10 April

Dear, Aggie

Sorry about yesterday's letter. What a moaning, whinging baby I was. Truth is, I cocked up and I just couldn't bear it.

I phoned home today for the first time since I got here. They've introduced a welfare package to provide us with a couple of minutes of satellite phone calls per week. Poor Dad. I thought he was going to have a heart attack when he heard my voice. He just started screaming, 'Marge, Marge, it's our Rosie, quick!' And I was trying to tell him there was no time to get Mum and not to waste the call, and so I spent the first minute speaking to no one - typical. Mum's voice was shaking a bit but she was calm, then Dad grabbed the phone and said, 'I've had a terrible nightmare! Under no circumstances are you to get on a helicopter – promise me, Rosie!' What a ridiculous thing to say. And the worse thing is, I AM getting on a helicopter, about an hour from now, so I feel vulnerable today, which is not how I've been feeling at all lately.

I want to put my hands up and say, 'This is madness. I want to go home immediately.' But there's no getting off this bloody fairground ride once you're on it and to be perfectly honest, even if someone pitched up in the next ten minutes and said, 'OK love, there's been a huge mistake, you shouldn't be here, I'm taking you home,' I still wouldn't go because how can you leave your mates once it's started? How can you not stay as part of the team until the bitter end? Gethyn and I were sarcastic, opinionated onlookers before the war started. But now we get it.

Reading your letters is like hearing your voice again, and you'll never know (except for the fact that I'm telling you now) what a comfort you have been. So many memories of the two of us have come flooding back, memories of the little things, like sitting at my house watching films, usually with me laying on the settee and you sprawled across Mum's sheepskin rug (do you still sit on the floor rather than a chair?). Do you remember that year your mum gave you a spy set for Christmas and you persuaded me to hide behind the bins in Janey Peters' back yard to see if she was having a fling with that bloke your mum was knocking about with – can you actually believe she really was? Your poor mum was heartbroken.

With much love, Rosie

Bluey
From: Rosie
To: Josh

Date: 11 April

Hi, Josh
Thanks for the apology, but you were probably right.
Can you do me a favour, please? Could you possibly sort out all of Dad's tools we've borrowed over the years? He's getting himself into a pickle because he can't find a few bits and bobs and is worried Alzheimer's is settling in. If anything is broken just replace it. I think we have the sander, the matik (from when you dug out the drains for the new septic tank) a trestle table (from the wall papering fiasco) and a battery-powered drill (from when you built my raised beds).
I'd forgotten how much work you did. I'm not sure

what I was doing while you were doing all these jobs? If I never said thank you for all the hard work you put into the cottage, I'll say it now. You created a beautiful home for us and, for what it's worth, I loved it.

Rosie x

Bluey
From: Gethyn
To: Aggie

Date: 11 April

Hi, Aggie

I'm in love with Appledart and want to fly there immediately. But there is one thing I don't understand. In your letter you said you all travel to the pub on horseback, but you have two horses to share between three people, and one of the horses is a pony – do you and Anya share?

Speaking of Anya, a few nights ago Rosie and I were laying in our bunks in the dark in the tent, hoping the scud alarm wouldn't go off, and Rosie told me she had been to Appledart with her ex-husband (you probably already know this). But what you may not know is that Anya read Rosie's cards for her (if that is the correct terminology). In fact, Anya's presence at Appledart is the reason Rosie chose to go there. Rosie wanted to ask Anya

227

if she would ever have a child. Anya didn't answer Rosie directly, instead she told her that her future would not turn out as she might expect at that moment and that she had some challenging times ahead. Anya said Rosie would travel to a hot country – to a desert - and her life would turn in an entirely different direction, but that in the desert she would finally find peace.

I've often wondered if people actually find a way to act out the prophesies they are given. Take Rosie, for example. Would she have accepted the offer to work with the army if Anya hadn't predicted she would go to the desert and find peace? Maybe Rosie's future changed the very moment she stepped through Anya's front door.

My personal journey into the desert was less intense, but has a similar theme. I've journeyed from regular moments of melancholy before the war started, to the depths of despair when it began. But now I feel a greater force is pulling at me – pulling me out of myself. When I leave here I want to be a reborn version of a man others once knew – a phoenix out of the ashes. I'm babbling.

Write soon.

G

Bluey

From: Rosie

To: Oliver

Date: 11 April

Dear, Oliver.

How was The Huge Write – did you hate it? Why don't you ask your teacher if you can do some of your class work on a computer? You write my letters on a laptop, so why can't other long pieces of writing also be written on one? Can't you ask for a scribe? You said in your letter you like maths – me too. My dad always told me to, 'play to my strengths'. If your strengths are maths and fishing, then maybe focus on them. Maybe one day you will live near the sea and be a commercial fisherman? Or you could be a maths teacher? In answer to your questions:

I don't mind that my best friend is a boy. I'm beginning to realise that special friends appear from nowhere just when you need them the most, a bit like angels. Some of them will stay for life and, sadly, some of them won't, but you will always carry them in your heart. Do you think you could try to believe that the right friend is going walk into your life sometime soon? I discussed this exact issue a few evenings ago with my friend, Gethyn, and he said, 'like attracts like'. So, for example, if you are feeling down and low, then you may attract the same type of person into your life (someone without much joy about them) but if you dig deep and find joy and start to transmit joy from your soul, you will bring something – someone - more positive into your life. Will you try a little experiment for me? Will you please try to smile (for no particular reason) several times per day, and then see if things start to change – I bet they will! My friend Agatha thinks that if you wish for something hard enough (and write your wish down to make especially sure) then the universe will eventually provide it for you, one way or another. Even if you don't believe in my theory, isn't it worth giving it a try? I'm being a hypocrite in writing this, because I'm smiling on the outside rather than on the inside at the moment but smiling through the heartache is something I promised my dad I would do.

I want to come home but I can't. Once you are away with the Army you have to stick it out.

You said you wanted a dog - do you like animals? I haven't got much time today as we have just set up a new base and it's a bit hectic, but I'll write again soon, and do let me know how the smiling goes (don't worry if people think you look a bit daft).

Rosie

'E' Bluey
From: Aggie
To: Rosie

Date: 12 April

Hi, Rosie

Guess what? I was right after all, our Isabella has indeed got a bit of history with the infamous Nathan Browne. Sadly, my idea that they may have slept together after some foodie shindig in New York (leading to the conception of her first child) was entirely unfounded (note to self – try to keep imagination in check).

No, the truth (according to Isabella who I suspect could be a fairly unreliable witness) is this: ten years ago, at the height of his food-critiquing days, Nathan Browne criticised Isabella's signature dish by saying (in a Sunday supplement) that he didn't care a tot if her plums *were* smeared with amaretto and served with a sour juice, anything less than a mouthful was not worth the bother. I think Nathan served this comment with a side order of harmless fun-poking, but Isabella did not see the funny side and Alice's old friend Time has not softened the blow.

The media had a field day with his comment and her insistence on wearing chicken-fillet bras now makes sense. I tried to limit the damage by insisting that, person- ally, I found small plums were often more sought after as they can be particularly juicy but coming from me - the woman who personifies excess – my words didn't help. Anya isn't convinced by Isabella's distaste of Nathan and feels there is more to the Nathan Browne story than tiny plums, and she may have a point. The amount of blushing and stuttering issuing from Isabella when we told her Nathan was coming to Appledart, followed by a violent episode of cursing that her hair hadn't been coloured prior to her rapid deployment, leads me to believe there may be more to this than she's letting on. She asked Anya for a revitalising face treatment and has begun resting cold teaspoons under her eyes throughout the day.

Anyway, we've put Hector (the boat man) on lookout duty and have given him strict instructions to telephone from the pub the moment anyone called Nathan (or anyone who looks like Nathan because he'll possibly travel under a pseudonym) arrives. When asked by Hector to describe Nathan, Isabella shrugged and said, 'I suppose he's ok-looking. A bit rough round the edges, though. He often wears a woolly green hat, and he's got a bit of a limp. Oh, and the last time I saw him, he had an eye patch'. She glanced out of the window at the gentle ebb and flow of the sea kissing the sand and as her eyes softened she said, 'Lovely smile, though'.

On that basis, Shaun and Hector had been told to look out for a man who is a cross between Long John

Silver and Benny from Crossroads, who is travelling alone. Hector thought this wasn't much to go on (what the fuck?).

Anyhow, the whole of Appledart (twenty people max) have been instructed to waylay any man with a nice smile and only arrange for his passage to the café once we have given them the go ahead by telephone. What can possibly go wrong?

Ta ta for now, Aggie

Bluey
From: Rosie
To: Aggie

Date: 14 April

Hi, Aggie

How is the writing going? Should I even ask? Do you want me to drop asking about it or do you want me to nag you? Just in case you want me to nag, I'll admit that I'm worried you are getting bogged down sorting out someone else's business to the detriment of your own. You have always been so imaginative and able to dream up all kinds of wonderful (successful) schemes and when Casey comes back I'm sure her café will be on the road to being uber successful. But what about you? Will you be back at square one without having written a word?

I'll stop worrying because presumably at some point Isabella will shoo you away from the café and back to the house, so you can write her next best seller (although she sounds to be a few whisks short of a meringue herself at the moment, so maybe not).

You'll be pleased to know I survived the helicopter trip. Dad's nightmare (the one where I'm guessing I died) was clearly a load of bollocks. I'm not particularly keen on travelling by helicopter anymore. Night time, low level, evasive helicopter transits are the pits, we all just sit there and pray that the pilot won't hit an electricity pylon or get shot down. Bearing this in mind, you'll perhaps understand why our arrival at the airport was a surreal experience. The ramp opened and we all walked off the back of the helicopter onto the tarmac. Having seen nothing but sand for the past few weeks, it was odd to stand on firm ground and to see proper buildings rather than tents. I'm not sure I liked it. In fact, I am sure, I didn't like it. We were anonymous travellers in the desert, like a nomadic tribe. But here at the airport, we're fixed, firm, settled – trapped. The experience of arriving at the airport became even more surreal when we jumped onto the airport bus (which someone had either found the keys for or hot-wired) like tourists, which we are, I suppose.

So, HQ is now established inside the airport terminal and what a mess this airport is. We're working and sleeping in an air-tight concrete fortress in forty degrees of heat with no air-conditioning. Life was much more hygienic in the desert. The toilets leave a lot to be desired as they constitute a dug-out trench with a plank over the top. There is a waste-high screen between the gents and the ladies, but when I sat down for my ablutions this morning and looked to my right, a man was on the other side of the screen doing the same thing. I looked away quickly and said, 'If we both keep looking forward and just get on with it, we'll be OK.' But I'm honestly not complaining.

The heat is now like nothing I've ever known, but at least it's predicable, which is handy for a met woman. Oh, but the good news is there's talk of an RAF mobile met unit being deployed here from Ali Al Salem (an airbase in Kuwait). Can you imagine how frustrating it has been finding out that the RAF has had a met unit in Kuwait for all of this time and yet I've had no communication with them, at all? But, enough self-pity because more importantly, if the RAF come, I think I'll be able to go home! No one seems to know much at the moment, but let's pray they pitch up. Now we're here we seem to be in limbo. The war seems to have entered into a lull and I can't help but wonder at what point someone will declare we have won and we can all go home.

Lots of love,
Rosie
P.S. We have email now. My address is rosie-of-arabia@

yahoo.com. Gethyn is sitting next to me and asked me to say that his address is gethyn-of-arabia@yahoo.com (we weren't particularly individual in the creation of our email addresses).

'E' Bluey
From: Mrs Hughes
To: Rosie

Date: 15 April

Dear, Rosie

I got your letter about how difficult you are finding your job at the moment and I want you to take notice and believe what I'm about to say.

You have nothing to prove, my love. What I want you to do is to imagine your future self - the woman you want to be twenty years from now - and she's looking back at you. Your future self (who is going to be an amazing woman) is calmly explaining that you need to be proud of yourself. She's telling you to stay composed, graceful and feminine. To remember how much inner strength, you've found already. She's telling you that you DO have a role to play out there, but the bigger picture is yet to reveal itself.

I've talked things over with Dad, and I've finally admitted you've been writing to me separately (he says to say, don't be a daft sod, he's stronger than you know). He also said to tell you he read something in a magazine at the doctors the other day and wants to pass it on - life is 10% what happens to us and 90 % how we react to it. Stay calm, stay strong, and above all else, stay safe, my love.

Lots of love,
Mum (and Dad) xx

From: aggieb@yahoo.com
To: rosie-of-arabia@yahoo.com
CC: gethyn-of-arabia@yahoo.com

Date: 18 April

Hello, you two.

You have email! Fabulous. Be careful, you may become spoiled. This is my email address. More soon, off to the café.

Love, Ag

From: gethyn-of-arabia@yahoo.com
To: aggieb@yahoo.com
Subject: Nirvana

Date: 20 April

Dear, Aggie

That's it! I just have to visit Appledart now. Ishmael

and Anya sound to be exactly the sort of people I'd like to knock back a bottle of whiskey and chat with into the wee hours of the morning.

My news from here is uncertain. I may only have one more week with Rosie because it's likely I'm moving to work with one of the brigades for a few weeks, after which time an army doctor will come out to replace me. Now the heat of the war has dampened, my appointing officer says the RAF want me home, although, at the risk of sounding trite, when I say home, I have absolutely no idea where my home is anymore. It's exactly a month since the war started but it feels like a year. Everything is different now. Based at the airport, I believe that we (the original Headquarters staff) feel our job is done here – that we no longer belong in Iraq. We fought a war in four weeks and we're exhausted. Our uniforms are as tired as we are and it's time for a new tranche of soldiers to come to Basra to make their mark, although God knows, I pity them. Unlike those who will replace us, during the war there was a forward line of troops – an objective – which was relatively clean-cut. Now we want to befriend the enemy. But this is the Middle East, not the West, and I can't help but wonder about so many things, and worry. Back to my original point, that being the realisation that I have no notion of where to call home anymore. I will leave Iraq having found and lost myself in the desert. We have lived as a collective, thinking of nothing but survival – eating, sleeping and working together. Tomorrow didn't really matter, and although I had huge crisis of morality, I felt centred, and when busy, my mind did not think about anything beyond the present moment (especially when I was lost in one of your books, of course). But now we're at the airport, my thoughts are confused, and I have to dig deep and admit some truths. But that's enough about me, you still haven't given me any decent gossip on the customers.

G

From: aggieb@yahoo.com
To: gethyn-of-arabia@yahoo.com
Subject: Re: Nirvana

Date: 20 April

Dear, Gethyn
Email is great! It's wonderful to be able to respond on the same day. I'm sorry you are feeling a little lost. I'll send some sticky chocolate fudge brownies – it's my go-to food in times of uncertainty.

Aggie x
P.S. Sorry for the short email, I'll do better tonight. Shaun has just phoned and we have reports of a lone man with silver hair and posh shoes at the jetty and we need to go to action stations.

P.P.S. I cannot possibly divulge the secrets of the confessional (did I say confessional, I meant café). But – we did have a woman in last week who I suspect may have murdered her husband – honest to God, not kidding. She said her husband went missing two years ago and it's a real mystery. But I swear there was an evil glint in her eye (and almost a twitch) AND when she laughed with another customer, she had one of those evil villain, throw your head back laughs. And that is the case for the prosecution, me lud.

P.P.P.S Violin dispatched. Not sure if it's a good one. I bought it off the fiddler who plays at the pub.

'E' Bluey
From: Oliver
To: Rosie

Date: 25 April

Dear, Rosie

Thank you for your letter. Miss says I can't use a laptop in class. I need to practise my handwriting because of spelling and all the other kids will want one and she can't afford it. I type your letters by myself, now. My typing is very slow because I don't know where all the keys are so Miss still helps. I like the idea of being a fisherman to make money but no offence, why do grown-ups always talk about what kids will do when they grow up? Why is it one of the first questions I'm asked by strangers? I do like animals. I once had a dog. Last year I lived in a house that had a little dog called Scamper. She ran out of the garden and I found her on the road squashed and now when I think of Scamper, I can't breathe, so I don't think about it at all if I can. I tried to smile this week like you said, but Matt in class said he'd kick my brains out if I kept smiling at him, so I stopped. I don't think wishing works. I wished Matt was nicer to me, but he never was and I wished I got an XBox for Christmas and that didn't happen either. Have you used your gun yet? I prayed for you in assembly again. A woman is thinking of adopting me. It would be nice to stop moving around but why would someone want to adopt someone else? Why would someone want me in their house all the time?

Oliver

From: rosie-of-arabia@yahoo.com
To: percynmadge@hotmail.com
Subject: Thanks

Date: 28 April

Hi, Mum and Dad
No, you aren't seeing things, we have email now. But

no need to panic. We're safe as houses and snug as a bug. It's becoming unbearably hot, but we have electricity and have been given electric fans to cool us down, although we decided to turn them off as they just blow burning-hot air into your face. Thanks again for all the parcels you've been sending – keep them coming. Aggie has been sending books, which I've passed onto my friend Gethyn as I don't seem to be able to concentrate on reading a novel at the moment, but magazines are a nice, bite-sized respite. Are you having much rain? I would love to feel the rain on my face and walk barefoot on the grass and surround myself with the colour green - heaven. I don't believe there is any place more beautiful than home in the spring. Please enjoy it on my behalf by having some fabulous trips away in the caravan. Do you remember that trip we made to Tenby when I was twelve, or maybe I was a bit older? It was such a fabulous holiday. Maybe we could all go to Tenby when I come home? Maybe we could persuade Simon to take a special trip back, just so we can all be together again?

Please don't worry too much. I'm absolutely fine – get yourselves off to the caravan – life is for living.

Love you all so much, Rosie x

P.S. I haven't forgotten about the school, but I'm not sure about the best step forward.

Dear Rosie Hughes

From: rosie-of-arabia@yahoo.com
To: aggieb@yahoo.com
Subject: Feeling Better

Date: 29 April

Hi, Aggie

Oh my God! A violin came through the post for me today. The thing was, the sender hadn't put their sender's details or a description on the box, so the Army were going to blow it up. And then Gethyn dashed in and said, 'Stop! It's not a gun, it's a violin' - and it was. A bloody violin – in the desert. Despite being anonymous, this kind of antic has your name written all over it – was it you? Gethyn won't say. If so, thank you, I love it.

I'm feeling more upbeat today. I got an email from Mum recently saying that I should imagine my future self and imagine her talking me through my life. I'm not sure this kind of thing works for me, but it's promising that she feels positive enough to give firm advice.

I've yet another favour to ask, but it's on behalf of someone else – someone in need - so I hope you don't mind. Do you remember lovely Mrs Cartwright, our headmistress at primary school? You may know this already, but she's still the headmistress (she must be about a hundred and ten by now). The thing is, she wrote to me on the day the war started attaching a lovely letter from one of the kids at school. He's called Oliver. He has learning difficulties and is in foster care. I want to get him a laptop, but I think Mrs Cartwright is reticent. I know you'll be reticent, but the bucket list did say that we should help one person and make a difference to their lives – Oliver is my person. Can you possibly investigate so see if there are any specific typing programmes to help children who have writing difficulties? I will pay for everything. Can you phone Mrs Cartwright and ask, please?

Lots of love,
Rosie

From: percynmadge@hotmail.com
To: rosie-of-arabia@yahoo.com
Subject: At Last!

Date: 29 April

Dear, Babe

Email at last? Fantastic! Well, if you're sure you're safe then we may get off to Whitby tomorrow and air the van.

We remember the trip to Wales – of course we do! We stayed at a lovely campsite near St Davids. You insisted I pull into a layby as we headed down the hill towards the caravan site to look at the sunset across the bay. It's where Simon taught you to surf. You fought like cat and dog over that bloody surf board for the rest of the week, God only knows why we didn't buy two – oh, Mammy just said there was only one blue one in the shop and you both wanted it. There was a lovely fish and chip shop in St Davids. She remembers that you insisted on battered sausage, awkward little bugger! Oh, she's just lifted her head from her book to say you were definitely thirteen when we went to Wales because Simon had just finished his exams and went into the lower sixth that September.

I don't know what's got into Mammy these past couple of weeks but she's changed – much more positive. I don't think she's changed her medication, though. Anyway, you know where we are. Mobile will be on. Phone when you can.

KYHD.

Love you babe, Dad xx

From: rosie-of-arabia@yahoo.com
To: josh71@yahoo.com
Subject: Email

Date: 2 May

Josh

I wanted to let you know that we have email now. This is my email address (obviously). Probably best if we correspond via email from now on as it will be more immediate for sorting everything out.

Rosie

From: aggieb@yahoo.com
To: gethyn-of-arabia@yahoo.com
Subject: Bits and Bobs

Date: 3 May

Dear, Gethyn

Sorry I didn't write back when I promised. I fell into bed, shattered.

Oh dear. I see what you mean about people acting out their tarot card readings, but having spent some time with Anya, she doesn't seem to be a con-woman, in fact, she never touts for business and I don't believe she has ever sought out customers (perhaps 'clients' would be a better term?). But maybe that's the point with a master of deception, you'll never know if you've been deceived. One universal truth I do know is this: I always know when it's one of Anya's clients who arrives at the café because, on the whole, they carry a tangible sadness with them – you can see it, and that must be a kind of energy, surely. But when they leave, they seem much lighter of spirit. So perhaps, whether there is truth in the cards – or the stars – or anything else a lost soul might turn to

246

in time of need, Anya does provide comfort, but I do agree with you that it could possibly lead a person in a certain direction. I suppose it depends how the individual concerned interprets her words. Perhaps you should cross her palm with silver, too? You could make a better judgement then.

In other news, hopefully Rosie will have filled you in with all the latest goings on in the café and our impending visit by Nathan Browne (or have I done this already? I'm forgetting which one of you I have told what). Regarding my latest dreaded manuscript, I haven't written a word and have finally properly fessed up to Isabella and seem to have been given some breathing space. Also, my friends who own the café are fully engrossed in their life in Antarctica. They seem almost disinterested in Appledart, but that's what happens when you find a new and exciting love, the fickle heart can forget how much it adored its previous lover. In the deepest, most secret recess of my heart, I hope they stay away for good - then perhaps *I* could buy the café? Now wouldn't that be heavenly, although, to return to the analogy of the lovers, perhaps I want and appreciate Appledart all the more because I know I can't have it forever. Perhaps if my dream was granted, I wouldn't want it after a while; the chase would be gone (I've gone and depressed myself now).

In your last letter you seemed a little lost. Do you have a particular dream? Something you want to do in the future? Perhaps you could focus on that, and every time you feel down, bring the image of the dream back into your head and focus on your future. I know we should live for today and not for tomorrow, but sometimes, when your day-to-day is shitty (and there is no point pretending life in Iraq is anything but shitty) then it pays to focus on the future. Rosie tells me you're in a relationship? Maybe you could focus on your future with your partner? Sorry if this advice is nonsense. I cannot begin to fully comprehend what it's like to go to war. I'm sure you will look back and remember some happy times, like dancing with Rosie in your tent, but on the whole, it's probably something you just get through and then move on from. Finally, don't be deceived by Rosie's angelic face and thousand-watt smile, she was struggling to cope until you appeared in her life. You should take great heart knowing that you have been a light-worker, conjuring up joy where Rosie had found only sadness.

Yours, Aggie

P.S. Keep away from the booze (it's easy to turn to demon liquor at times like this).

P.P.S. Regarding the 'two horse, one rider' question, Ishmael and Anya ride on Jekyll together (he's a massive shire horse so can easily take the weight). Why did you ask?

P.P.P.S. What did one saggy boob say to the other saggy boob? If we don't get some support soon, people are going to think we're nuts.

From: gethyn-of-arabia@yahoo.com
To: aggieb@yahoo.com
Subject: Re: Bits and Bobs

Date: 4 May

Hi, Aggie

If only we *did* have booze to turn to (although we do still have that one bottle you sent). How are the customers? Still confessing their sins?

G

P.S. I didn't ask about the horse for any particular reason, just nosy.

P.P.S. Did Nathan pitch up?

From: aggieb@yahoo.com
To: gethyn-of-arabia@yahoo.com
Subject: Re: Re: Bits and Bobs

Date: 5 May

Dear, Gethyn

False alarm on the Nathan front. He was a double glazing salesman. I'm afraid I have no gossip today (note to self, must try harder in café to prise juicy bits out of customers!). As the café is (relatively) expensive to reach (train, accommodation, boat transfer) my congregation tend to be a middle-class bunch and my 'confessional over coffee' concentrates on stereotypically middle class woes. You know – affairs, debt, murder (the usual). You're up late again?

Ag

From: gethyn-of-arabia@yahoo.com
To: aggieb@yahoo.com
Subject: Re: Re: Re: Bits and Bobs

Date: 6 May

Take it from a doctor who has heard many a confessional, woes are woes, and they usually boil down to the following issues; abandonment, control, deception, money and grief. But when you really get down to the nitty gritty of any kind of emotional angst, you may find that only word to surmise any problem is this – fear.

G
P.S. It's only 1a.m. in Iraq. That's early for me.
P.P.S. Any writing done? I'm waiting for the next book to come out!

From: aggieb@yahoo.com
To: gethyn-of-arabia@yahoo.com
Subject: Re: Re: Re: Re: Bits and Bobs

Date: 5 May

Early? I'm usually out of it by 9.30p.m.

No writing done. I seem to be listening to stories rather than writing them and finding it even more difficult to return to my novel because I'm getting so confused about people – no one seems to be as they appear, and it worries me regarding my writing. Since our communication has begun, every time I sit down to write, I'm overthinking everything. On the plus side, I'm finding taking a break from my imaginary friends quite refreshing – they're a needy bunch!

A

From: gethyn-of-arabia@yahoo.com
To: aggieb@yahoo.com
Subject: Re: Re: Re: Re: Re: Bits and Bobs

Date: 6 May

Hi, Aggie

I wish I had never said anything about your books and cringe when I think of that first letter, but to be fair, do remember that I was writing for the first time to a real author, and I confess that I was trying to impress you (it's just typical that I made a hash of it).

In terms of character, I think most of us do blunder

from one page in our lives to the next, in the most part with good intentions, even if we cock up and are selfish sods along the way. We can't ever all know each other completely (would we even want to?), so why should you know your characters' innermost thoughts – give them some space. Most of the people I know are just ordinary folk getting on with their lives, and other than the occasional eccentric millionaire, the people in your books are just ordinary folk too, not mass-murdering psychopaths. Don't overthink it (and yes, I know I'm going against my initial advice, but that was all a load of crap). Perhaps allow other authors to enter into the darker side of the species and stick with romance, i.e. 'Let other pens dwell on grief and misery' (how on Earth do I remember that quote?).

Your books sell well, and I've loved all of them. Don't change, and more importantly, don't worry – it's only words!

G

From: aggieb@yahoo.com
To: gethyn-of-arabia@yahoo.com
Subject: Re: Re: Re: Re: Re: Re: Bits and Bobs

Date: 5 May

You are not only quoting Austen but the Bee Gees now, too! And you've proved my point, exactly. I am flabbergasted you can quote Austen – should a doctor from the valleys be able to do so? This is madness.

From: gethyn-of-arabia@yahoo.com
To: aggieb@yahoo.com
Subject: Re: Re: Re: Re: Re: Re: Re: Bits and Bobs

Date: 4 May

Don't worry. That Austen quote is the only line I can remember from my O Level English Lit (and I've been waiting twenty years for a conversation to develop in such a way to allow me to use it!).

By the way, I've done as you said and written down my dream. Whenever I feel low, I take the piece of paper out of my pocket, imagine the scenario and smile. Maybe one day my dream will come true, but for now, it's bed time for me.

Good night, Agatha Braithwaite

From: aggieb@yahoo.com
To: gethyn-of-arabia@yahoo.com
Subject: Re: Re: Re: Re: Re: Re: Re: Re: Bits and Bobs

Date: 5 May

Sweet dreams. Gethyn Evans

From: simonday14@hotmail.com
To: Rosie-of-arabia@hotmail.com
Subject: I'm a Dick

Date: 9 May

Hi, Rosie-anna Fish-face

What's my little sis doing in the big bad desert, then? Dad tells me you're in Iraq, which means I can't leave you alone for two minutes without you getting into trouble. Life in Australia is great. Loads going on. Just in case you're too busy to reply (you know how unreliable you are) I've written a reply email for you. All you have to do is delete the words that don't apply then cut and paste onto a new email. Here you go:

Hi Simon, my *beloved/adored/despised* brother

I *miss/hate/want to kill* you so much. Life here in Iraq is *great/shit/abysmal*. I've *found/shagged/shot* Saddam Hussein and I'm ready to go home to Blighty for tea and *cake/medals/defleeing*. I have *missed/adored/wanted to kill you* every day since you left home. I'm *happy/pissed off/ suicidal* at the thought of carrying the burden of looking after Mum and Dad in their dotage and all I want is for you to be *happy/sad/dead* in your new life. On the whole I'm a *happy/carefree/lonely* single woman without Josh and I'm having the *best/worst/most horrific* time of my life.

Love you, you're the *best/worst/most mediocre* brother in the whole world.

Your *adoring/irritated/insane* sister, Rosie-anna Fishface

Take care and don't get blown up!
Love ya, Si

From: rosie-of-arabia@hotmail.com
To: simonday14@hotmail.com
Subject: Re: I'm a Dick

Date: 9 May

Hi Si

Well, it's about time. Yes, you are a dick. Here's my reply. I've added a few bits:

Hi Simon, my beloved brother

I miss you so much. Life here in Iraq is abysmal. I've not seen Saddam Hussein and I'm ready to go home to Blighty for tea and de-fleeing. I have wanted to kill you every day since you left home.

I'm happy at the thought of carrying the burden of looking after Mum and Dad in their dotage (but I would rather do it with you) and all I want is for you to be happy in your new life (in England). On the whole I'm a lonely single woman without Josh and I'm having the most horrific time of my life. I miss my brother more than he could ever know.

Love you, you're the worst brother in the whole world (because you left me).

Your adoring sister, Rosie-anna Fishface

Yep, that just about sums things up. So, how's it really going for you, down under? No bullshit this time.

Rosie

From: gethyn-of-arabia@yahoo.com
To: aggieb@yahoo.com
Subject: On the move

Date: 12 May

Dear Aggie

I have news. I'm definitely going to Basra Palace next week and then I'm flying home, date TBC. I'm pleased, but I will miss my little friend, Rosie.

What's the weather like these days in Scotland? Who have you had in the café this week? Rosie was laughing because we were talking about you taking a self-imposed Hippocratic oath as a café owner, but she reckons you won't be able to resist spilling the beans; so come on, who have your most entertaining customers been to date, and what's the latest on Nathan Browne?

G

From: josh71@hotmail.com
To: rosie-of-arabia@hotmail.com
Subject: Lazy Bones

Date: 13 May

Hi Rosie

You're welcome regarding the house renovations, but if you really want to know what you were doing while I was lost in DIY SOS, then I'm afraid you were devouring *25 Beautiful Homes* magazine while drinking coffee and resting your arse on the AGA. I didn't mind. You looked happy during those times.

Josh

From: aggieb@yahoo.com
To: rosie-of-arabia@yahoo.com
Subject: My Future

Date: 13 May

Hi, Rosie

Violin? Not guilty. What kind of an imbecile would send a violin to a soldier in the desert?

Anyhow, your letter got me thinking about my future – what type of a woman will I be when I'm sixty? Where will I be?

You'll love this – I closed my eyes and a really clear image came to mind – it was awesome. I was standing outside my villa in Spain with a glass of wine in my hand, a loving partner cooking up a storm in the kitchen and lots of lovely guests arriving for a party. Future me is cool, she doesn't sweat the small stuff. She exercises regularly (a yoga buff, I think) but eats well and when she eats she enjoys every mouthful. She's still sexy at sixty, and she's sexy because she's full of joy. In sum, I LOVE me at sixty. What about you? Who will you be at sixty?

But back to now, is it all over now you're settled? I thought we were still at war? Gethyn wrote that he's moving on. One minute you were in the midst of battle and the next it all seems to have ended? I'm confused.

Life in Appledart continues in the same vein - peaceful. I'm considering turning in my quill and inkpot for good, selling up in Yorkshire (sod Mum) and building a house next to Ishmael overlooking the beach. We've had two false alarms on the Nathan Browne front, but at least Shaun and Hector are keen to help out. The second false alarm was indeed a silver fox type chap and was fairly good-looking, but he was on a pilgrimage to the café because (wait for it); he'd lost his job, his wife had recently had a wild affair and left him for his brother and taken everything with her, and he is now living in a bedsit in Wolverhampton. To add insult to injury, while sitting in the doctor's surgery waiting for the results of a testicular cancer test (I know, this man has seriously shit-out) he was chatting to a woman who had visited Anya two years before and her life had been on the up ever since. So, he spent the last cash he had on giving Anya a go. He was too depressed to notice he had been held hostage in the pub by Shaun for four hours, and, thank the Lord, he left Anya's house with a smile on his face and a spring in his step.

The other false alarm was a double glazing salesman who also spreads the word of our Lord during his travels. Poor chap was on the cusp of losing his faith. He spent several hours with Ishmael in the café and, not surprisingly, left even more of a confused man (Ishmael is particularly well-read and can bamboozle even the best of us with his unique mix of spirituality, science knowhow and – occasionally - common sense). So, we're still on the lookout for Nathan, but at least Isabella has stopped crying and has started to dress well rather than impersonate a bag lady. Ta ta for now.

Aggie
P.S. Any details on Gethyn's relationship? Obviously, I'm just interested, not 'interested'. He seems like a nice chap.

From: rosie-of-arabia@yahoo.com
To: josh71@yahoo.com
Subject: Re: Lazy Bones

Date: 14 May

Lazy bones? Arse on the Aga? Is that really how you remember me? I'm sure I did some decorating?

From: josh71@yahoo.com
To: rosie-of-arabia@yahoo.com
Subject: Re: Re: Lazy Bones

Date: 14 May

Yes, on the Aga – and occasionally on the settee (in front of the fire). I'll take a trip to Yorkshire in June, I'm due some holiday. I'll take all the tools back then. Hope all is good your end?

Josh

From: gethyn-of-arabia@yahoo.com
To: aggieb@yahoo.com
Subject: Bored

Date: 15 May

Hi, Aggie

I'm bored. Did you ever find out if Ishmael and Anya are close?

G

From: aggieb@yahoo.com
To: gethyn-of-arabia@yahoo.com
Subject: Re: Bored

Date: 15 May

Dear, Gethyn

In order to answer your question, first I need to ask you a question. I know you hate superfluous use of quotation, but are you asking if Ishmael and Anya are 'close' or just, close?

A

From: gethyn-of-arabia@yahoo.com
To: aggieb@yahoo.com
Subject: Re: Re: Bored

Date: 15 May

OK, you win. Are they 'close'?

From: aggieb@yahoo.com
To: gethyn-of-arabia@yahoo.com
Subject: Re: Re: Re: Bored

Date: 15 May

Ah, now I understand. See, without the use of inverted commas I was unsure as to your meaning. The answer is: I still don't know for sure, but I'm pretty certain they're shagging.

Speaking of Ishmael, he is now called Moses and I fear this may be my fault. We had a few too many whiskeys at the pub last week and Ishmael and I got talking about the importance of awarding the right name to the characters in my books. This led onto discussing how, in choosing a baby name, parents almost certainly dictate the path of a child's life. You know the sort of thing, 'would a rose under any other name smell so sweet.' Would someone called Posy Piper ever be Prime Minister? Or in my case, would Agatha Braithwaite ever be a best-selling novelist? No, but Isabella Gambini would. Ishmael violently disagreed (it was a little bit tense for a while). Eventually, he confessed that, in fact, his name is not Ishmael at all, it's Marc. But he likes to say to people, 'Call me Ishmael,' which is the first line in *Moby Dick*. I said that if I changed my name to Summer Santiago, I could write books of great spirituality and import, which led us on to discuss the idea of reinvention of character, and we asked ourselves this question: could we, by a simple change of name, clothing and even accent, truly reinvent ourselves, or would our basic (at the core of the soul) personality, give us away in the end?

We argued it down to the bone and arrived at no final conclusion, but the next day, Ishmael walked into the café and, just as I was about to say, 'Good morning, Ishmael', he put his hand up and said, 'For the next month, I'm called Moses.' Unfortunately, I was unable to get into a deep discussion regarding the choice of this particular name because Shaun pitched up with a couple of lobsters (did you know they're deep blue before they're cooked?). However, I did discover that Moses (Ishmael) believes that Moses (the fella with the burning bush) is a misunderstood anti-hero with a speech impediment, so I'm looking forward to delving into that particular topic of discussion next time we're at the pub. But if Moses takes his new role too far, for example, if he adopts a stutter, renames Ben Nevis as Mount Sinai and tries to lead us away from Appledart over the hills to redemption, I shall have to slap him (we can only hope he isn't summoning up a flood as I type – or was that Noah?).

Speaking of mountains, I'm climbing one tomorrow – with Moses.

More anon, Aggie

From: rosie-of-arabia@yahoo.com
To: aggieb@yahoo.com
Subject: Future Self?

Date: 15 May

Hi, Ag

I'm confused. I've tried to imagine my future, like Mum said. Where will I be? What will I be doing? Nothing came to mind – no image at all. Is this bad? Oh, and Gethyn says you're climbing a mountain tomorrow – at least that's something else ticked off the list!

Rosie

From: gethyn-of-arabia@yahoo.com
To: aggieb@yahoo.com
Subject: Flying Home

Date: 16 May

Hi, Ag

Just a thought. Maybe I could take some R&R at Appledart next month? Is there a B&B? Let me know when you get back from the mountain safe and sound.

Gethyn

Dear Rosie Hughes

From: aggieb@yahoo.com
To: rosie-of-arabia@yahoo.com
Subject: Gethyn

Date: 16 May

Hi, Rosie

Don't worry about it. Imagining your future self when you're at a crossroads is a daft idea. Mine was just a load of far-fetched nonsense. You'll get there. You're in the middle of a war. It's confusing. Just get yourself home in one piece, come to Appledart and we'll sort everything out then.

So, here's the big question. Is Gethyn handsome? You still haven't told me the latest situation on the girlfriend front? Answer this email immediately.

Love, Ag

P.S. Please let Gethyn know I'm back safe and sound from the mountain hike. In all honesty it wasn't an actual 'mountain' but it was a bloody big hill and a VERY long walk (so I'm still ticking it off the list). Next item – sleeping under the stars!

From: rosie-of-arabia@yahoo.com
To: aggieb@yahoo.com
Subject: Re: Gethyn

Date: 17 May

Hi, Aggie

So, you are 'interested'. Fabulous. Well:

It turns out that Gethyn phoned his girlfriend last week, but neither one of them had anything to say. They emailed each other after the call and both decided the best course of action was to let each other go. It would be unfair to discuss this further, but needless to say, he's not heartbroken. He feels free and optimistic. Perhaps your books have worked their magic on him. I think he feels the need for adventure, fun and, dare I say it, a little romance? His ex-partner, although a very talented doctor, would apparently have scorned if he had revealed a romantic/devil-may-care side to his personality.

Is he handsome? What a question! Come on, Ag, beauty is in the eye of the beholder, you know that.

Love, Rosie

P.S. I've told Gethyn you're back safe and he says to say that you CANNOT class a hill as a mountain, you lazy cow!

P.P.S. Have you slept under the stars yet? I have bagged this one to death and I can honestly say it's over-rated – I'd kill for a squidgy double bed and a cosy duvet right now!

From: aggieb@yahoo.com
To: rosie-of-arabia@yahoo.com
Subject: Re: Re: Gethyn

Date: 17 May

1. Have not slept under the stars. We tried to but lasted only two hours before we heard the voices of a thousand demons. Also, when I went for a pee, Isabella said she saw a shooting star, which was intensely annoying. If anyone deserved to see a star and make a wish it was me (it was my idea, after all!).
2. Shall I send a duvet? Best not, it would be too hot. How about a bed sheet made of purest Egyptian silk?
3. Beauty is in the eye of the beholder my arse! Haven't you got a photo you can scan?

From: rosie-of-arabia@yahoo.com
To: aggieb@yahoo.com
Subject: Re: Re: Re: Gethyn

Date: 17 May

OK, let's say I send you a photo and you don't like the look of him, what then? Will you stop emailing him, or will your tone change in your letters? Looks aren't everything.

From: aggieb@yahoo.com
To: rosie-of-arabia@yahoo.com
Subject: Re: Re: Re: Re: Gethyn

Date: 17 May

Do not even think about going moralistic on me Rosanna
Hughes. You dumped Jack Peterson when he fell off his
bike and smashed his teeth in and I didn't judge you
then! Physical attraction to your partner matters – fact.
Also, Gethyn has the upper hand as he has seen a photo
of me. I want to redress the balance.

From: rosie-of-arabia@yahoo.com
To: aggieb@yahoo.com
Subject: Re: Re: Re: Re: Re: Gethyn
Date: 18 May

I don't have a photo.

From: aggieb@yahoo.com
To: rosie-of-arabia@yahoo.com
Subject: Re: Re: Re: Re: Re: Re: Gethyn

Date: 18 May

Fuck's sake! On a sliding scale of one to ten, with ten
being Jonny Depp and one being the Hunchback of

Notre dame, where does Gethyn sit? Also, would you imagine him to be a good kisser? Kissing is more important than shagging.

From: rosie-of-arabia@yahoo.com
To: aggieb@yahoo.com
Subject: Re: Re: Re: Re: Re: Re: Re: Gethyn

Date: 18 May

I'm not being drawn into this. A five for me could be a ten for you. And how can I possibly know if he's a good kisser? He's like a brother.

From: aggieb@yahoo.com
To: rosie-of-arabia@yahoo.com
Subject: Unbelievable!

Date: 18 May

I sent you a fucking MP3 player AND got your dad a snow shovel!

From: Rosie-of-arabia@yahoo.com
To: aggieb@yahoo.com
Subject: Re: Unbelievable!

Date: 18 May

OK!!! I'll see what I can do. And stop swearing at me, for fuck's sake!

From: aggieb@yahoo.com
To: rosie-of-arabia@yahoo.com
Subject: Re: Re: Unbelievable!

Date: 18 May

Right ho!

From: rosie-of-arabia@yahoo.com
To: aggieb@yahoo.com
Subject: Photo

Date: 19 May

Hi, Ag
   Sorry, no can do on the photo. I did try.

   Love, Rosie

From: aggieb@yahoo.com
To: rosie-of-arabia@yahoo.com
Subject: Re: Photo

Date: 20 May

Ok, I'll believe you – this once!

From: rosie-of-arabia@yahoo.com
To: aggieb@yahoo.com
Subject: Re: Re: Photo

Date: 20 May

Are you interested in Gethyn? Genuinely, not a passing fancy?

From: aggieb@yahoo.com
To: rosie-of-arabia@yahoo.com
Subject: Re: Re: Re: Photo

Date: 20 May

Yes

From: simonday14@hotmail.com
To: rosie-of-arabia@yahoo.com
Subject: The Truth

Date: 21 May

Hi, Rosie
    You know me too well. OK, so here's the truth. Australia
isn't working out too well for me. I've lost my job at the
theatre. I was dating the director's daughter (she's in the

show) and before I could blink we'd got a flat together and she was planning baby names. For Christ's sake! Why do chicks always want to move in so quickly? My visa runs out in six months, but I haven't the money to fly home. Sophie (the director's daughter who's pissed at me because I started seeing someone else) has kept the flat on and muggings here is still paying for it. So now I'm skint and sleeping on a mate's sofa. I've got a job in a club to tide me over cash wise. It's all a bit shit but I'll work my way out of it, always do.

Si

P.S. If I don't respond straight away to your email it's not because I'm ignoring you so don't be mad. I can only access email at my mate's computer and I'm working all hours God sends at the moment to claw back some cash. And please don't nag in your reply. I already know I'm a cock.

From: rosie-of-arabia@yahoo.com
To: simonday14@hotmail.com
Subject: Re: The Truth

Date: 21 May

Simon

I'm not sure what to say, except:

When will you learn?! You're a grown man, for goodness sake. Stop thinking with your dick!

Nag complete. Why do you always let women push you into a firm commitment before you're ready? This set of circumstances happens every single time you meet a woman. You fall head over heels for a pretty face and long legs, you shower her with compliments until you're sure she's crazy about you, then, when you know she's a done deal and the chase is over, you lose interest. If you want to jump from woman to woman and shag your way around Sydney then that's up to you, but perhaps you could stop committing so quickly and leading them to believe that you're their 'happy ever after'.

I haven't been able to spend any money for a few months, so I could easily cobble together about £3,000 from my current account and get it transferred over to you. This would help get you a ticket home, at least? Despite the fact that you're a dickhead, for what it's worth, I don't think you're a cock (there *is* a difference). And I want to talk to you about Aggie Braithwaite, but I'll do that next time I see you.

Rosie

From: simonday14@hotmail.com
To: rosie-of-arabia@yahoo.com
Subject: Re: Re: The Truth

Aggie who?

From: rosie-of-arabia@yahoo.com
To: aggieb@yahoo.com
Subject: Great News

Date: 22 May

Hi, Aggie.

Great news! I've been given another job. Thank God, I was so desperately bored. I still do the bloody sodding weather forecast (this job has put me off the weather for life) but I'm now the Visits Officer, too. 'What's that?' I hear you say. Well, now that the war is over (Gethyn says it's far from over and this is only the beginning of a massive bloody mess and that we NEVER EVER learn), but anyway, now the war is 'pretend over' we're going to start receiving lots of visitors (AKA glory hunters) to have a nosy around Basra and I will organise the visits.

Visitors this month are mainly Brit politicians (watch the news and you'll see who). I'll be driving around Basra with them. Am I nuts? The answer to that is, yes! Definitely. I hate driving around Basra. We're in this phase called 'hearts and minds' which means we're now showing the Iraqis that we're here with all good intentions and only want the best for them (even though we knocked ten bells of crap out of them for the last couple of months) and that we're actually the good guys.

To show our trust in them and promote a reciprocal attitude towards us, we wear berets rather than helmets and have abandoned the body armour (not that I have any since I gave mine away in March).

I still carry only ten rounds of ammunition, but I'd be useless with a gun anyway so the fact that I have so little ammo is immaterial. Having said that, Gethyn double-checks my pistol for me before I go out into the city. I think he's more worried about me being out and about than he lets on. But honestly, I think I'll be fine, and it's better for my mental health to get out of HQ for a bit. I know I'm no soldier, but I genuinely believe that being at war is much worse than being in prison – in prison I would at least have a shower, a flushing toilet, visitors and the possibility of an early release for good behaviour.

I'll tell you one thing, though, I agree with Gethyn that it was a nicer environment when we were out in the desert. Oh, I know I bitched about the sand for weeks, but the problem with living and working at the airport is that it just feels so unhygienic and it's unbear-ably hot. The air-conditioning and sanitary provisions are shot through (literally) and so our work space is full of stagnant, stifling air (getting up to 50 degrees). There also seems to be more cases of diarrhoea and vomiting since we moved to the airport. So, yes, I preferred living in the middle of the desert, it was cooler, cleaner and freer (told you, no matter how shitty you think your life is, it can always get worse! You've got to laugh).

Bye for now.
Love, Rosie

Bluey
From: Rosie
To: Oliver

Date: 23 May

Dear, Oliver

No, I haven't fired my gun, thank the Lord. We're now in Basra at an airport terminal. It's not a civilian airport anymore with normal aeroplanes coming and going. The Chief of Staff is a very important Army Colonel. He has set up his office in a room that used to be the airport shop. There is a sign above his door that says, 'Duty Free'. Don't you think that's funny?

I know what you mean about wishes. I spent several years wishing for something to happen to me, but my wish never came true and that made me very sad, and then I got my wish, but it was taken away from me. But I think the important thing is to never stop wishing for something – anything – that brings you joy, even if it's not what you originally imagined it would be. I wouldn't have thought this way a couple of months ago, but I do now.

You said someone was thinking of adopting you? Isn't that a good thing? Didn't you wish for it? Let me know how it goes.

Rosie

From: aggieb@yahoo.com
To: rosie-of-arabia@yahoo.com
Subject: Oliver

Date: 24 May

Hi, Rosie

I researched computer programmes for Oliver. There are a couple you can buy that teach children touch-typing. I phoned (and persuaded) Mrs Cartwright to let Oliver have one. However, she does insist (and I agree with her) that Oliver should only use it when writing long pieces of work and that he shouldn't use the spell checker facility – his spelling requires a great deal of improvement. Mrs Cartwright (I'll never be able to call her Angela) thinks you are, perhaps, under a false impression of Oliver's literacy skills. She helps Oliver write his letters to you and it takes him absolutely ages to type them out and, because he wants his letters to seem grown up, she helps. But anyway, I'll get him a laptop and put the typing programme on there and you can settle up with me later. Also, tell me to mind my own business, but there was something else I discussed with Mrs Cartwright and I feel the need to pass it on to you (don't be mad).

For child protection reasons Mrs Cartwright reads all the letters you send to Oliver before she passes them on to him, which is perfectly understandable. One thing she is slightly concerned about is that you may be setting Oliver up with false hopes for the future. I haven't read your letters and so can't comment. But she feels that children like Oliver just don't get the breaks you and I had and that you may be setting him up for a fall in the long-run, even if you have all the best intentions. Anyway, I'll sort out the laptop which hopefully will improve things for him in the class.

Love, Ag
P.S. Mrs Cartwright also said please don't feel tempted to buy Oliver a dog

From: percynmadge@yahoo.com
To: rosie-of-arabia@yahoo.com
Subject: Back Home

Date: 25 May

Dear, Babe
We're back from Whitby – lovely weather, only a bit of rain. Bad news on the metal detecting front, I'm afraid. The farmer who owns the field near Holmfirth doesn't have any time for us metal detecting types and he's refused access. It's a blow. I'd have loved to get my hands on that field. Ah well, I'll find that pot of gold one day, babe. Your old Dad hasn't given up yet. Back to Whitby day after tomorrow probably. Love ya babe

and don't become complacent – remember what I've told you,

KYHD!
MumnDad x

'E' Bluey
From: Oliver
To: Rosie

Date: 26 May

Dear, Rosie

I'm getting adopted by a couple who live in Darlington. I'm pleased but I do mind a little bit because I will have had to leave school in a couple of weeks and that means I can't write to you and I want to write to you until you come home safe. I hear you're getting me a laptop. Thank you. I'm going to come to school early every morning and sit with Mrs Cartwright and she's going to teach me how to type (she's doing it right now). What does Iraq look like? Mrs Cartwright said it is a place from the bible and that the river was important. Do you believe in Jesus? I'm more of a big boom boom person myself. I don't think it's possible for there to be a man with a beard looking down on us and knowing what every single person is doing every minute of the day. This is a Christian school so we have to learn about the bible.

Mrs Cartwright says to say she's told me that even if I don't believe in God and stuff I can still learn from the bible stories. I told her I would try. Matt is nicer to me now because I told him I'm getting a laptop and he wants to have a go on it.

Oliver

From: igambini@hotmail.com
To: rosie-of-arabia@yahoo.com
CC: gethyn-of-arabia@yahoo.com
Subject: Agatha

Date: 27 May

Dear, Rosie and Gethyn

My name is Isabella and I'm a friend of Agatha's. I've accessed Aggie's emails so that I can contact her friends and family to pass on the unfortunate news that poor Aggie has had quite a serious fall from a horse. She was galloping on the beach and the horse ran away with her. Her injuries are not as bad as first suspected, but she has a broken wrist, broken ribs and a cut and bruised face and concussion. She is expected out of hospital tomorrow and is returning to the café, insisting we do not inform Casey of the fall. Agatha wanted you both to know that you are not forgotten, and she will return to letter writing duties as soon as possible. I have emailed Agatha's mother but received only a curt response. I'm sure Agatha will email you with all the details as soon as she is fit.

With very best wishes,
Isabella

From: gethyn-of-arabia@yahoo.com
To: igambini@hotmail.com
Subject: Re: Agatha

Date: 28 May

Dear, Isabella

Thank you for your email. Please give Agatha my best wishes and tell her I hope for a speedy recovery. Out of interest, and please don't think I'm interfering as I'm sure you will have everything organised, but as Agatha has suffered concussion, will someone be on hand to keep an eye on her? Also, speaking as a doctor, please can you pass on my advice to Agatha that she does not resume duties at the café for a little while – she needs bed rest. The reason I say this is because I am aware that she is waiting for a food critic to arrive and I fear she will exert herself ensuring the café is at constant readiness.

Kind regards,
Gethyn

From: igambini@hotmail.com
To: gethyn-of-arabia@yahoo.com
CC: rosie-of-arabia@yahoo.com
Subject: Re: Re: Agatha

Date: 28 May

Dear, Gethyn

I completely understand your concern, but rest assured, Agatha will not be baking up a storm this week but has been informed she must tolerate bed rest. The food critic's first day at Appledart was, in fact, the day Agatha had her fall. Our spies had failed to inform us of his arrival because he was not travelling alone. In fact, Nathan and his assistant (who seems to have taken more than a shine to Agatha), have decided to stay on in Appledart for a week or so for a holiday, which means I have plenty of help at the café and Agatha has a companion waiting on her every need (his assistant). I'm sure Agatha will fill you in on the bizarre events of the day in question once she is up to emailing again.

Best wishes,
Isabella

Bluey
From: Rosie
To: Oliver

Date: 29 May

Dear, Oliver.

You're welcome. I hope it helps. Be sure to keep up with your spelling and handwriting practise or you'll get me into trouble! I have email now. If Mrs Cartwright doesn't mind you can email me at: Rosie-of-arabia@ yahoo.com

I'll probably leave Iraq in early July. Maybe we can keep in touch when I get home? You'll have to ask your new parents though (how completely exciting!).

Rosie

From: rosie-of-arabia@yahoo.com
To: aggieb@yahoo.com
Subject: Are you OK?

Date: 29 May

Hi, Ag

Not sure when you'll read this but I'm so worried – are you OK? It's supposed to be me in the wars, not you. Please get well soon and email as soon as you can to let us know you're OK.

Love, Rosie

From: percynmadge@hotmail.com
To: rosie-of-arabia@yahoo.com
Subject: Whitby

Date: 30 May

Dear, Babe
We're going back to Whitby the day after tomorrow.
Your mother has a hair appointment in the morning but
if we went straight back after that we'd have to contend
with the problem of the racket from the disco which
defies description, so we'll miss a day.

Everything's OK at this end. One slight hiccup is that
Aunty Joan's got to go back to the hospital and have a
knee scan, but her mind's being taken off it to some
extent because she's just won £500 on Radio Sheffield
– jammy bugger.

KYHD.
Luv ya babe
Mumndad xxx.

From: josh71@yahoo.com
To: rosie-of-arabia@yahoo.com
Subject: Shells and Stuff

Date: 31 May

Hi, Rosie

I went into your box of special things today and I found a shoe box full of our shells. I had no idea you'd written the date and location on each one and saved them. The shell with the seaweed attached to it we found at Findhorn still has the seaweed attached! You drew a frowning face on it and said it looked like my Mother. Do you mind if I keep it? I love the photo of the two of us sat on the ferry to Appledart, too – you always came up with such great places to go. I've left the lamp in the box. It's yours and I should never have asked for it back.

Our divorce is finalised tomorrow. I hope you find great joy in the future, where ever life takes you.

Take care.
Josh

From: simonday14@hotmail.com
To: rosie-of-arabia@yahoo.com
Subject: What a nag!

Date: 31 May

Hi, Rosie

And this is why I don't tell you anything. What a nag!

Anyhow, thanks a gazzilion for the offer, sis, but I can't take your money. Don't worry, your 'ol brother will sort himself out before too long, and I'll have enough cash to come home and take you and that chesty mate of yours (I remember who Aggie is now) up town to get pissed like the old days and then leg it into Huddersfield for a kebab and a new tattoo.

Gotta go. Got a shift at the club.

Stay safe kiddo. Si x

P.S. Shame things didn't work out between you and Josh. That guy really loved you. Is there no hope?

From: rosie-of-arabia@yahoo.com
To: josh71@yahoo.com
Subject: No Subject

Date: 31 May

Dear Josh

I didn't sleep very much last night, not because of the stifling heat, but because of the noise coming from the engines of an RAF C17 that had its engines running while parked on the apron all night. I'm not angry about it, just very sad. We repatriated some soldiers who were killed the day before onto that same aircraft yesterday evening, but it couldn't take-off until this morning, so the air-conditioning had to stay on all night for obvious reason – I lay listening to the hum of the engines, thinking of the people inside. It was an all-night reminder of the truth of this war. But this terrible sadness has urged me to do something in this letter that is more frightening to me even than going to war, but if I can face jumping into a trench and drive around Basra without a helmet or body armour, then I can do this.

For the past few years, my every waking thought has been occupied with Angelica. Next time it's raining, sit and look at the window – not out of the window, but at the window pane itself - and follow the slow pattern the rain makes as it works its way down the glass. That slow trickle of water is the best way I can think of to describe my previous feelings, a never-ending supply of tears that just kept falling, except the tears fell on the inside because I just couldn't cry. When I closed my eyes, I would imagine Angelica clinging to me, or crying for me in the night or (my favourite image of self-harm) I would imagine her as a toddler, looking up at me with her arms outstretched and a great big smile on her face. I've brought this sorrow onto myself every day in a kind of masochistic ritual. But now that I've had my whole life stripped away to nothing – no possessions, no freedom and no guarantee of waking up tomorrow – I realise how much I have to be thankful for and, most of all, as melodramatic as it sounds, I realise that I lost the most precious gift of all – you. I'm sorry if this sounds as if I've had a clichéd epiphany, but I have, truly. That fortune teller told me I'd find peace in the desert, and I have.

But although I may have found peace, I've lost my future. I've tried to imagine myself – my life – ten years from now, but it's impossible, not without you. Can we please try again? We once told each other we were two little soul mates that had found each other, and that we would always find each other, from one life to the next, for eternity – remember? And remember our song, *La Vie en Rose* (I know I'm throwing every bit of emotion at you now but it's all I've got). Imagine I'm singing it to you now – in my best fake French accent, in lacy underwear!

We – you and I – are enough for me. I don't want to try for another baby. I accept my life as it is. Please don't say goodbye. I understand everything now. I love you, and that love, I promise, is enough.

With all of my love, always.
Rosie

From: rosie-of-arabia@yahoo.com
To: percynmadge@yahoo.com
Subject: Coming Home

Date: 1 June

Hi Mum and Dad

Not sure when you'll get this as you're probably at the coast but I'm coming home on 2 July, which is a good thing as Basra is turning a bit nasty. I'll probably have spoken to you on the phone by the time you read this.

   Love, Rosie x

From: acartwright1@yahoo.com
To: rosie-of-arabia@yahoo.com
Subject: Best Friend

Date: 2 June

Dear Rosie

   I've got a best friend. It's Matt. I went round to his house. We played in the garden but I had to leave when his dad came home from work because he was tired and didn't want the noise in the house but we were in the garden, so I didn't understand. His Mum took me back to my foster house. He says I can have a go on his XBox next week. Miss Cartwright thought you'd want to know.

   Oliver

From: rosie-of-arabia@yahoo.com
To: josh71@yahoo.com
Subject: ???

Date: 3 June

Hi, Josh
   You haven't answered?

   Love, Rosie x

From: josh71@yahoo.com
To: Rosie-of-arabia@yahoo.com
Subject: Re: ???

Date: 3 June

Sorry, but I need some time to think.

From: percynmadge@hotmail.com
To: rosie-of-arabia@yahoo.com
Subject: Coming Home

Date: 5 June

Dear, Babe
   We got back from the coast late last night. There
were a few messages on the phone, including your

quickie from Tuesday. All we could make out was 'Mum, it's me', the rest was broken up by static or whatever.

So, you're finally coming home – fabulous news! Basra doesn't seem to be as friendly as you first thought? What a bloody awful state of affairs this lot is developing into. Josh came round this afternoon to bring all my tools back. He's taken a couple of week's ad hoc leave – not like him? Such a shame about you two. Nice lad, but it's your life, love. I told the dog when I took her for her walk this morning, I said I knew in my soul you'd be home soon. Just keep your head down in this final few weeks, that's the only pathetic bit of advice I can give.

The dog spent the afternoon with me cutting the hedges and tidying the garden in readiness for our next trip off. If the forecast is good, we'll probably push off back after tea tomorrow; it all depends on how your mother feels.

Nothing else to report right now. News on the school is grim. Looks like they won't rebuild. Such a shame.

Talk to you soon. Don't forget, KYHD

Luv ya - MumnDad. x

From: rosie-of-arabia@yahoo.com
To: aggieb@yahoo.com
Subject: On Tenterhooks

Date: 5 June

Hi, Ag

How are you? I know your wrist is broken but could you get Isabella to write a letter for you, just so we know you're OK?

Guess what? I've asked Josh if we can start again. He's taking his time to think about it. At least he didn't say no, which can only be a good thing, can't it?

Life in Basra is the pits. I took a foreign diplomat out into the city yesterday with his close protection (CP) team to look at a house that might be suitable as an embassy. We drove into this street and the diplomat and the CP team went into the house leaving me sitting in a Land Rover with two TA guys.

All of a sudden, all these Iraqi men carrying rifles started coming out of their houses and stood on the street, watching us. It was horrible. I honestly thought I was a goner. Anyway, the CP guys and the diplomat came out of the house, jumped into their vehicle and we all shot off, but I genuinely thought the Iraqis were brewing for a kick off and I may well be the luckiest woman on the planet today. To sum up, I can't wait to get out of this stifling hell hole and back to England. I will never

ever complain about the rain or my country again. I was a naive fool (again) to think that being Visits Officer would be enjoyable. Yet another life lesson for silly Rosanna.

Thanks for the brownies by the way – you must have sent them before your accident. Gethyn devoured them.

Again, what's this about an admirer?

Lots of love,
Rosie

From: aggieb@yahoo.com
To: rosie-of-arabia@yahoo.com; gethyn-of-arabia@yahoo.com
Subject: Miss Me?

Date: 6 June

Hello! And how are my two heroes today?

I'm typing this email one-handed on a laptop balanced across my knee while lying on the settee in front of the fire with a crocheted rug draped over my bruised and battered body. But don't worry, I have at least five people calling in at regular intervals acting as my personal Punkah Wallahs – fabulous! Poor Anya was most upset at my accident. And so she should be! What's the use of having a fortune teller as your best buddy if she can't prevent you from falling off a horse? She looked horrified and said, 'And that, Agatha, is why I don't read the cards of friends!' but I think she was a bit shaken.

I know you'll be desperate to know what happened on the day Nathan arrived, but I'm afraid you're going to have to wait a bit longer as I can barely keep my eyes open (must be the painkillers) but I'm sure I'll be back to normal soon and able to tell you everything. But please do both write and tell me your news as I'm keen to hear that you are both safe and well. Lots of love,

The Queen of Sheba (I may drag this out a bit).

From: aggieb@yahoo.com
To: rosie-of-arabia@yahoo.com
Subject: Proud of You!

Date: 6 June

Hi, Rosie

I've just written a combined email to you and Gethyn but having just read your email about Josh, I wanted to make the effort to write straight back because I wanted to say how proud I am of you for putting your heart on the line – go Boudica! I really hope he decides to take you up on your offer and have another stab at marriage. Let me know what he decides. Whatever the decision, you deserve to be happy and I'm sure, either way, you'll find oodles of love and joy when you come home. We must have celebratory night out when you get back. Do you think you could come and see me in Appledart for a few days? I am injured, after all.

Love, Ag

From: rosie-of-arabia@yahoo.com
To: aggieb@yahoo.com
Subject: Shit Day

Date: 7 June

Hi, Aggie

Today is not a good day. No news from Josh and to top it all, Gethyn has gone to work somewhere else for his last two weeks. It's like I've lost a part of my soul. But at least I ticked off another a few things on the list. Gethyn and I drank the wine you sent and watched the sunset while lying on the airport roof last night (you've got to stay incognito to prevent getting shot at). We're not allowed booze but we thought, 'sod it!'. Then, at 3a.m., we went into the silence of the terminal building and Gethyn danced a river dance – giggling like a child - on the General's planning table (it's covered in Perspex so it was fine) while I played an Irish jig on the violin. He said he felt like he was dancing a jig on Tony Blair's grave, which cheered him up no end! Quick as a flash, we took my violin, shot back up to the roof and waited for the sunrise. I played *La Vie en Rose*. It was wonderful.

Regarding Appledart. I don't need a reason to come, you idiot, I want to. So, yes, please, can I come to your café? Will you feed me cake till I pop? I do expect you to keep writing while I'm there, however.

Speaking of writing, don't be angry, but I thought of something regarding your work: You and I must have watched *Little Women*, what? one hundred times? You were Jo (obviously) and I was Meg (even more obviously). You'll remember that Jo only settles into her writing career once she writes about her dead sister, Beth. In other words, once she writes truly from the heart, about a place and a time and people she knows and loves and understands, she's happy, and realises that, even if no-one else reads or likes her book, it doesn't matter, because it's something she's proud of in her own right, without requiring approval from anyone else.

Why don't you do the same thing? You could write about the two of us; two childhood friends who lost touch through heartbreak and a misunderstanding, and who rekindle their friendship during difficult times and discover, through the course of their correspondence, that nothing in life is so utterly unbearable or totally unfathomable, when shared between friends. You can have all my letters – from you, from Dad, from everyone – and you could write a story just for me (exaggerate and drag it out a bit if necessary). During these past months I've grown to realise that partners – and even some family – come and go, but best friends, well, they last a lifetime, don't they?

It's just an idea.

Love,
Rosie

From: josh71@yahoo.com
To: rosie-of-arabia@yahoo.com
Subject: No subject

Date: 7 June

Dear, Rosie

I'm sorry it's taken me a while to respond, but I'm on leave at the moment doing a little travelling, so I haven't always got access to the Internet. Also, I needed time to think about your letter and what my answer should be.

I find this is such an unfortunate letter to write given your situation, but the truth is, I think it's too late for us to start again. I think your present state of mind is achievable only because you are in Iraq and, like you say, life has been stripped down to basics and you're able to see things differently. But I know you, Rosie, I really do. And I know that once you're home, once you're seeing children and mothers on the streets again and you're back at work and other women are going off on maternity leave, you'll soon yearn for a child and we'll be back to square one. For the past few years, seeing your face weighed down with sorrow, has been hellish. And then losing Angelica ... it's a place I don't want to go back to. I don't need to look at a window pane in the rain to understand your sadness because, trust me, I felt every inch of your pain for years and it was my pain too. I'm sorry to say this, but I hadn't realised how unhappy I was in our marriage until I was free of it.

The main reason I'm saying no to a reconciliation, though – and the difference between us – is despite everything we've been through, I would *never* have left you. I loved you. You broke my heart, Rosie, and I just can't imagine jumping on the hamster wheel again. I felt like you only wanted me in your life to provide you with a baby. But I wanted to spend my life with you with or without a baby, even though I really did desperately want to be a Dad – that's the difference between us. You miss me now because you're in Iraq, but deep down, I don't believe anything has really changed. I wish you all the very best in the world, but I need to start again. I know it's a cliché, but I mean it – be happy.

Josh

From: simonday14@hotmail.com
To: rosie-of-arabia@yahoo.com
Subject: Cash

Date: 7 June

Hi, Rosie
  Can I change my mind about the offer of the borrowing some money? A mate leant me some cash a few months ago to tide me over and he's being arsey about getting it back. Can you manage that three grand? I'll pay you back as soon as I can, promise.

  Si

From: rosie-of-arabia@yahoo.com
To: josh71@yahoo.com
Subject: No subject

Date: 7 June

Josh
  I understand.

  Rosie

Melanie Hudson

From: rosie-of-arabia@yahoo.com
To: simonday14@hotmail.com
Subject: Re: Cash

Date: 7 June

Hi, Si
Email me your bank details and I'll find a way to get it transferred.

Rosie

From: simonday14@hotmail.com
To: rosie-of-arabia@yahoo.com
Subject: Re: Re: Cash

Date: 8 June

Thanks a million, Rosie. I'll make it up to you – and that's a promise.

From: percynmadge@hotmail.com
To: rosie-of-arabia@yahoo.com
Subject: It's Hot!

Date: 10 June

Dear, Babe

Roll on July - what do you say?

I don't know how you cope with the heat. We've had an unseasonable hot spell here and we're struggling – it's 25 degrees! The dog tries to keep cool by lying in the shade underneath my car on the cold concrete, which means we've got to keep checking to make sure she's not slipped through a hole that the cat's made in the hedge on to next door's drive – she's a bugger for doing that. Mind you, we've got her cunning little plan sussed out now, so she'll have to think up a new ruse. Would you believe, it's starting to rain: let's hope it doesn't thunder or else I'll have a nursing job on my hands.

The big news is that they've caught the school arsonist. It's shocking state of affairs but one of the pupils – a foster kid – set the place alight. What's the world coming to, eh?

Mammy went to Shirley's for her hair doing this morning, but as usual, she came back chuntering because she'd had a slightly darker colour put on and still can't decide if it looks better or worse – at least it's not green. Do you remember that little episode?

KYHD
Luvya, Mumndad. Xxx

From: rosie-of-arabia@yahoo.com
To: acartwright1@hotmail.com
Subject: Arsonist

Date: 10 June

Dear, Mrs Cartwright

I've had a letter from my father with a throwaway line stating that the arsonist at the school is a child in foster care. Was it Oliver? If it was (and I hope and pray it wasn't) can you please let me know what the situation is and if there is anything I can do to help him.

Best wishes,
Rosie

From: acartwright1@hotmail.com
To: rosie-of-arabia@yahoo.com
Subject: Re: Arsonist

Date: 11 June

Dear, Rosie

I'm sorry you heard the news from your father, but I'm afraid he is correct, Oliver did, sadly, set fire to the school. He was seen in the school grounds on the night of the fire and when challenged, admitted he set his classroom on fire. I believe he put a match to his year group's creative homework. He has been suspended from school pending investigation and is in the care of social services. I'm afraid I cannot facilitate your continued correspondence with Oliver, but if it is any consolation, his letters to you opened a window regarding how he felt about his situation and this will act in his favour.

Take good care.
Best wishes, Angela

From: rosie-of-arabia@yahoo.com
To: acartwright1@hotmail.com
Subject: Re: Re: Arsonist

Date: 11 June

Dear, Angela
Thank you for letting me know. What will happen regarding his new adoptive parents – will the adoption still go ahead?

Best wishes,
Rosie

From: acartwright1@hotmail.com
To: rosie-of-arabia@yahoo.com
Subject: Re: Re: Re: Arsonist

Date: 11 June

Dear, Rosie
I believe Oliver will not be adopted at this time.

Best wishes,
Angela

From: rosie-of-arabia@yahoo.com
To: aggieb@yahoo.com
Subject: For Fuck's Sake!

Date: 12 June

Hi, Aggie
Josh doesn't want me back. I don't want to write about it. Also, it seems that Oliver, the boy at Midhope Primary I've been writing to, is the school arsonist. I'm gutted. And it's so frustrating because I genuinely don't believe he's a bad kid, but he's had a shit start to life. He was just pulling his life together, too. I was hoping he would be my, 'make a positive change to someone's life' person, but in actual fact it looks like that person will be my brother who needs some money to get home. I've saved

quite a bit being away with the Army so I'm going to give it to Simon. I know he'll pay be back as soon as he can.

Poor Oliver, though, and what a mess we can get our lives into within just a few moments of recklessness. The old me would want to rock in a corner. But not anymore. I've had a day of hard, devastating knocks, but I'm alive. We did yet another repatriation ceremony an hour ago and I thought I was going to vomit. As per the Chief of Staff's instruction, I played the *Last Post* on the violin while six coffins were carried onto an aircraft draped in union flags. Then, thinking of us, I played *La Vie en Rose*.

And from somewhere, finally, I cried.

Today, as clichéd as it sounds, I finally found Life in Rosie Hughes, and I felt ashamed that it's taken a war to appreciate the preciousness of my own life. I'll come home and fight for my future – I owe that to the people who haven't made it home. I'll pull myself back bigger and better than ever before. I may not be able to see my future self in a particular setting or doing a particular job, but she'll be a warm, gentle, confident woman, and if I get that right, surely the rest should follow?

Love, Rosie

From: aggieb@yahoo.com
To: rosie-of-arabia@yahoo.com
CC: gethyn-of-arabia@yahoo.com
Subject: That Fateful Day

Date: 14 June

Hello, you two.

I'm managing to sit up a little easier today, so I thought I write to let you know what happened on 'that fateful day'. I'm able to sort of type with both hands now (shhh, don't tell Isabella).

Where to begin:

It was a gloomy spring day consisting of only one season – winter. We were all taking shelter in the café. Even Moses had been driven inside by the force of the wind and icy rain. The radio was on and I was huddled in front of the wood-burner reading *Moby Dick* out loud (it soothes Moses ... don't ask). Anya was cleansing her chakras laying across a table next to the window in a meditative trance, and Isabella, who had moved the chairs and tables to the edge of the café to provide a little elbow room, was teaching Moses how to Argentine tango while I read aloud (I'd taught her some moves during a tango workshop I ran the week before).

Just as Isabella hooked her leg around Moses' thigh for the last time and shouted, 'Ole!' the café door opened with a bang and a windswept alpha male blew in wearing

306

an expensive waterproof jacket, a green woolly hat and a magnetic smile. Isabella froze in position, but what was fabulous was, on noticing Isabella, Nathan Browne (for it could only be him) also froze on the spot, and his jaw (with rain dripping from his silver stubble) dropped. We all remained suspended in animation for a few seconds before Isabella un-hooked her leg, smoothed her top over her jeans and, with the poise and grace of royalty, held out her hand, smiled and said, 'Hello, Nathan. May I offer you some tea?'

Seconds later, another soaked soul walked through the door – Nathan's assistant, Jack – and the realisation dawned on me that Nathan Browne had found his way to the end of the road on the very day we had decided it not worth the bother of baking – we hadn't even both-ered to get supplies, such was the ferocity of the weather. We had just about enough of the basics to knock up a Victoria sponge, but it wouldn't be triple layer. I could have spit feathers! Rather than accept defeat, I kicked the table on which Anya was still laying comatose, and she awoke in the manner of Sleeping Beauty waking after her long sleep. Nathan was lovely, if a little dumbfounded, and his underling, Jack, was very pleasant and easy to talk to. Isabella made the tea. When asked how on earth she had found herself at The Café at Road's End, she explained in a deadpan face that she had come to Appledart for the weather. Everyone laughed, and Nathan waited for the real explanation, which wasn't forthcoming.

Watching Isabella interact with Nathan was a masterclass in how to maintain a mysterious air with an attractive man – but I've written too many love stories to be under any illusion: they fancied the pants off each other. I seemed to be the only person who remembered the real reason for Nathan's visit and, not knowing how long he intended to stay, indicated that Isabella should keep him talking while I shot off to Morir. I decided to take a shortcut across the beach and nail the bucket list, 'ride a horse on the beach'. Jekyll, sensing the urgency of the trip, shot off in a gallop, but I have not yet learned to gallop properly and was thrown – some considerable way - and ended up in a ditch unconscious. It's a good job I'm well-padded because I lay there for three hours before Ishmael (I can't get used to calling him Moses, it just doesn't suit him) found me. Apparently, Anya had felt a shiver and dispatched a search party. After that there was much commotion and, by hook or by crook, four hours later I was in a cottage hospital and then transferred to Inverness for X-rays and spent a couple of days under observation.

I arrived back in Appledart expecting Nathan to have left the peninsula taking our chances of getting into the guide with him, but I was wrong (and you're not going to believe this) but the real reason Nathan had come to Appledart was to see Anya – to have his cards read (even though I speculated this might be the case,

I was only joking). Despite many attempts at bribery, Anya will not divulge the nature of his reading. Also, and this is the best bit, Nathan and Jack decided to stay on for a few days to help Isabella run the café and to have a little holiday – they've been bunking up with Ishmael. It's all a bit nuts, but Isabella has never looked so radiant (she seems to have forgotten all about the small plums). Nathan and Jack are great company and although I've returned to Appledart a broken woman, I've had my every need catered for and – get this – that knock on the head must have done me some good because I feel like writing again. Hurrah! But, I'm going to take your advice, Rosie, and write a story about love and friendship – about us. And I'm going to write it in my own name, just for me and you. Are you sure that's OK?

Love to both of you, Aggie

From: aggieb@yahoo.com
To: gethyn-of-arabia@yahoo.com
Subject: Urgent!
Date: 15 June

Hi, Gethyn

Very quickly – you need to stop Rosie from lending money to her brother. She will never get it back! He's not a good man. He still owes me £800 – since we were eighteen, it was my university savings. Rosie doesn't know this – don't tell her. She adores him.

Thanks, Aggie.

From: rosie-of-arabia@yahoo.com
To: aggieb@yahoo.com
Subject: Stuff

Date: 15 June

Hi, Aggie

Thank God you're back on form – I've missed you. And of course it's OK to fictionalise our story, I wouldn't have suggested it if not.

It's more or less a full moon tonight so I've taken a leaf out of your book and written my dreams down on a piece of paper. I'm going to burn the paper, just as you did, and send a prayer up to the Universe. I actually only have one dream – for peace.

Why aren't you telling me about your admirer, Jack? Have you found the man you dreamt up in your ritual after all?

With oodles of love,
Rosie

Dear Rosie Hughes

From: aggieb@yahoo.com
To: rosie-of-arabia@yahoo.com
Subject: Re: Stuff

Date: 15 June

Oh, Rosie. You're so right. Peace is everything. I'm so sorry about Josh. Focus on the wonderful life you have to look forward to. You're an amazing woman – just look at what you've just gone through. We've got a hell of a lot of laughing and dancing to do, you and I. So, pack your coat and grab your hat, leave your worries on the doorstep,. and come to Appledart for a holiday as soon as you get back.

I got to thinking about our bucket list today. Did you notice that as eighteen-year-old women, on the whole, we sought out adventure together – as friends - beyond romance? When did I lose that certainty of independence? Also, in terms of the fulfilling of these adventures, I see that it can easily become a list to be 'ticked off' before moving swiftly onto the next adventure. Surely, for the bucket list to be of real value, I should meet my need for adventure only when, in doing so, I'm experiencing a true human connection with the thing that I'm doing. In the case of the beach ride, as I was not connected with the horse, with nature or with myself, is it surprising that I fell?

So, I'm taking my fall as a sign that I need to put the

bucket list to one side for a while and that I should, instead of dashing here there and everywhere, consider rooting myself in this time and this place. I feel a sudden urge to force my feet into the Earth, stand tall, and allow myself to develop roots – imagine them sprouting out from the souls of my feet. Big fat anchoring roots and mini, tendril, feeding ones. I want to become fixed, tree like, stand tall (and be just a little bit lofty). Maybe then, I'll stop falling.

As for my admirer, he's very sweet and very smitten, even though I look like I've been through a mangle and I haven't encouraged him AT ALL. I only had an hour in the café with him and Nathan before I shot off on Jekyll, but he keeps popping round because he feels like a gooseberry in the café with Nathan and Isabella. In fact, I really am turning into a tree because I'm quite standoffish with him and haven't put a brush through my hair in a week (why are men much more interested in you when you are less interested in them?). I haven't kissed him (which is a first for me), much as I think he would like to, my excuse being that my mouth is too bruised from the fall. In summation, he's handsome, kind, caring, quite funny and affable – he's a nice man. A few months ago, I would probably have gone for it, but a switch has been turned in my head, and I don't feel a desperate need to be in a relationship with just anyone, anymore. He's not for me.

Love, Ag
P.S. Gethyn suggested visiting me.

From: rosie-of-arabia@yahoo.com
To: aggieb@yahoo.com
Subject: Re: Re: Re:

Date: 16 June

Hi, Ag

You passed up on a snog with a handsome man and now you want to be a tree? That's it, I need to get to Appledart sharpish before you turn into Yoda!

Did I tell you I fly home on 2 July? I'll be homeless initially, but at least I'll be home in Blighty. I've got a month's post-deployment leave and so I'll probably look for somewhere to rent in Exeter, but I don't want to work at the Met Office anymore. What should I do with my life, Aggie? Maybe we'll come up with something when I'm in Appledart. Can't wait.

Love, Rosie

From: aggieb@yahoo.com
To: rosie-of-arabia@yahoo.com
Subject: Gethyn (again)

Date: 17 June

OK, so I know I'm a lofty independent tree, blowing gracefully in the breeze now, but should I follow up on

313

Gethyn's request to come to Appledart? He said he wanted to visit. Am nervous. I don't want him to think I'm 'loose'. Also, I look like shit.

From: aggieb@yahoo.com
To: rosie-of-arabia@yahoo.com
Subject: Re: Gethyn (again)

Date: 17 June

No offense, Ag, but you flew to Venice to shag a total stranger; just saying. Let him come.

From: aggieb@yahoo.com
To: rosie-of-arabia@yahoo.com
Subject: Re: Re: Gethyn (again)

Date: 17 June

But that's exactly the point. Paddy was a *stranger*. This is Gethyn and I don't want to mess it up. Shit, you haven't told him about Venice, have you?

From: rosie-of-arabia@yahoo.com
To: aggieb@yahoo.com
Subject: Re: Re: Re: Gethyn (again)

Date: 17 June

Of course not. By the way, what's the latest with Isabella and Nathan?

From: aggieb@yahoo.com
To: gethyn-of-arabia@yahoo.com
Subject: Appledart

Date: 17 June

Hello, Gethyn
    Sorry about the abrupt last email, and sorry I was unable to reply to your previous email straight away. Of course you can come to Appledart, you could stay at the pub or with Ishmael. I'm sure he would be happy to have you to stay.
    Let me know what you decide. I'd love to meet you.

    Aggie

From: aggieb@yahoo.com
To: rosie-of-arabia@yahoo.com
Subject: In Other News ...

Date: 18 June

Hi, Rosie
    Oh, yes, Isabella.
    Well with me laid-up and useless, Isabella took to the helm at the café. Nathan decided to extend his stay at

the pub (with Jack) so he could help Isabella run the café (and get his leg over in the process). Nathan has risen in the ranks from 'shithouse' to white knight. I could drag out the whole nitty gritty of it, but in a nutshell, they're shagging, which means – fabulously – that the café's place in the almanac is secured.

The other fantastic news is that Casey has asked me if I'd like to lease the café from her for the next year. We're sorting out the details, but I've said yes. I'm going to rent out my place at Midhope to raise the money – the one will offset the other. I'm not telling Mum. She hasn't written or phoned to check that I'm OK after my fall, but I will continue to send love in her direction.

Well, ta ta for now.

A

From: gethyn-of-arabia@yahoo.com
To: aggieb@yahoo.com
Subject: Re: Appledart

Date: 18 June

Hi, Aggie

I thought you were getting a bit cocky on a horse for a beginner, you daft mare! Some good news. I'm booked onto an RAF aircraft for the 22 June – I've got a one-way ticket home!

Regarding Rosie's brother – I mentioned that perhaps it wasn't a good idea to give him the money she's saved, but she seems to have a higher opinion of him than you. She told me why you don't like him, but maybe you're being a bit harsh. Young hearts break hard!

Anyway, that's about all from me, Thanks for the offer to come to Appledart, but I may do something even more radical and take the rare opportunity of having a month off to go further afield. Also, I hear you have someone staying with you while you're ill and it's probably best if I don't get in the way. For what it's worth, just in case we lose communication for a while, I think there's something wonderful about you. You're an incorrigible romantic and you deserve to be romanced. I hope your new admirer knows that.

Take care,
G

From: aggieb@yahoo.com
To: rosie-of-arabia@yahoo.com
Subject: No Subject

Date: 18 June

Does Gethyn know about Jack? And how come he knows about Simon??!!

From: aggieb@yahoo.com
To: rosie-of-arabia@yahoo.com
Subject: No Subject

Date: 18 June

Stop what you're doing and answer my email! I need an answer right now – ROSIE!

From: rosie-of-arabia@yahoo.com
To: aggieb@yahoo.com
Subject: Re: No Subject

Date: 18 June

OK, steady on. I only get chance to log on to a computer every so often. Yes, Gethyn knows about Jack but it's not my fault. Isabella sent us both the same email and said you had an admirer. And I told him about you and Simon a long time before I knew you were interested in him – I was explaining how we'd lost touch.

From: aggieb@yahoo.com
To: rosie-of-arabia@yahoo.com
Subject: Re: Re: No Subject

Date: 18 June

FOR FUCK'S SAKE, Rosie!!

From: aggieb@yahoo.com
To: gethyn-of-arabia@yahoo.com
Subject: Abroad? Why?

Date: 19 June

Pray, sir, what pleasures are to be found abroad that cannot be found here? (I may have stolen that line from an Austen film). And, just for your info, I'm not wrong about Rosie's brother. I found him in bed with my Mother. Just saying.

   Ag

From: gethyn-of-arabia@yahoo.com
To: aggieb@yahoo.com
Subject: Re: Abroad? Why

Date: 19 June

Oh my God, your Mother?! Does Rosie know? And as for your original comment, let's see – diverse culture, language, temperament, climate (need I go on). But honestly, Ag. You already have plenty of company.

Melanie Hudson

From: aggieb@yahoo.com
To: gethyn-of-arabia@yahoo.com
Subject: Re: Re: Abroad? Why?

Date: 19 June

Yes, I have company, but I don't have 'company' if that's what you mean. That's the problem with The Café at Road's End, people come and never want to leave.

No, Rosie doesn't know. Her Mother does. Do not tell her.

Ag

From: gethyn-of-arabia@yahoo.com
To: aggieb@yahoo.com
Subject: My Foolish Heart

Date: 20 June

Dear, Aggie

It's late and I'm all knackered out, so I'm sorry if this letter is to the point, but I'm just going to empty my head into this email and press send, then it's done.

Although Jack twat-face has the lead on me, deep, deep in my soul I feel that you and I are supposed to meet. I know you may not find me attractive, but what if, by chance, you do? I want to do all the things I read about

320

in your books. I want to squirt honey out of a bottle in the shape of a heart onto your porridge, I want to come to your home and find the door wide open and a note on the kitchen table that reads, 'Upstairs, now, you beast!' I want us to have dinner parties and to look across at your smiling face as you converse merrily with someone (who is actually very annoying) at the table and know exactly what you're really thinking behind the smile – 'he's a cock'.

And I know you'll be thinking that I've been drawn-in by all the sex scenes, which, I admit, you do write particularly well. But honestly, it's not that at all (well, not entirely). It's difficult to describe, but I *know* you, Aggie – the real you – the generous you, the you that sits alone at night, providing so much joy for others while taking very little back yourself. I know the angry you, the passionate you, the zesty you, the hilarious you.

Basically, all I want to do, Agatha Braithwaite, is run away from this hell hole and keep on running until I step off that little boat onto that funny little crag of Scottish wilderness you call home, and if I'm really lucky, we won't feel a moments awkwardness, but look into each other's eyes and just know that everything we've both been searching for will manifest in each other.

But whatever you do, don't fall in love. Wait for me.

Be my Scheherazade, tell me your stories.

Yours, Gethyn

P.S. Oh, and for some final doctorly advice, do yourself

a favour and get your arse off that settee, stride out onto that beach and get some fresh air.

From: aggieb@yahoo.com
To: gethyn-of-arabia@yahoo.com
Subject: Re: My Foolish Heart

Date: 21 June

Dear, Gethyn.
  Jack has gone.

  Ag

From: gethyn-of-arabia@yahoo.com
To: aggieb@yahoo.com
Subject: Re: Re: My Foolish Heart

Date: 21 June

Good. Why?

From: aggieb@yahoo.com
To: gethyn-of-arabia@yahoo.com
Subject: Re: Re: Re: My Foolish Heart

Date: 21 June

He wasn't you.

From: gethyn-of-arabia@yahoo.com
To: aggieb@yahoo.com
Subject: Happy Ending?

Date: 21 June

What if I disappoint you?

From: aggieb@yahoo.com
To: gethyn-of-arabia@yahoo.com
Subject: Re: Happy Ending?

Date: 21 June

Dear, Gethyn

So this is how I feel.

I don't want to rush into a relationship or have sex with you or experience anything more than friendship, at the moment.

Yes, my gut feeling is that you may just be the person I've been waiting for all of my life. But here's the rub: in some of my novels, I have absolutely no doubt that, after the last turn of the page most of the relationships wouldn't last the year out. But what if you and I really could live happily ever after? I believe this will only happen if you come to Appledart as a friend and with no expectations. If we are to fall in love, then let's fall in love over time – gently, tenderly (you do realise that I've turned into you and you've turned into me?)

Who is Gethyn Evans? Who is Agatha Braithwaite, for that matter? Our letters could hide a myriad of lies and yet, I don't care, because I feel that perhaps I've seen a side of you that no one else has seen. What I know for absolute certainty is that you're a man I would be honoured to meet because:

- You're the man who stole a tent, so my friend could have some privacy in a world where every scrap of womanhood was taken from her.

- You're the man who took her a bowl of water, so she could clean herself during her lowest days.

- You're the man who made a football out of a sandbag to cheer her up.

- You're the man who danced to the Bee Gees during a scud attack.

- You're a man with a moral conscience.

- You're also the man who got me to strip away my ego, see myself as the heroine in my own novel, rip apart my story and write a new and better one.

Come to Appledart and have some fun, you deserve it.

Yours, Agatha

P.S. If I'm your Scheherazade, does that make you my Arabian knight?

From: gethyn-of-arabia@yahoo.com
To: aggieb@yahoo.com
Subject: Re: Re: Happy Ending?

Date: 22 June

I'll see you next Saturday – armour and all.

G

From: aggieb@yahoo.com
To: gethyn-of-arabia@yahoo.com
Subject: Re: Re: Re: Happy Ending?
Date: 22 June

There's no boat on a Saturday.

From: gethyn-of-arabia@yahoo.com
To: aggieb@yahoo.com
Subject: Re: Re: Re: Re: Happy Ending?

Date: 22 June

I'm a knight. The lack of a boat won't stop me.

From: sexymamma@yahoo.com
To: aggieb@yahoo.com
Subject: Hello Darling

Date: 23 June

Dear, Agatha

How are you, my darling? Terrible news about the horse fall. Sorry I haven't been in touch since you went away. My computer crashed just after you left, and I've only just got it back from that chap on the high street. I've been so very busy, though, the time has just flown by. But I'm back online now so do let me know how you're getting on at that sweet little café of yours.

I wanted to tell you that a journalist from *The Sun* contacted me a couple of days ago. He asked me all kinds of questions about you, my daughter, the secret author! I have absolutely no idea how the word got out, but I was very subtle. I think they are running an article on you this Sunday – I thought you'd want to know. Well, must dash. Do let me know when I can visit. I do miss you, darling.

Mamma x

From: aggieb@yahoo.com
To: rosie-of-arabia@yahoo.com
Subject: You'll Never Fucking Believe This!

Date: 23 June

Hi, Rosie

Total frigging nightmare! I think my complete imbecile

of a mother has let it slip in the village that I ghost write for Isabella, the upshot being that someone has tipped off the press (probably Mum, come to think of it) and Isabella will be 'outed' in the papers this Sunday. We didn't even know anything about it until Mum emailed to tell me (she certainly chose her moment to get in touch).

All hell has been let loose with Isabella's agent – who wanted to sue me for breach of contract - but bizarrely, Isabella herself doesn't seem to care. It seems the only absolute truth in life is this: when you're shagging like a wombat, nothing in the world can bother you!

But back to you. If you don't want the Met Office job you could set sail for absolutely anywhere you choose, but if you're not sure, maybe go back to your old job for a while, just to get your feet back on terra firma, then why not just see which way the wind blows you (as a met woman at least you'll know which direction you're headed).

Regarding Jack, the problem is that I seem to have fallen for Gethyn – I know, madness - and I know I've never met him, but I genuinely do believe there is a connection that common sense cannot explain. Perhaps we find our soulmates via routes we could never possibly have expected, but that route was pre-ordained the whole time? Take Isabella, for example. Who would ever have foretold her great luck – not even Anya, I reckon.

So, I've invited Gethyn to stay. He's coming next week. But here's some news: I have no intention of jumping into bed with him, no way. It's easy to get carried away in an email, but we've never met, and we may not fancy each other and I don't want to ruin his time here by flirting wildly on email and then doing to him what I did to the jockey in Venice. No matter what, though, he's going to have a wonderful time, and so are you when you come to stay. Can't wait to see you, Rosie. And this time, we're never going to lose touch again.

Love, Ag

From: rosie-of-arabia@yahoo.com
To: aggieb@yahoo.com
Subject: Re: Coming Home

Date: 24 June

Oh, Aggie

I'm thrilled to bits Gethyn is coming to stay. I think you'll fancy him though, no question, and he'll definitely have the hots for you. It's all just perfect and exactly as I planned (cue villainous laugh). I know I was supposed to learn from *Emma* and not meddle, but after the Simon disaster, I wanted to make amends. I hope I'm finally forgiven now.

But back to me. You're right. It's time to set sail and leave my failed marriage in the past. But I may not need to go back to the Met Office as I've got an idea (and I got it from your friends from the café) – and my idea is – go to Antarctica!

I know! Crazy!

I had an email from work to say that the British Expedition Force are looking for a meteorological observer to join their team for six months – it can't be a coincidence. I've put my name down and I've got a good chance of getting it.

What do you think?

Love, Rosie

'E' Bluey
From: Andrea Evans
To: Rosie

Date: 24 June

Dear, Rosie

I wanted to write you a quick note to say thank you so much for suggesting I follow my heart. I've enrolled on a nursing course starting in September. Mum's going to have the kids for me and I'll be able to keep some hours at the shop. I can't wait. It's like a whole new life is about to start. Get in touch when you get home. I'd love to see you. Thanks again.

Take care, Andrea

From: aggieb@yahoo.com
To: rosie-of-arabia@yahoo.com
Subject: Re: Re: Coming Home

Date: 24 June

Antarctica? Not you too? It's a bit extreme, Rosie, but fuck it - great idea. Go for it! We never know what lies round the corner, do we?

In your last letter you said you want to put your failed marriage behind you. This got me thinking about the world 'failure' and I realised that relationships that come to an end should not automatically be regarded as failures. I think we should stop associating the ending of things with failing, full stop. Many people who live alone have a sense of having failed in some way, which categorically is not the case (and if a woman does not have a baby, this is not a case of failing, either). I would have been much more content as a single woman in Yorkshire if I hadn't known the tongues of the women at the shop (OK, one woman at the shop) were casting aspersions. But was she, really? And so, what if she was? Similarly, some women are predisposed to be genuinely motherly, while others, like my own mother, have no concept of selfless nurturing. But again, does this mean that she too is a failure? (I can't believe I'm giving her some slack bearing in mind her latest exploits).

We are all only failures if viewed in a certain light. Yes, I would love to have a monogamous relationship ('it's better with two, said Poo') but even if Gethyn and I hit it off, I will never again allow myself the horror of being without close friends – especially female friends. How many times have I listened to women in this café cry their hearts out, usually saying that their man doesn't understand them, but seriously, *of course* men don't understand us, they aren't women!

The most useful thing Anya has taught me is that most of the upset in my life has been caused through my own thought processes – through my own imagination. Yes, I would like to love and be loved – it's a wonderful thing – but I should not expect that if I can just find a man he'll be delivered with an unlimited supply of happiness. I don't think one man can possibly provide me with everything I desire; and I won't expect Gethyn to either; laughter, DIY, sympathy, financial security, foot warmer in bed.. Also, my partner shouldn't expect me to be all kinds of a woman in one, either.

And here endeth the sermon, by Agatha Braithwaite.

Ciao, Bella. Safe trip home, lovely lady.

From: percynmadge@yahoo.com
To: rosie-of-arabia@yahoo.com
Subject: Antarctica

Date: 25 June

Dear, Rosie

I've not been able to settle since your phone call, so I got Dad to log me onto email because I needed to write to you straight away. I've been thinking about your application to go to Antarctica and wondering if it's the right thing to do. I agree you need to take charge of your life and go out and grab it by the tail, but do you realise you'd be jumping from a sandy desert to an icy one. Are you deliberately placing yourself outside normal life – normal society – as a means of running away? I can understand this, but what happens after Antarctica? Will you move on to the jungle, or the outback, or Alaska? You say you've found peace, but have you if you're still running?

    With love, Mum x

From: aggieb@yahoo.com
To: rosie-of-arabia@yahoo.com
Subject: Deliriously Happy!

Date: 27 June

Hi, Rosie

Oh my God! Gethyn arrived yesterday, and I've just had THE BEST twenty-four hours of my life.

But oh, the best bit is the story of how he travelled to Appledart. He walked (yes, walked) across the Appledart mountains (twenty miles of hard-walking in horrendous weather) to get to me because the boat doesn't run on a Saturday. He'd joked that he'd find a way to get to me as soon as he could, but I never for one second thought he would walk here. When he stepped through the door of the café - wet through and a bit out of breath, with his paunch popping out of the lower buttons of his shirt and the rain shining off his head - I was sat at a table in front of the fire playing cards with Anya. When I turned around and looked at the person who had dropped his rucksack on the floor I knew it was him. I tried to learn from Isabella and be as cool with Gethyn as she was with Nathan, but of course, I could *never* be that cool. I rushed over to him and tried to speak but turned into a tongue tied, blithering fool. Gethyn took my hands in his and bid me to be quiet a moment and said, 'I've walked a long way but I'm hoping this is the end of the road, and if you're Agatha Braithwaite, I'm sure it will be.'

Oh, my Jesus Christ – how romantic was that!

Gethyn said it was you who persuaded him it was the right move to come and visit - thank you, thank you, thank you, my sweet, amazing friend! And don't worry your head about anything at all, because I'm absolutely certain that your life is going to have a miraculous change of direction any moment, I just feel it in my bones.

Love, Ag

P.S. I may have invited Gethyn back to my place after all – Agatha Braithwaite, you're such a devil!

From: rosie-of-arabia@yahoo.com
To: aggieb@yahoo.com
Subject: Re: Deliriously Happy!

Date: 27 June

Hi, Ag

That's wonderful news. I'm so pleased for you both. Send Gethyn my love. Have a fabulous time. See you very soon.

Love, Rosie

From: aggieb@yahoo.com
To: sexymamma@yahoo.com
Subject: Re: Hello Darling

Date: 27 June

Dear Rosie Hughes

Hello, Mamma

It was lovely to hear from you. Everything is good at my end but I'm keeping a low profile with the press and I strongly suggest you do the same. I'd love for you to visit, but I wonder if we could keep my location a secret. Like you used to say, Mamma, it's just me and you in this life together and no one else needs to be involved.

Let me know when you want to come, and I'll book your tickets. I could fly you to Inverness and have you picked up in a car? Would you like that?

    Love you, Agatha x

Bluey
From: Rosie
To: Mrs Hughes (via the Post Office)

Date: 28 June

Hi, Mum

The Internet is down, but I wanted to write a letter just to you before I leave to say thank you so much for everything while I've been away. The packages, the letters, everything. I stood on the banks of the Euphrates today. It was amazing - a lush oasis of hope in the middle of an arid hellhole. The Euphrates is very special, spiritual almost. I brought Angelica's tiny knitted hat to Iraq in my rucksack, the one she wore in intensive care, just after she was born. I'm going to put the hat and a message in a bottle, take it to the river tomorrow and let it all just flow away.

Love you, Mum.
Your, Rosanna xx

From: josh71@yahoo.com
To: rosie-of-arabia@yahoo.com
Subject: Appledart

Date: 28 June

Hi, Rosie
   Me again.
   Guess where I am? You never will. I'm in Appledart. Is that spontaneous enough for you? I'm writing to you from your friend Agatha's laptop. I hope you don't mind but I've been chatting to her and your friend Gethyn for a few hours and they seem to have set me straight. I'd better explain:
   After I looked in your chest of special things for the lamp I felt so confused. Then I got your letter and my head went into meltdown. I decided to bring my holiday forward a week, put on my walking boots, packed a bag, jumped in the car, went to your Dad's to drop off his tools, felt even more confused, then hit the road with the express purpose of getting away from everything

– especially from mobile phones, email and from the bloody media pushing out images of Iraq all the damn time. When I left your Mum's house I checked into a hotel, logged onto a computer and emailed you my first response. Ten minutes later I knew I'd made a mistake but didn't know what to do. So, I carried on travelling north, not entirely sure where I was headed and bounced from one hotel to another. And then I got an email from your friend, Agatha, inviting me to Appledart, and before I knew it, I was here.

Agatha has been fantastic, and in talking to her, I finally let go of all my pent-up emotion and the long and short of it is this: all I know is life is shit without you and I've changed my mind. So yes, I agree, if you'll have me, let's try again. I don't know why I sent that bloody letter saying no. I was an arse. Come home to Dartmoor. I've called off the exchange of contracts on the cottage, it's ours and no one else's and I promise I'll be more spontaneous in future and I'll work less.

Finally, in the closing words of Edith Piaf; *give your heart and soul to me, and life will always be, La Vie en Rose.*

Rosie Hughes, will you marry me? Phone as soon as you can with your answer.

Love, Josh x

From: rosie-of-arabia@yahoo.com
To: gethyn-of-arabia@yahoo.com
Subject: Thank You

Date: 28 June

Hi, Gethyn

I'm just about to head into the city, but I wanted to send you a quick message to you to say what I failed to say on your last night in Basra – thank you.

You and I will always know what we've seen and what we've done, but I don't know that I'll ever want to talk about it. I don't want to let the moment pass without making sure you know that the day you walked into HQ and smiled that fabulous smile was one of the most blessed moments of my life. I will never forget dancing in the desert. Thank you a thousand times over, my wonderful friend. I surely would have been lost in hell without you.

Love, Rosie
P.S. I hid the little ornament of Big Ben that came with Aggie's hamper in your Bergen before you left – it's to remind you of our time together (the good bits).

From: aggieb@yahoo.com
To: rosie-of-arabia@yahoo.com
Subject: My First Chapter!

Date: 28 June

Hi, Rosie

I know I'm going to see you next week, but I had to write straight away and tell you that I've completed chapter one of my new novel – and it *flew* onto the page! Oh, I know it will probably be cut to pieces in the edit, but all I can say is, 'Thank Christ for that!'

And so thank you, my wonderful friend, for allowing me to tell your story. I promise to take the very best of care of it. I'm wetting myself with excitement about writing the final chapter, which is going to be so blooming heart-warming, there will not be a dry eye in the house. Just imagine the scene: two old friends meet up for the first time on an achingly beautiful Scottish beach, one having just come back from a war zone in the desert, the other having finally found a purpose to her life, after years of being lost in a desert of her own. We lost many years of friendship (and all because of a man and a misunderstanding – women will never learn!) but once you get home, we can crack on with a new bucket list and pledge (in blood, if necessary) never to lose touch again. Anyway, enough mush. I'm sending the blurb for the book. Let me know what you think!

With all the love in the world,
Aggie (AKA Stella Valentine – I told you I'd find a use for the name)

West Yorkshire Herald Headline
Date: 30 June 2003

Local Woman Killed in Basra

A Royal Naval Reserve Officer was gunned down in Basra yesterday, next to the River Euphrates, in an ambush that left two service personnel dead and two in a critical condition. Rosanna Hughes, a thirty-four-year-old Meteorological Forecaster, originally from West Yorkshire. . .

Epilogue

Bluey
From: Rosie
To: Aggie

Dated: 29 June
Read: 3 July

Hi, Aggie

The Internet has crashed again and won't be up and running for a couple of hours so, for old times' sake, I thought I'd return to the good old Bluey system for my last letter before I go home.

Home! Imagine that?

Firstly, I want to thank you for inviting Josh to Appledart (I take it you got hold of him through Dad?). You're an incredible woman, Aggie, really, you are. I also wholeheartedly give my blessing for the book, but more of that in a minute, because I have to tell you something

of great importance and you'd better sit down because–
I can bloody well flick-flack!

I know, incredible!

Gethyn had been helping to support my back while
I practised, but I never quite committed to really going
for it and failed every time. And then, after I got the letter
from Josh asking me to marry him, I just went for it and
Ta Da! Tis done.

But flick flack aside, you're right about not seeing the
bucket list as something to be ticked off as quickly as
possible, and honestly, I don't care if I never swim with
dolphins (actually, I do, they are truly amazing), or count
to ten in Russian backwards, or basically tick my life
away on a wish list of doing things for the sake of it.
My home, my family and my friends really are all I need
– this life, the one I already have, it's enough. So now
my bucket list reads like this:

1. Hug Mum, Dad and the dog.
2. Show Josh the warmth of my love.
3. Go metal detecting with Dad. He's never given up
   on finding that elusive pot of gold, and if we believe
   strongly enough, together, maybe one day we'll find
   it.
4. Play a duet with you.

That's it.

But oh, yes, your book: I loved the blurby thing, and
for once, I'm delighted by your mother's behaviour
because it's about time you wrote a novel in your own

name. Agatha Braithwaite is a great name and it suits you. Oh, and feel free to go crazy with the romance stuff and give me a fabulous, over-the-top, happy ending. I know Gethyn gave you some grief over this, but sod it. Mum said I was to imagine my future life in a glowing, positive way, so let's go for full technicolour (just like when Dorothy enters Oz in the Judy Garland film).

This is what I want:

At the end of the book I should travel to your café (all upset because my marriage is over – my face stained with mascara smudges) and then you smile at me (knowingly), wipe my face clean, brush my hair and lead me out to the beach for a walk (because I've been travelling for days and I need fresh air). But, would you believe it, Josh is waiting for me on the jetty, standing in the rain. I run up to him cautiously, because I'm not sure what he is going to say to me (can a person run cautiously?) and he tells me how he loves me and asks me to marry him - all over again – and I say, 'Yes, please' and we kiss and the waves brush across our feet (maybe we need to be on the beach, not on the jetty for the kiss). Having watched the scene from a distance, you meander back into the café and sit on Gethyn's lap, who's waiting by the fire, and he smiles up at you and you tell him you're pregnant (I thought I'd throw that little showstopper in there) and it suddenly stops raining, and Josh and I walk off into the sunset together, and we all live happily ever after. The end.

Author's Notes

Knoydart:
There is a very special place on the west coast of Scotland called the Knoydart Peninsula. Anyone who has been there will know that my fictional haven, Appledart, is based very closely on Knoydart (let's face it, Appledart is more or less a carbon copy). I wrote part of this novel during my brief stay on the peninsula, during which time I walked to the hamlet of Airor and visited the Road's End Café and realised – with great whoops of delight – that it was the perfect location for Aggie's new home. I'm grateful to the owner for allowing me (so blatantly) to steal Road's End Café for my novel.

https://en-gb.facebook.com/The-Roads-End-Cafe

Iraq:
Although I served with the 1st (UK) Armoured Division in Iraq during the conflict in 2003, Rosie and Gethyn are not a representation of either myself, or anyone I met

during that time. Rosie and Gethyn have their own unique, fictional story. I have, however, drawn on my experiences during the war to add reality to Rosie's experience.

Fell in love with *Dear Rosie Hughes*?

Keep reading for a sneak peek at Melanie Hudson's
gorgeous next novel...

'Like a breath of wind gone in a fleeting second,
only the memories now remain.'

Prologue

Read Me

This is a note to yourself, Juliet.

At the time of writing you are ninety-two years old and worried that the bits and bobs of your story have begun to go astray. You must read this note carefully every day and work very hard to keep yourself and the memories alive, because once upon a time you told a man called Edward Nancarrow that you would, and it's important to keep that promise, Juliet, even when there seems to be little point going on.

In the mahogany sideboard you will find all the things you will need to keep living your life alone. These things are: Bank details; savings bonds; emergency contact numbers; basic information about you - your name, age and place of birth; money in a freezer bag; an emergency mobile phone. More importantly, there are also your most precious possessions scattered around the house. I've labelled them, to help you out.

Written on the back of this note is a copy of the poem Edward sent you in 1943. Make sure you can recite it (poetry is good for the brain). And finally, even if you forget everything else, remember that, in the end, Edward's very simple words are the only things that have ever really mattered.

Now, make sure you've had something to eat and a glass of water – water helps with memory – and whatever happens in the future, whatever else you may forget, always remember ... he's waiting.

With an endless supply of love,
Juliet

Chapter 1

Exeter, 2019

It was a bright Saturday lunchtime in early December. I'd just closed the lounge curtains and was about to binge-watch the first three series of *The Crown* for the fourth time when a Christmas card bearing a Penzance postmark dropped through the letter box.

Uncle Gerald. It had to be.

The card, with an illustration of a distressed donkey carrying a (somewhat disappointed-looking) Virgin Mary being egged on by a couple of haggard angels, contained within it my usual Christmas catch up latter. I wandered through to the kitchen and clicked the kettle on - it was a four pager.

My Dear Katherine

Firstly, I hope this letter finds you well, or as well as to be expected given your distressing circumstances of living alone in Exeter with no family around you.

355

Melanie Hudson

Cheers for that, Gerald

> But more of your circumstances in a moment
> because (to quote the good bard) 'something is rotten
> in the state of Denmark' and I'm afraid this year's
> letter will not burst forth with my usual festive cheer.
> There is at present a degree of what can only be
> described as 'Civil Unrest' breaking out in Angels Cove
> and I am at my wits end trying to promote an atmos-
> phere of peace and good will in time for Christmas.
> I'm hopeful you will be able to offer a degree of
> academic common sense to the issue.
> Here's the rub: the Parish Council (you may
> remember that I am the chair?) has been informed
> that the village boundaries are to be redrawn in
> January as part of a Cornwall County Council admin-
> istrative shake-up. This simple action has lit the touch
> paper of a centuries-old argument amongst the resi-
> dents that needs – finally - to be put to rest.
> The argument in question is this: should our village
> be apostrophised or not? If 'yes' then should the apos-
> trophe come before or after the 's'?
> It is a Total Bloody Nightmare!

It really isn't, Gerald.

> At the moment Angels Cove is written without an apos-
> trophe, but most agree that there should be an apostrophe

356

in there somewhere, but where? The argument seems to rest on three questions:

1. Does the cove 'belong' to just one angel (the angel depicted in the church stained glass window, for example) or to a multitude of angels (i.e. the possessive of a singular or a plural noun).

2. Does the cove belong to the angels or do the angels belong to the cove? (the minority who wish to omit the apostrophe in its entirety ask this question).

3. Does the word angel in Angels Cove actually refer, not to the winged messengers of the Devine, but to the notorious pirate, Jeremiah 'Cut-throat' Angel, who sailed from Penzance circa 1723 and whose ship, The Savage Angel, was scuppered in Mounts Bay (not apostrophised, you will note) when he returned from the West Indies at the tender age of twenty-nine?

As you can see, it's a mess.

Fearing the onset of a migraine I stopped reading and decided to sort out the recycling, which would take a while, given the number of empties. An hour later saw me continuing to give the rest of Gerald's letter a stiff ignoring because I needed to get back to *The Crown* and plough my way through an ironing pile that saw its foundations laid in 1992. Just at the point where Prince Phillip jaunts off solo on a raucous stag do to Australia (and thinking that I really ought to write a letter to the Queen to tell her how awesome she is), I turned the iron off (feeling a pang of guilt at leaving a complicated silk blouse alone in the basket) and with Bublé's Christmas album on shuffle, poured a glass of Merlot, popped a Tesco 'extra deep' mince pie in the microwave for ten seconds and returned to the letter ...

I expect you will agree that this is a question of historical context, not a grammatical issue.

I don't.

As the 'go to' local historian (it must run in the family!) I attempted to offer my own hypothesis at the parish meeting last week, but can you believe it, I was barracked off the stage just two minutes into my delivery!

I can.

But all is not lost. This morning, while sitting on the loo wracking my brains for inspiration, I stumbled across your book, From Nob End to Soggy Bottom, English Place Names and their Origins *in my toilet TBR pile (I had forgotten you have such a dry wit, my dear) and I just knew that I had received Devine intervention from the good Lord himself, because although the villagers are not prepared to accept my opinion as being correct, I do believe they would accept the decision of a university professor, especially when I explain that you were sent to them by God. So, I have a proposition for you.*

Time for that mince pie.

In return for your help on the issue, please do allow me the pleasure of offering you a little holiday here in Angels Cove, as my very special present to you, this Christmas. I know you have balked at the idea of coming to stay with me in the past (don't worry, I know I'm an eccentric old so-and-so with dubious bowl control and disgusting toenails)

True

but how do you fancy a beautiful sea view this Christmas?

Well, now that you mention it ...

The cottage is called Angel View (just the one angel, note) and now belongs to a local man, Sam Lanyon (Royal Navy pilot – he's away at sea for Christmas, poor chap) He says you can stay as long as you like – I may have mentioned what happened to James as leverage.

Gerald!

Melanie Hudson

The cottage sits just above the cove and has everything you could possible need for the perfect holiday (it's also a bit of a 1940s time capsule because until very recently it belonged to an elderly lady - you'll love it).

The thing is, before you say no, do remember that before she died, I did promise your mother that I would keep an eye on you ...

It was only a matter of time

and your Christmas card seemed so forlorn it set me off worrying about you being alone again this Christmas, and I thought this would be the perfect opportunity for us to look out for each other, as I'm alone too – George is on a mercy mission visiting his sister in Brighton this year. Angels Cove is simply beautiful at Christmas. The whole village pulls together (when they are not arguing) to illuminate the harbour with a festival of lights, and the school children have a few tricks up their sleeves too. It's magical.

But?

But ... with all the shenanigans going on this year, I'm not sure the villagers will be in the mood for celebration and I'm concerned the children are going to suffer. Please do say you'll come and answer our question for us, and in doing so, bring harmony to this beautiful little

360

cove and save Christmas for all the little children.

Surely this kind of thing is right up your Strasse!

My idea is that you could do a little bit of research then the locals could present you with their proposals for the placement of the apostrophe in a climatic final meeting. It will be just like a Christmas episode of the Apprentice – bring a suit!) and meanwhile I'll have whole programme of excitement planned for you – a week of wonderful things - and it includes gin!

Now you're talking

Do write back straight away and say you'll come, because by God, Katherine, you are barely forty-five years old, which is a mere blink of an eye, and it is not an age where a person should be sitting alone with only their memories to comfort them, and if anyone deserves it a little comfort this Christmas, it's you. I know you usually visit the grave on Christmas Day, but please, for the build-up week at least (which is the best part of Christmas after all) come to Cornwall and allow yourself to be swaddled by our angels for a while (they're an impressive bunch).

I am happy to beg.

Yours, in desperation,

Uncle Gerald.

P.S. Did I mention there would be gin?

I tore of a square of kitchen towel off the roll and dabbed my eyes. Dear Uncle Gerald. You see, that's the thing with random acts of kindness, they knocked you sideways when you were busy looking the other way.

Sitting back in a kitchen chair I'd ruined by half-arsedly daubing it in powder blue chalk paint two weeks before, I glanced around the room and thought about Gerald's offer. On the one hand, why on earth would I want to leave my home at Christmas. It was beautiful. But the energy had changed, and what was once the vibrant epicentre of Exeter's academia, now hovered in a haze of hushed and silent mourning, like the house was afraid of upsetting me by raising its voice.

A miniature Christmas tree was sitting on the edge of the dresser looking uncomfortable and embarrassed. I'd decorated it with a selection of outsized wooden orna-ments picked up during a day out to Ikea in November. Ikea in Exeter was my weekly go-to store since James had gone. It was a haven for the lost and lonely. A person (me) can disappear up their own backsides for the whole morning (literally) in an unpronounceable maze of fake rooms, rugs, tab-top curtains, plastic plants and kitchen utensils (basically all the crap the Swedes don't want) before whiling away a good couple of hours gorging themselves on a menu of meatballs and cinnamon swirls, and still have the weirdest selection of booze and confec-tionary Sweden has to offer (what on earth is Lordagsgodis, anyway?) to look forward to at checkout.

And we wonder why the Swedes are so happy!

But did I really want to spend the run-up to Christmas in Ikea this year? (Part of me actually did - it's *very* Scandi-chic Christmassy). But to do it for a third year in a row, with no one to laugh out loud with when we try to pronounce the unpronounceable Swedish word for fold-up bed?

(That was a poor example because a futon is a futon in any language and I really did need to try to control my inner monologue which had gone into overdrive since James died - I was beginning to look excessively absent minded in public).

But did I want to spend Christmas in Ikea this year?

Not really, no.

But the problem (and Gerald knew this, too) was that if I left the house this Christmas, then it would mark the beginning of my letting go, of starting again, of saying that another life – a festive one – could exist beyond the mourning of James. What if I laugh and forget him for a moment? I might start to forget, but if I stay here, and keep thinking of him, if I keep the memories alive, if I re-read the little notes he left me every morning, if I look through photographs on Facebook, replay scenes and conversations in my mind, then he's still here, alive, in me. But if I go away, where would that lead? I knew exactly where it would lead - to the beginning of the end of James. To the beginning of not being able to remember his voice, his smell, his laugh – to the beginning of moving on.

And I wasn't sure I was ready for that.

I knocked back the last of the Merlot while Googling train times to Penzance, and in a moment of abandoned frenzy, fished out the last card in a box of Ikea Christmas cards I'd abandoned to the dresser drawer the week before. It was the exact replica of the one I'd already sent him, a golden angel. I took it as a sign and began to scribble ...

Dear, Uncle Gerald

You are quite correct. This kind of thing is indeed 'right up my Strasse'. Rest assure there will be no need to beg – I shall come!

I arrive in Penzance by the 1830 train on the 17th and shall stay (wait for it) until Boxing Day! By which time I am confident that, one way or another, I will have found a solution to your problem. DO NOT, however, feel that you have to entertain me all week. It's very good of you but actually – and quite selfishly - this trip could be a blessing in disguise. I have been wracking my brains for an idea for a new book – a history project to keep me going through the rest of the winter – and I have a feeling that hidden deep within the midst of Cornish Myth and legend, I might find one.

Please thank Mr Lanyon for the offer of use of his cottage – I accept!

How are the cataracts, by the way? Are you able to drive? If so, I wonder if you could meet me at the station?

With oodles of love,
Your, Katherine

P.S. *Wouldn't it be funny if 'The Cataracts' were an old couple who lived in the village and I would say, 'How are the Cataracts, by the way?' And you would answer, 'Oh, they're fine. They've just tripped off to Tenerife for Christmas.'*

P.P.S. *Take heart in knowing that there is nothing simple about the apostrophe. It is punctuation's version of the naughty Cornish pixie, and seems to wreak havoc wherever it goes. There is a village in America, for example, where the misplacing of the apostrophe led to full-scale civil unrest and ultimately, the cold-blooded murder of the local Sheriff. Let us hope for your sake that the situation at Angels Cove does not escalate into a similar scale of bruhaha!*

P.P.P.S. *Gin? I love you!*

Chapter 2

It turned out that the residents of Angels Cove were expecting not one, but two Katherines to arrive in Penzance on the evening of 17th December. My namesake *Storm Katherine* – a desperate attention seeker who had decided to make a dramatic entrance - would arrive late with the loud and gregarious roar of an axe-wielding Viking. Trees would crash onto roads, chicken hutches would be turned upside down, and the blight of every twenty first century garden - the netted trampoline - would disappear over hedgerows never to be seen again (it wasn't *all* bad, then). I hoped Uncle Gerald wouldn't see my concurrent arrival with *Katherine* as some kind of omen, but really, how could he not?

Stepping onto the train in Exeter, despite the forecast weather, I was excited. By Plymouth I was beginning to wonder if it had all been a dreadful mistake – the locals would want to chat, and the woman in the shop (there was always a chatty woman in a shop) would glance at my wedding ring and pry into my life with a stream of double negatives: 'Will you husband not be joining you in the cottage for Christmas, then? No? Well, it's nice to have some time away from them all, eh? And what about your children? Will they not be coming down? No children? Oh, dear. Well, never mind ...'

That kind of thing.

By Truro I'd decided to turn back, but *Katherine's* advance party had already begun to rock the carriages, and by the time St Michael's Mount appeared through the late afternoon darkness – a watered down image of her usual self, barely visible through the driving rain and sea fret - my excitement had vaporised completely. Gazing through the splattered carriage window, I was startled by the sight of my mother's face staring back at me. Only it wasn't my mother, it was my own aged reflection. When had *that* happened? Anxious fingers rushed to smooth the lines on my mother's face, which could only be described as tired (dreadful word) and I realised that, just like St Michael's Mount in the winter rain, I too was a watered-down image of my usual self, barely visible through a veil of grief I had worn ever since the morning James had gone.

*

I hadn't needed an alarm call that morning. I'd been laying on my side for hours, tucked into the foetal position, the left side of my face resting on a tear-stained pillow, my eyes focussed just above the bedside table, fixed on the clock.

I watched every movement of Mickey Mouse's right hand as it made a full circle, resting, with a final little wave, on the twelve.

Mickey's voice rang out –

'It's time, time, time, to wake up! It's time, time, time to wake up!'

I'd never known if Mickey had been supposed to say the word 'time' three times, or if at some point over the past umpteen years he had developed a stutter, but I silenced him with a harsh thump on the head and lay staring at the damp patch on the ceiling we'd never gotten to the bottom of, just to the right of the light fitting.

I wanted to lay there and consider that phrase for a moment – 'it's time'. Two little words with such a big meaning.

It's time, Katherine.

How many times had I heard those words?

My father had said them, standing in the kitchen doorway on my wedding day. He'd taken my hand with a wonderful smile and walked me to the car, a happy man. We were followed closely behind by my Aunt Helena, who was frothing my veil and laughing at Mum – who did not approve of the match - and who fussed along behind us, arguing about ... I think it was art, but it might have been cheese. And now, twenty years later, the exact same words were used by Gerald, to direct me out of the house. To force me, my insides kicking and screaming for release, to slide into the long black car that

369

waited in the yard - the car that would take us to James'
funeral, the sort of funeral that has the caption 'But dear
God, why?' hovering in the air the whole day.

I turned my back on Mickey and ran my arm across
the base sheet on the other side of the bed. If only there
was still some warmth there. His arm to curl into, his
woolly chest to rest my head on. But the sheet was cold,
and like everything else in my house in Exeter, retained
the deep ingrained memory of centuries of damp.

But if I just lay there and let the day move on without
me ...

It's time, time, time, to wake up!

Mickey again.

I stretched. Ridiculous thought. Mickey was right. The
day wouldn't move on, not if I didn't wind the cogs and
drop-kick the sun through the goal posts. I threw my
legs out of bed, sat up, patted Mickey on the head,
apologised for hitting him on the head and I kissed him
on the face. Poor thing. It wasn't his fault James had been
killed, even if he did insist in shouting at me every
morning in his sickening, overly polite, American way.

It's time, Katherine.

*

But that was the thing with travelling alone on a train,
there was simply too much time to think. Trains were
just one long rolling mass of melancholy, the carriages
filled with random, interconnected thoughts. Travel alone
on a train with no book to read and an over-thinker can

spend an entire journey in the equivalent of that confused state between sleeping and waking.

And then the guard broke my reverie.

Ladies and gentlemen, we will shortly be arriving in Penzance. Penzance is the last station stop. Service terminates at Penzance. All alight at Penzance.

It was pretty obvious I needed to get off.

As the train slowed to a final halt at the station, the last of the passengers began to stir. I grabbed my laptop case, put on my winter coat, hat and gloves and trundled to the end of the carriage in the hope that my suitcase would still be there. It was time to step out onto the platform, find uncle Gerald, and head out into the storm.

Chapter 3

I stepped down onto the platform and stood still for a moment, my eyes searching through a river of passengers, before catching sight of Uncle Gerald, who was waving his multi-coloured umbrella like a lunatic and working his way upstream.

My heart melted. Uncle Gerald had been a steady presence in my life as a child, and although I'd hardly seen him during my adult years, the bond that was formed during those childhood visits - nothing overly special, just a kind smile and couple of quid for sweets tucked into my sticky fingers - had never gone away. It was a bond that represented the safety and easiness of family. A bond that is usually lobbed into the back of the dresser drawer, stashed away, forgotten and allowed to loiter with the unused Christmas cards, nutcrackers and Cellotape, until the day came along when you actually needed it, and you opened the drawer with a rummage saying to yourself, 'I know I left it in there somewhere.'

Gerald rested his umbrella against my suitcase and put his arms around me.

I wasn't expecting the sudden onset of emotion, but he represented a simpler time. A happy time. A time of singing together in the kitchen with Mum. Usually the Carpenters.

Rainy Days and Mondays.

I started to cry.

He patted.

'Now then, none of that, none of that.'

'Oh, don't mind me, Uncle Gerald,' I said, trying to smile while rifling through my handbag and coat pockets for a tissue. 'Train stations and airport lounges always do this to me. I swear they're the portals used by the tear fairies to tap directly into the tender places of the soul.'

Gerald handed me a folded faded blue handkerchief.

I blew my nose.

He smiled. 'Still over-dramatic then?'

I nodded.

'That's my girl!'

We both laughed and sniffed back our emotion before heading out into the wind and rain. We dashed to the car and he handed me the keys. 'You wouldn't mind driving, would you? Only I spent the afternoon in the Legion ...'

The drive to Angels Cove took less than half an hour. It was a fairly silent half hour because Uncle Gerald slept while I battled the car through the beginnings of the storm, luckily satnav remembered the way. The road narrowed as we headed down a tree-lined hill. I slowed the car to a halt and positioned the headlights to illuminate the village sign through the driving rain.

I nudged Uncle Gerald.

'We're here.'

He stirred and harrumphed at sight of the sign.

'Perhaps now you can see why I asked for your help,' he said.

I failed to stifle a laugh.

The sign had been repeatedly graffitied. Firstly, someone had inserted an apostrophe with permanent marker between the 'l' and the 's'. Then, someone else had put a line through the apostrophe and scrawled a new apostrophe to the right of the 's', which had been further crossed out. The crossings out continued across the sign until there was no room to write any more.

'This all started at the beginning of November, when the letter from the council arrived. I've got my hands full with it all, I can tell you. Especially on Wednesdays.' He nodded ahead. 'Drive on, straight down to the harbour.'

'Wednesdays?' I asked, putting the car into gear.

'Skittles night at the Crab and Lobster. It's a whole village event.'

'Ah. I can imagine.'

We carried on down the road, the wipers losing the battle with the rain, and I tried to remember the layout of the village. I recalled a pretty place consisting of one long narrow road that wound its way very slowly down to the sea. Pockets of cottages lined the road, which was about a mile long in total, with the pub in the middle, next to the primary school which was a classic Victorian school house, with two entrances. 'Boys' was written in stone above one entrance and 'Girls' written above the other.

The road narrowed yet further before opening out onto a small harbour. I stopped the car. The harbour was lit by a smattering of old-fashioned street lamps. We watched waves crash over the harbour walls. Although Katherine had not yet arrived with the might of her full force, the sea had already whipped itself up into an excitable frenzy.

Gerald pointed to the right.

'You can't make it out too clearly in the dark,' he said, staring into the darkness. 'But the cottage you're staying in is up this little track by about two hundred meters.'

I glanced up.

'You ready?' he asked.

'Ready? Ready for what?'

'Oh, nothing. It's just a bit of a bumpy track, that's all.' He tapped the Land Rover with an affectionate pat, as if he was praising an old Labrador. 'No problem for this little lady, though. Been up that track a thousand times, haven't you, old girl? Onwards and upwards!'

I set off in the general direction of a farm track. The

car took on an angle of about forty-five degrees and began to slip and slide its way up the track. Waves crashed against the rocks directly to my left.

'Shitty death, Gerald! What the -?'

But then, to my absolute relief, a little white cottage appeared under a swinging security light like a shimmering oasis. We pulled alongside and I switched of the engine, left the car in gear and went to open the door.

'Don't get out for a moment,' Gerald said. 'I'll go in ahead and turn on the lights. It'll also give me time to shoo the mice away and make it nice and homely, that kind of thing.'

'Mice?'

He winked.

'Well, only a few, and they're very friendly.'

'Don't be too long.' I wiped condensation from the window and tried to peer out into the storm. 'I feel like I've stepped through one of the seven circles of hell!'

The tour of the cottage was very short but very sweet. When Gerald mentioned that an elderly lady had left it as a 1940s time capsule, he was right. There were three upstairs bedrooms, which were pretty but functional, a downstairs bathroom, a good-sized kitchen and an achingly sweet lounge. Gerald lit the fire while explaining that he'd stocked the fridge with enough food, milk and mince pies, to take me through to the New Year, just in case.

I took off my coat and lay it across the arm of a green velvet chaise longue, then crossed to the window to close the curtains. I picked up a photograph frame that sat on the windowsill. The black and white image and was of woman standing in front of a bi-plane, holding a flying helmet and goggles, smiling brightly, if squinting slightly against the sun. There was a tag attached to the photo. I read it.

Summer 1938. Edward took this. Our first full day together. Two days in one - fantastic and tragic all at once. Why can we never have the one, without the other. Why can't we have light without shade?

'Juliet was a pilot,' Gerald said by way of explanation, turning to face me briefly while attempting to draw the fire by holding a sheet of newspaper across the fireplace. 'She flew for the Air Transport Auxiliary during the War.'

I nodded, still looking at the photograph.

'Juliet handed the old place to Sam Lanyon, but he hasn't got around to sorting through her belongings yet,' Gerald added, rising to his feet. He screwed up the paper he'd used to draw the fire and threw it onto the flames.

I put the frame down, closed the curtains and looked around the room ... photos, books, paintings, odds and ends of memorabilia. I stepped across to a 1920s sideboard and opened a drawer, it was full of the same forgotten detritus of someone else's life.

This was no holiday cottage, this was a home.

Gerald turned his back on the fire a final time. It was blazing.

'You've a good supply of coal and logs so just remember to keep feeding it, and don't forget to put the guard up when you go to bed - this type of coal spits!'

He made a move towards the door. His hat and scarf were hanging on a peg in the little hallway. He grabbed them and began to wrap his scarf around his throat.

'Are you sure it's ok for me to stay here, Gerald?' I was standing in the lounge doorway. 'Only it seems a bit ... intrusive.'

'Nonsense! It was actually Sam's idea! He's happy that it's being aired.'

Gerald turned to leave and attempted to open the door. The force of the storm pushed against him. My unease at the prospect of staying alone in an unfamiliar cottage on a cliffside, unsure of my bearings, during one of the worst storms in a decade, must have shown on my face. He closed the door for a moment and walked into the lounge, talking to himself.

'On nights like this, Juliet always put her faith in one thing, and it never let her down.'

I followed him. 'God?'

He opened the sideboard door and peered inside.

'Ha! No,' he answered, taking out a bottle. 'Whiskey! And there's a torch in there, too.' He put the whiskey back and walked into the kitchen. I heard him open and close a few drawers before reappearing in the lounge with half a dozen candles. He handed them to me.

'Just in case the electricity goes out. And the matches are on the fireplace so you're all set.'

The lounge window started to rattle.

He straightened his hat and headed to the backdoor. 'This cottage might seem rickety, but it's the oldest and sturdiest house in the village.'

I picked up the car keys from the hall table and grabbed my coat from the lounge.

'I'll drive you home.'

'No, no. I'll walk back,' he said, pulling his scarf tighter.

'In this weather?' I asked, only half concentrating as I was now searching in my handbag for my phone. 'Mercy, me! I have a signal!'

Gerald paused at the door.

'Put the keys down, Katherine. I'll be fine. Listen, why don't you leave your coat on and come to see my friend, Fenella, with me. I promised her I'd pop in on my way home. She's had a bit of a bereavement and isn't coping very well.'

'Oh, dear. Husband?'

'No. Dog. Her cottage is just behind the harbour. We can nip in and pay our respects and then make our excuses and go back to mine ... via the pub. You might as well meet the enemy straight off!'

I wanted to say, 'Thank Christ for that. Yes please.' But

the curse of the twenty first century independent woman prevented me from throwing myself at his mercy. And I didn't fancy the pub.

'Don't be silly,' I said with a blasé shoulder shrug and taking my coat off one final time. 'I'll be absolutely fine.' (which is the exact phrase everyone uses when they are, in fact, sure that they will not 'be absolutely fine').

He put his hand on the door handle.

'Well, if you're sure, I'll be off. Just phone me if you need reassurance. Oh, and there's WiFi here!'

Result.

'The code is ...' Gerald paused and delved into his coat pocket. He took out a scrap of paper. '... tiger moth, all lowercase. And try not to worry. I wouldn't leave you here if I thought it wasn't safe.'

Gerald kissed me on the cheek and stepped out into the wind.

'I'll pop up tomorrow morning,' he shouted. 'I've got a fabulous programme of events all worked out! And lock the door behind me straight away. It'll bang all night if you don't.'

'I will,' I shouted down the lane. 'And, thank you!'

With the door locked and bolted, I walked into the lounge, sat on the sofa for a moment and stared into the fire, unconsciously spinning my wedding ring around my finger. Alone again.

The lights began to flicker and somewhere in the

kitchen, another window rattled. I grabbed my laptop from the hallway, logged onto the WiFi and - for at least five seconds – thought about doing a little 'Angels Cove' research (or any research that might lead me in the direction of a new project and take my mind off the storm). I closed the laptop lid.

Tomorrow. I'd do the research tomorrow.

I grabbed the remote control, flashed the TV and Freeview box into life and pressed the up button on the volume. The closing scenes of a *Miss Marple* rerun sounded out most of the noise of the storm. Now all I needed to do was make a cup of tea, rustle up a spot of dinner and settle down to a spot of *Grand Designs* on Freeview (the harangued couples who had mortgaged themselves to the hilt and lived in a leaky caravan during the worst winter on record with three screaming kids and another on the way while trying to source genuine terracotta tiles in junk shops for a bathroom that wouldn't be built for another five years ... they were my favourites).

With the closing credits of *Miss Marple* rolling down the screen, I walked through to the kitchen to make dinner. It was the real deal on the quintessential cottage front – not a fitted cupboard in sight - and very pretty, with French doors at the rear. A circular pine table with two chairs sat at the opposite end of the kitchen to the French doors, underneath a window. A golden envelope addressed to *Katherine Henderson, C/O Angel View*, sat on the table. Assuming the coincidence of there being another Katherine Henderson associated with the cottage being slim, I guessed the card was for me, opened the envelope and took out the Christmas card. Another angel, they were everywhere this year.

> *Dear Katherine*
> *Just a quick note to welcome you to Angel View and explain about the house. Until recently the house belonged to a very special lady called Juliet Caron – my amazing Grandmother - and you will find that her spirit is still very much alive within the cottage walls. Most importantly, please make yourself at home and have a very happy Christmas.*
> *Yours,*
> *Sam Lanyon*

I rested the card against a green coloured glass vase filled with yellow roses. A few half-burned candles were scattered on the worktop and the windowsill. I found the matches in the lounge and lit a couple of them. There was a notepad and pen on the worktop, too, as if waiting for the occupier to make a list, and a very pretty russet red shawl was draped over the back of one of the chairs.

I picked up the shawl and ran it through my fingers – it smelt of lavender and contentment. I wrapped it around my shoulders and began to put together the makings of dinner – cheese on toast with a bit of tomato and Worcester sauce would do. I took an unsliced loaf out of the breadbin and opened the drawer of a retro cream dresser looking for cutlery. Sitting on top of the cutlery divider was a hard-backed small booklet with a large label attached to it. Another label? I took out the booklet and ran a finger over the indented words, *First Officer Juliet Caron, Flying Log Book*.

I turned the label over. With very neat handwriting, it read:

> *This is your flying logbook, Juliet. It is the most significant document of your life. If you read between the lines you'll remember the times when you were happy (Spitfires), the times when you were stressed out (Fairey Battle - awful machine) and the times when you had no idea how you survived to fly another day (like that trip in the Hurricane when the barrage balloons went up). This is your most treasured possession.*

I sat at the table for a moment, my hunger pangs momentarily forgotten, and flicked through the logbook - one of the most intimate historical documents I'd ever read, and wondered about the lady who had once lived here, and about Sam who, I had the distinct impression, did not want this place to change.

My rumbling tummy brought me back to the moment.

I filled the kettle, stepped over to the fridge and noticed a laminated note stuck to the door with 'Read Me' written on the top. It was probably instructions from Sam, or Gerald.

It wasn't.

While the kettle was boiling, I read a letter which began:

This is a letter to yourself, Juliet ...

I couldn't resist taking it off the fridge. I turned it over and read the poem.

Where Angels Sing, by Edward Nancarrow, March 1943

When from this empty world I fall
And the light within me fades
I'll think, my love, of a sweeter time
When life was light, not shade

With bluebirds from this world I'll fly
And to a cove I'll go
To wait for you where angels sing
And when it's time, you'll know

To meet me on the far side where
We once led Mermaid home
And finally, my love and I
Will be, as one, alone

And at that moment, after pouring water from Juliet's kettle into Juliet's cup, sitting in Juliet's house and wearing – presumably - Juliet's shawl, for the first time in three years I felt an overwhelming sensation of being swaddled, that my grief was shared with the grief of another, and I had the notion that Juliet and I were somehow linked, that I was *supposed* to come to Angels Cove this Christmas, that some other - greater - force had guided me here, and not simply for the positioning of an apostrophe.

With my dinner quickly made and eaten, I set up camp in the lounge and, trying to ignore the other Katherine who was hammering at the door to get in, I decided it was time for a spot of Grand Designs ... and a tot or two of that whiskey! Glancing into the sideboard I was mesmerised – it was an Aladdin's Cave of memorabilia – and call it historical research rather than blatant nosiness, but next to the whiskey was a wad of faded A4 paper, held together by green string. The top sheet had the simple typewritten words, *Memories*.

A sudden crash outside coincided with the onset of a veil of darkness. The electricity supply must have fallen foul to the storm. The glow from the fire provided sufficient ambient light and I reached into the sideboard again and found the torch, but the battery must have been an old one because the torchlight was weak and to my disappointment, within a few seconds, petered out.

Determined to take on some of the inner strength of

the remarkable woman who had written a note to herself at ninety-two years old to never give in, I surrounded myself with candles and wrapped the russet shawl around my shoulders. And despite knowing that I shouldn't waste my phone battery on a little light reading, not tonight of all nights, I enabled the torch and began to read.

A Q&A with Melanie Hudson

What was your inspiration for _Dear Rosie Hughes_?

I was sitting in my parents' house a few years ago, drinking tea and munching my way through a packet of Jaffa Cakes, when Dad wandered down the stairs from the back bedroom and handed me a large buff envelope. He'd been having a clear out and had come across the letters – placed in date order – I'd sent during my time in Iraq. They were difficult to read, but sparked within me a desire to tell a story. I wanted to show – in their own words and point of view – the effect the war had on friends and family at home, albeit fictional ones. The epistolary format was the perfect medium for this.

Have you always wanted to be a writer?

Yes. It was never in question. I just needed to do a bit of living first.

How do you find time to write? And where do you write when you do?

To get me started on a new project, I generally opt out of life for a week or so and write the first 30,000 words – I also write pages and pages of notes during this time to be used later as the story progresses. If I don't do this – live and breathe the story until it is firmly entrenched – then I find it difficult to become completely invested. My characters need to make me laugh out loud one minute and move me to tears the next, and they can't do this if I'm not giving them my full attention. Other than that, I write when my son is either at school or in bed, although I do find it difficult to write at home. Big-brand coffee shops are a lifesaver. You can literally sit there all day with one Americano and your headphones on and nobody bats an eyelid!

What would you like readers to take away from *Dear Rosie Hughes*?

This is a tricky question for me because as a reader I like to take complete ownership of any novel I read, so I don't want to be prescriptive, especially given the sensitive nature of the story. I suppose Rosie's final letter probably says it all.

Dear Rosie Hughes

Who are your favourite authors and have they influenced your writing in any way?

My favourite authors are those wonderful women who penned what are now known collectively as the Virago Modern Classics. I also adore Nora Ephron, Maria Semple and Joanna Cannon. In terms of influences on my writing, everything I've ever read – from Louisa May Alcott to Agatha Christie – has played its part in developing the writer within. And even though my voice is very much my own, and is suited to the modern women's commercial fiction market, these women have all been inspirational, especially Elizabeth Von Arnim.

If you could run away to a paradise island, what or who would you take with you and why?

Rosie Hughes would definitely take her family with her, so I'd do that (and my battered copy of *The Enchanted April*). But having gone through an early menopause, I would also have to take a good supply of HRT tablets with me too, or my husband and son would probably refuse to come!

HELP US SHARE THE LOVE!

If you love this wonderful book as much as we do then please share your reviews online.

Leaving reviews makes a huge difference and helps our books reach even more readers.

So get reviewing and sharing, we want to hear what you think!

Love, HarperImpulse x

Please leave your reviews online!

amazon.co.uk   kobo   goodreads   L♥vereading   iBooks

And on social!

f/HarperImpulse   🐦@harperimpulse
📷@HarperImpulse